He was a warrior figh

She was his e

Laird Brandon Sinclair has given his life to the Scottish cause. Swearing fealty to Robert the Bruce, he will stop at nothing to see oppression end.

Lady Mariana wants nothing more than to break free of the tyrannical hold the English king has on her. When he sends her to Scotland with a message for the rebels, instead of obeying his orders, she finds herself submitting to her desires. After one sizzling, life-altering night, Brandon and Mariana must part ways. But Mariana has no intention of betraying her heart again.

And Brandon is determined to get her back. Stealing Longshank's secrets felt like victory, but taking his woman will be this Highlander's ultimate triumph.

The Highlander's Triumph

Book Five: The Stolen Bride Series

By
Eliza Knight

****

FIRST EDITION
June 2013

Cover Design by Kimberly Killion @ Hot Damn Designs

****

Also Available by Eliza Knight

The Highlander's Reward – Book One, The Stolen Bride Series
The Highlander's Conquest – Book Two, The Stolen Bride Series
The Highlander's Lady – Book Three, The Stolen Bride Series
The Highlander's Warrior Bride – Book Four, The Stolen Bride Series
Behind the Plaid (Highland Bound Trilogy, Book One)
A Lady's Charade (Book 1: The Rules of Chivalry)
A Knight's Victory (Book 2: The Rules of Chivalry)
A Gentleman's Kiss
Men of the Sea Series: Her Captain Returns, Her Captain Surrenders, Her Captain Dares All
The Highland Jewel Series: Warrior in a Box, Lady in a Box, Love in a Box
Lady Seductress's Ball
Take it Off, Warrior
Highland Steam
A Pirate's Bounty
Highland Tryst (Something Wicked This Way Comes Volume 1)
*Highlander Brawn (*Sequel to *Highland Steam)*

Coming soon…
The Rebound Pact – A Sexy Contemporary Novel
The Highlander's Sin – Book Six, The Stolen Bride Series
The Highlander's Temptation – Prequel, The Stolen Bride Series
Bared to the Highlander (Highland Bound Trilogy, Book Two)
The Dark Side of the Laird (Highland Bound Trilogy, Book Three)
My Lady Viper – Tales from the Tudor Court
Prisoner of the Queen – Tales from the Tudor Court

Writing under the name Annabelle Weston

Wicked Woman (Desert Heat)
Scandalous Woman (Desert Heat)
Notorious Woman (Desert Heat)
Mr. Temptation
Hunting Tucker

****

Visit Eliza Knight at www.elizaknight.com or www.historyundressed.com

Dedication

To my family, who makes every day a dream come true.

Acknowledgements

Once again, special thanks to Andrea, Vonda and all of my loyal and new readers. These books would not be possible without you! Also, many thanks to my realtors, and now friends, Denise and Rich, who not only made the selling/buying process smooth so I could keep working, but have spread the word about my books!

Chapter One

Nearing spring, 1298
Highlands, Scotland

Smoke filled Laird Brandon Sinclair's lungs as he rode on horseback with his men toward the north of Kinterloch Village.

High above the wooden wall, flames burst in hungry orange licks. A vengeful fire that would turn everything in its path to ash. The late afternoon sky was already overcast, but the smoke of the blaze made it nearly black.

No villagers ran from the fire. No animals screamed. The chaos that should be erupting with the flames was non-existent—as if deserted. But he knew it couldn't be. The people, the animals, were either trapped or had managed to get out from a different gate.

The Scottish troops' fearless leader, William Wallace, had already charged through the front gates into the inferno as if he were a man with a death wish. He'd ordered Brandon and his men to check the north side for survivors. Brandon's cousin,

Ronan Sutherland, had taken his warriors to the west side near the loch.

Far from his castle and lands in the north of the Highlands, Brandon had traveled to Eilean Donan the month prior to help his cousins Daniel Murray and Ronan along with William Wallace and Robert the Bruce in the war against the English. But it seemed now it wasn't only the English they were fighting—but traitor Scots too.

A loud crash reverberated through the air as another building collapsed behind the wall. A rush of heat surged his way, and a cloud of dark smoke billowed into the sky, in stark contrast to the world around them, a peaceful, beautiful place with lush pine trees and gorse bushes, even in winter. Hell set in the middle of heaven.

Doubt darkened his mood. There would be no survivors. Not in a raging inferno like this—one that rivaled Hades. He shook his head and spurred his horse forward. His chestnut colored warhorse, Checkmate, pounded the earth with his massive hooves.

If only they'd been able to get to the village before Laird Ross—traitor to all Scots and their ancestors. The damned bastard had defected to the English, and since doing so, had laid a path of destruction across the Highlands. There wasn't a man Brandon knew that hadn't been affected by Ross' treachery. Hell, it seemed like the man was on a mission to make enemies with everyone of true Scottish heart.

Brandon's thoughts were cut midway when they rounded the burning wall on the north side.

"Halt!" he shouted to his men, reining in Checkmate.

A woman burst through the wooden gate, exposing the interior angry flaming village. Hair black as a midnight sky, skin covered in soot. Her dark green gown was covered by a singed, once high-quality, wool cloak. She tripped, falling onto her hands and knees, coughing, yet she did not stop. The lass crawled forward, every move beleaguered in her attempt to escape the flaming village.

Without a thought, Brandon jumped from Checkmate, and ran toward her.

"Lass, are ye all right?"

He knelt before her and she practically fell into his arms, her breath coming out in a rush against his face. Her eyes closed, then fluttered open. She grasped onto him with weak, trembling fingers.

"Oh, *monsieur…*"

French. Brandon quirked a brow, trying not to be completely infatuated with the way her words rolled seductively off her tongue. What was a woman of French descent doing in Kinterloch? The lass clutched at the front of his cloak and glanced up, hair falling onto her soot covered face. He swiped the strands away and was startled by a pair of lovely, sparkling blue eyes. The color of the sky on a cloudless summer day. Like blue diamonds. But they were filled with fear, pain.

Brandon's hands skimmed over hers—soft and small—then up her arms as he pulled her to standing. She wavered on her feet, and glanced around as if she expected the devil to burst from the earth and drag her down into the depths of his hellish domain.

"Lass, ye're safe now. Tell me, are ye hurt?"

She shook her head, licked at her cracked, red lips. "No. I'm not hurt, other than my lungs—they burn with each breath." Her voice was hoarse, as though just a tiny hint of air passed through her delicate throat.

"Dinna speak then, if it pains ye." Brandon's hands slipped to her shoulders, automatically massaging the tense muscles there.

The woman sagged against him, a few tears spilling from her eyes. "Thank ye."

Brandon wiped at her tears with the pads of his thumbs. "Shh… I will ask ye a few questions, simply nod or shake your head. But first, tell me your name."

"Lady Mariana."

A name as pretty as a ballad. And she was a lady. He'd known that, and he suspected, though covered in soot, she was well off. Her cloak spoke of a high-quality fabric. He expected when she washed the grime from her hair it would shine, proof that it had been well kept. As it was the silken locks teased his skin and he longed to entwine his fingers within it. Where that desire came from, he didn't bloody well know.

"Lady Mariana, are ye alone?"

She nodded, her eyes locking on his with what looked to be a suspicious glance, and a peek behind him at his men had her paling.

"We'll nay harm ye, lass. We've come to help."

She shuddered in his arms.

"I promise no harm will come to ye." Brandon made his assurance loud enough for all his men to hear. "Ye are under my protection. I'll see ye to safety."

Mariana chewed her lower lip.

Turning to a few of his men, he ordered, "Check to see if there are others."

The men nodded and urged their horses forward, checking the north gate, then moving beyond it and out of sight.

"Were ye a guest?"

Her eyes crinkled up as she studied his face. Having plenty of experience judging people's expressions, he guessed she was trying to figure out how to answer.

"I know ye've no cause to trust me, but I assure ye, I'd never see ye harmed. I am Laird Brandon Sinclair and I am one of Robert the Bruce's men."

Her eyes lit up at that. "I trust ye."

Brandon didn't expect the sudden constriction in his chest upon hearing those words. He was a little taken aback by it. In fact, he was a little taken aback by this entire encounter. Lady Mariana was eliciting a reaction that no other woman ever had. Unable to quite describe it, Brandon could only call it awe. He was attracted to her; she was beautiful, delicate, exotic. But beyond that, he had a fierce need to protect her. And he didn't know why. He'd wanted to protect his cousins' wives, women in his village, his mother, but never had he felt the fierce need to pull a woman close so that no other could get near her.

It was almost possessive. And he needed to dismiss it with haste. His men made themselves still as statues behind him. Mayhap he should pass her on to one of the remaining retainers, just so he could get a breath of air without her scent—for indeed he could smell the sweet aroma of flowers beneath the smell of smoke. It was embedded in her hair, on her skin.

He cleared his throat. "Well, good. I shall take ye to safety."

Brandon took a step, intent on leading her toward his horse, however, Lady Mariana's legs were so shaky the simple task became labored. He swiftly pulled her into his arms, his muscles tightening at the feel of her supple curves.

"Will ye allow me to take ye to Eilean Donan?"

Mariana lowered her lashes, long black curly lashes that showed off the curve of her cheekbones. She nodded.

"Verra well." Brandon wanted to say something more charming, more comforting to a lass in such distress, but he could think of neither. Only that he never wanted to put her down—and how that made him want to toss her and run.

A woman would only slow him down. He'd seen that very thing happen to his cousins—Magnus, Blane, Daniel, Ronan—all tied to a woman. Brandon didn't ever want to deal with the fears that came with loving someone. He'd seen enough strife where love was concerned. His mother had not been a happy woman—save for when his own father passed.

Brandon grunted, pushing those unhappy thoughts aside. He lifted Mariana onto the horse and then climbed up behind her, putting his arm around her waist and pulling her securely against him. Her body melded to his, warm and lithe. Her head fell back and she breathed out a ragged sigh. Brandon ground his teeth, willing his body not to react to the soft curves pressed to his—the full derriere that if he allowed himself, he could fully imagine sliding his hands over as passion gripped him.

God's teeth, it was going to be a long ride back to the castle. Even still, he pulled her closer, feeling the brush of her breasts on his arm. Blood rushed through his veins, ignoring his warnings, and centered in his groin. A long ride indeed.

The heat of the flames washed over them in blistering waves. Sweat beaded on his brow and trickled down the sides of his face. How on earth was Wallace faring inside the blaze? Brandon blew out a breath and scanned the surrounding area. Beside the firs and pines, the trees were still winter bare, moss covering some of their trunks. He didn't see a glint of metal or out of place movement. Part of him suspected that Ross sat in the shadows watching, waiting, probably even stroking himself with glee at the destruction he'd caused, but Brandon knew better. The bastard wouldn't stick around. He'd hightail it to the next place he could barrel into and force a bed from.

But beyond Ross and his minions having disappeared, the lack of villagers was beyond disturbing. He hoped that did not mean they'd all perished, yet another crime against his own countrymen Ross could add to his long offensive list. Brandon wasn't the first in line to land a blow if the man were ever to be captured, but damn if he didn't want to be.

Despite the heat, Lady Mariana shivered. Brandon tightened his hold, wishing he could take away the fear that filled her. What a horror it must have been for her to be surrounded by fire within the village, to see one's life threatened. A near daily occurrence for him, but he was a warrior, trained for such, she was a lady, used to soft, fine, nice things.

Brandon tugged an extra plaid rolled behind his saddle and wrapped it around her shoulders, making sure to cover her legs.

"I thank you, my laird." Her voice was shaky, and he suspected she was on the verge of hysterics.

"Who were ye staying with? Have they…" He trailed off not wanting to ask if they'd indeed succumbed to the flames.

"I was staying with Sir Teirnan Barclay."

"Ross' cousin," Brandon growled. What the devil was she doing with him? Suspicion grew ripe in his mind.

Mariana nodded, her head bumping his chin. She turned up to him, her eyes red-rimmed, but fierce. "Is he your enemy?"

"Aye, Ross is my enemy." A sudden thought occurred to him—was Mariana going to pull a hidden dagger from beneath her skirts and attempt to strike him? "I've no quarrel with Barclay, *yet*."

After having witnessed Lady Julianna's fighting skills, he wouldn't put it past a woman again to be fully equipped with a blade. Julianna was the Bruce's half-sister and guardian—and his cousin Ronan's love.

Mariana nodded. "Ross is a bad man."

He didn't know whether or not to be surprised by her words. "Why do ye say that, lass?"

She gestured toward the fire. "All this."

"And Barclay?"

She shook her head, folded her hands in her lap. Long slim fingers, pale skin. She wore a beautiful ruby and gold ring on her right finger, but none on the left. Brandon hoped that meant she didn't have a husband waiting for her back in France—and he wasn't sure what difference it would make. He had no intentions of…

Of what?

Dammit, he was supposed to be worried over the blaze, over the safety of the townspeople, the Scots. Not whether the woman in his arms was spoken for.

"Tell me, lass. Does Barclay still live? I've need to hear who we're fighting."

"Barclay is alive. He's not a bad man in his own way. He's a follower. Caved when Ross first raised his fist."

Just as the Bruce suspected. Barclay was afraid of Ross. Not many weren't. Brandon and his cousins weren't. The Bruce wasn't. But that was because they'd already seen through the man. Knew they could beat him. Had been fighting against him for months. Others weren't as willing to put their necks out when a man, half-crazed, showed up on their doorsteps and demanded cooperation or death. Brandon was fairly certain that was the stipulation. While Ross was gaining much from his alliance with Longshanks, the English king, he wasn't one to pass it on to anyone else. Nay, Ross would hand out punishments if his wishes weren't followed.

"How long were ye here?"

Mariana shook her head. "Not long." Her voice was soft, but scratchy, a reminder of what she'd been through and Brandon's previous promise that she didn't have to talk.

His own throat was starting to feel scratchy from the smoke blowing on the wind. The fire had already conquered at least half the village, and the spots where it still blazed showed no sign of relenting.

Mariana coughed delicately, her shoulders quivering against Brandon's chest. He resisted the urge to stroke his hands over the gentle curve of her shoulders. Instead, he managed to do the gentlemanly thing and pulled his waterskin from its place attached to his saddle.

"Take a sip, lass."

Mariana turned her glorious blue eyes up to him, and gave a grateful smile. "My thanks, my laird."

Brandon gave a stiff nod. Wanted to tell her to call him by his name, but knew that would only seem odd to a lady he'd just met. She took hold of the waterskin, her cold fingers brushing his.

"Ye're cold," he muttered.

Mariana shook her head. "Just thirsty." She drew the waterskin to her lips, wrapping their pink, plushness around the rim and taking a deep pull.

Brandon's mouth fell open and his eyes were riveted to the sight—a number of sinful thoughts running wickedly through his mind.

"Thank you." She handed him back the skin, her eyes starting to droop.

"Are ye tired?" he asked, feeling as though he stated the obvious. Her lids were heavy, her face pale. The lass was completely worn out.

Mariana nodded. "I feel so weak."

"'Tis from the smoke. Rest, lass. I will wake ye when we make camp."

Mariana wiggled in his lap—driving him crazy with the way her bottom hit his thighs and groin—until she found a comfortable position. She laid her head against his chest and closed her eyes. How easily she found her ease in his arms. Brandon was stunned.

Before he could think more on it, his men returned from their search, no villagers with them. Brandon frowned, his anger growing.

"We saw no survivors, my laird."

Brandon gave a jerky nod, then turned his horse back in the direction they'd come. "Let us find the others." If Wallace wasn't back with Ronan and Julianna, then they might very well need to ride through the blazing village.

Ronan and Julianna met them halfway. No signs of their enemy and no signs of survivors either.

"Who is this?" Julianna asked Brandon.

Brandon opened his mouth to speak, but Mariana roused and lifted her head. She stiffened, her back becoming straighter.

"I am Lady Mariana," she said with her silky accent.

Odd how the sound of her tongue made Brandon want to pull her closer, touch her sensitive spots and hear her speak his name.

Julianna frowned. "What are ye doing here?"

"I was sent by His Majesty, King Edward."

Fire flashed in his cousins' woman's eyes, just as shock at her statement made his blood run cold. Longshanks had sent her? What in blazing ballocks was she talking about?

"Put her down. 'Tis a trick! We just left several others. The fire was a trap to lure us in. There are archers and warriors hidden in the woods to the west—most likely all around us." Julianna pulled her sword from her saddle.

Brandon pressed his lips firmly down in a frown and glanced at Ronan with question. Julianna acted as though Mariana might attack them. The lass stiffened further in his lap and again he wondered if she had a hidden dagger. Despite her omission, his gut told him she was not his enemy and he tended to trust his instincts. They weren't going to leave her out in the cold, or lynch her.

If Ronan didn't rein Julianna in, Brandon wasn't sure he'd be able to hold his tongue. Normally, Julianna was more cautious, gave no signs of her true feelings, but now she was acting completely different.

"Laird Sinclair, on behalf of my brother, your leader and future King of Scotland, I order ye to put the woman down. She is our enemy."

Mariana clutched her hands to Brandon's chest, her cupid lips forming a bow full of fear. "My laird, please dinna let her hurt me," she whispered.

Ronan reached out a hand and laid it lightly on Julianna's arm. The man certainly had patience when it came to his woman—and some sort of magical power. Julianna seemed to stand down.

"What is your purpose, Lady Mariana?" Ronan asked, the voice of calm and reason.

Brandon couldn't help feeling like they were interrogating the poor lass. Couldn't they see that she was struggling to breathe, to stay awake? Whatever her purpose, she wasn't a danger to them now.

Mariana shuddered. "I…I…" And the woman lost consciousness. Anger surged within Brandon. They'd scared her half to death.

Julianna bristled.

"We'll take her with us. She can give us the information we seek," Ronan said sternly. "Any sign of Wallace?"

Brandon shook his head, his grip tight on Mariana. He'd vowed to keep her safe, and damn if he wasn't going to see that vow through—even if he had to fight every man *or woman* to see it done.

Chapter Two

Hammering on the north wooden wall broke the stifling, tension-filled air. Mariana shivered, every muscle tightening. *Oh, mon dieu! Pray be survivors.* The horrifying memories of Ross and his men galloping through the village, flinging torches and oil onto the buildings burned with a vengeance throughout her mind. Their wicked smiles and laughter as the people screamed out in fear was an image of such wickedness, she was sure to never sleep well again.

At the sound, Laird Sinclair swiveled his horse around in time for her to see a large warrior and several men charge through an opening created in the burning wood. Mariana gasped at the horrendous sight, forced her eyes to remain open and braced herself for an oncoming attack. Who was the man barreling toward them?

"'Tis Wallace, my lady," her rescuer whispered, as though reading her thoughts. "Ye've no need to fear him."

Mariana relaxed, but only slightly. She truly had no cause to trust this man or the one charging toward them, but she did all the same. There was something about Laird Sinclair's eyes—

blue and flawless like a summer sky. His hair was dark, black and shiny like a raven's feather, giving him the look of a warrior god.

The moment he pulled her into his arms she'd felt safe. Felt a keen sense of awareness toward him, too. Every inch of her skin tingled, and where he touched grew hot. An instant attraction, one she'd never experienced before now. Instinctively, she knew the man would be intense and virile in the bedchamber.

Her skin heated at the thought. No maiden was she. Mariana had been trained as a young lady in the arts of pleasure. A lady she was—but was first the mistress to the French king at age fifteen. Her family hoped for an advantageous marriage by giving Mariana over to their sovereign's pleasure. Their ploy worked—except for her elderly husband's untimely demise. Since then, she'd been used as a mistress to men, a means to gain information, make peace. Indeed, she was a spy of sorts, and the good she'd been able to do thus far had been worth the unpleasantness of spreading her thighs for men she did not desire.

But Brandon Sinclair… This man she wanted, but she had no excuse to give in to her desires. Her body was not her own.

The warriors grew closer. This Wallace she'd heard much of from the English King. Edward hated him. Feared his power—though he'd never admit to it. Wallace and his men were covered in black soot. Like demons rising from the flames, the warriors rode toward them. Upon closer inspection as they neared, it was obvious the men were weary—much like herself. Breathing in the smoke as she removed blockades Ross' men had used to trap people, battered down dozens of doors and searched for anyone she could rescue, had taken much from her.

"Any survivors?" Brandon asked.

The rumble of his chest against her back startled her. Mariana sucked in a breath, frustrated with how meek she appeared. If King Edward knew she was this close to his enemy, he'd burst from his anger. What would he have her do? Gain information most likely. And he'd have her seduce Wallace to do it. Probably even issue her a command to take her knife to the rebel leader's throat while he slept.

She wouldn't do it—not the knife nor the seducing. For now, Edward had no idea that she was with these people, and she would like to keep it that way.

Wallace shook his head, disappointment etched in his brow. "Looks to have been torched purposefully as we guessed."

Laird Sinclair stiffened, most likely feeling his leader's discontent. Mariana felt it, too. How could one man be so cruel and evil? To torch a town, burn people, heedless of the lives he took or ruined. 'Twas a horrid way to die, and she could still hear the screams of those inside. Though she knew none of them personally, had only been a guest of the town for less than a sennight, that mattered little. Compassion and humanity compelled her to feel the loss of those lives, bound her to say a prayer for their souls and wish for Ross to die a most painful death.

"Aye," Ronan said. "We learned as much from a group by the burn. They were left to capture us. 'Twas a trap. Their group was shot dead, save for a couple of women and a child, by their own men."

"Damn," Brandon muttered, his expelled breath tickled the nape of her neck.

If possible, his muscles tightened more, his grip around her waist tense. Mariana's trade obliged her to study body language, and Laird Sinclair's wasn't hard to decipher—the man was filled with anger. How could she tell him she was in bed with his enemy's sovereign? He would surely kill her on the spot—after torturing her for information.

"Any sign of Ross?" Wallace asked.

The ones Brandon referred to as Julianna and Ronan shook their heads and said, "Nay," in unison. As they continued their report, they held hands, so very romantic and sweet. Was there any hope that one day, she might too find comfort in the arms of a man? Have someone she could turn to in times of need? A man to love and cherish and vice versa? 'Twas what she longed for most.

"The men said they'd been waiting for us. That Ross expected us to come. That he wanted me left alive," Julianna said. "But before we could gain more information, arrows flew from the woods hitting the men in their backs." The woman was beautiful. Not in the French elegant sort of way, but a rugged, earthy beauty. High cut cheekbones, large almond shaped eyes and blondish-red hair that shone. For all her rough exterior, the woman obviously took care of herself.

Mariana did what she did best, she listened intently while pretending to do anything but.

"Traitorous lot," Wallace said with a shake of his head.

"Aye," Julianna said. "We've no way of knowing their numbers or if Ross is among them."

"The lady will tell us," Wallace said with certainty, turning his attention back to Mariana and Laird Sinclair. Mariana held her breath, keeping her eyes lowered.

Laird Sinclair shifted, his thighs quivering beneath her bottom. She sensed his need to bolt, and with it, realized he truly did mean to protect her.

Under his breath he whispered, "They'll not put ye through the wringer, lass. Ye've already fought off a blaze and given me your trust. I willna let harm come to ye."

Mariana didn't want anyone to know what he'd said, so she squeezed his hand in reply, feeling the roughened skin beneath her softer fingertips. His hands were huge compared to hers—engulfed her completely. A hand that she could hold. Someone she could depend on. Her heart constricted, belly did a little flip. *Oui,* she could picture herself with Laird Sinclair. An odd thought considering they'd only just met.

"Aye, she will tell us," Julianna chimed in. 'Twas a dare. Through her lowered lashes, Mariana could see the challenge in Julianna's eyes.

Brandon squeezed Mariana gently on the waist. His gesture told her without words that it would be all right.

"Let us get to cover," Ronan said, eyes scanning the horizon. "We are being watched."

Mariana, too, felt the invisible eyes. Much like at court when she was with the king. From outward appearances they would be alone, but she could always feel several sets of eyes watching and she wondered from which cracks in the walls they spied. Her heartbeat quickened at the thought. Word traveled fast. Was one of Edward's spies now running to tell him that his mistress was in the arms of a Scot?

Mariana closed her eyes, letting the exhaustion she felt take hold. Pray let Laird Sinclair keep her safe.

If Ronan and Julianna had just witnessed people of Kinterloch being shot by their own people, there was no telling what any lurkers would do to them. Shot in the back might be a welcome end compared to other such evils Ross was likely to come up with—though they wouldn't go down without a fight. Brandon would hack down any enemy bastard he could, arrows protruding from his back and all.

Not willing to take his gaze from every possible hiding place—woods, boulders, shrubs, a few outbuildings, Brandon followed Wallace back onto the road toward Eilean Donan Castle. Mariana slept in his arms, mumbling between soft snores. He couldn't make out what she said, and a few times had to clench his jaw to keep from laughing for she sounded jovial and spoke gibberish in a high-pitched tone like a wee fairy.

Within a half-hour, feeling that they were a safe distance away, Wallace bade them to stop and make camp. He and his warriors had to be exhausted after going into the flames. They were still covered in soot—only now sweat made flesh-colored lines through the black.

Lady Mariana had fallen asleep in his arms but as soon as he pulled his horse to a stop, she shifted, stretched her arms and blinked up at him.

"We're going to make camp here," Brandon said softly.

Mariana nodded her acceptance, but glanced wearily around the camp. Wallace had yet to interrogate her, but it was coming soon. She most likely feared the questions, just as Brandon feared her answers. He'd yet to find out exactly what she was doing in Kinterloch, besides being sent by Longshanks to stay as a guest of Barclay.

"My lady…" Brandon shifted in the saddle and watched as those around them began to settle. "Is there anything I need to know before ye are approached by Wallace?"

Mariana shook her head a little too quickly for his liking.

"Are ye certain?"

She nodded.

Brandon frowned. She trusted him to keep her safe, but not with any information. Interesting.

He dismounted from the horse and reached up, hands settling on her delicate waist and lifted her down off the horse. Mariana's head reached to just below his shoulder. She gazed up at him with questioning eyes. Opened her mouth to say something, but then shook her head and looked away. He'd not pry it out of her. When a mare was skittish, one didn't pounce. Waiting patiently would often be enough for the mare to come forward. Mariana was no horse, but she was skittish. Mayhap waiting for her to open up would be enough, save for the fact that Wallace would soon be questioning her.

Mariana shivered, and wrapped her arms around herself. Spring was on the way, but winter's chill still made the air crisp. Her singed cloak and the plaid blanket he gave her weren't enough to keep her warm. They were far from the heat of the blazing village. Their breaths puffed out before them in white clouds, mingling. Brandon's eye was caught by the way Mariana bit her lip. He wanted to bite her lip, then lick the sting away.

"Can I offer ye my cloak?" He swung the wool fabric from around his shoulders, not giving her time to answer, and settled it around her form.

His cloak engulfed her completely, pooling around her feet.

"My thanks."

Brandon nodded, his body tense with desire and alert with a sense of danger. A danger that this woman presented even more so than their enemies.

'Twasn't that he thought her physically capable of harming him. Quite the opposite—she had a body built for pleasure and he couldn't stop thinking about all the sinful things he wanted to do with her. Nay, the danger she posed was entirely different. Danger to his peace of mind. His solitude. The life he'd carved out for himself. Aye, he was laird and chief of his clan and someday he would have to marry. But he'd no plans to do it now. Not when the country's stability hung in the balance. He refused to tie himself to a woman and produce heirs that would only suffer. Nay, he had to help rid Scotland of its enemies first. Then he could think about settling down with a wife and making bairns.

Indeed, he wanted a woman in his life when the chaos calmed. But the thought of her being in danger like this, of showing such displays as the ones he'd witnessed his cousins doing, hand holding, pain when their hearts were crushed, fear… That was not something Brandon thought he'd be able to endure. He couldn't judge his cousins, he accepted them and their right to love, and in fact respected them all for it. In his heart though, his gut, he knew it wasn't the right thing for him. Not yet, anyway.

Och! Why did looking at Mariana make him start questioning himself and his ideals?

"Come, let me find ye a place to sit afore the fire."

Mariana slid her arm through his—he ignored how right that felt—and he led her toward the fire the men had started. Two warriors lounged on a fallen, moss covered tree. One jerk of Brandon's head and they both scurried to find another spot.

"Oh, I couldn't take their place," Mariana said with a shake of her head.

"Nonsense," Brandon said gruffly. "They were happy to vacate for such a lovely lass."

Mariana's lip twitched, and she smiled at him. "You think me lovely, my laird?"

Brandon's chest seized. He had no skill with talking prettily to women. Never took an interest in flirting. Och, he could kiss the hell out of one, and he usually did let his prowess in the bedchamber speak for him. He gave her a curt nod, took hold of her shoulders and nudged her to sit.

"Stay here." He walked back toward his horse, feeling on edge and nervous. Lord, he hated being out of control. He took off his pack filled with food and drink, nodded to one of the grooms to take care of his mount, then returned to the fallen log.

Mariana pulled the plaid blanket from beneath her cloak and settled it on her lap. She looked down at her hands, picking at her manicured nails. Not too long, not too short. He could practically feel them scraping down his back. As he got closer, she jerked and looked up, relief filling her features at seeing it was him. Was she that terrified of speaking to Wallace? Brandon's senses went on alert. Something was not entirely right with that. Aye, could simply be fear, but what did she have to be afraid of?

Brandon sat beside Mariana, his thigh brushing hers. He ignored the spark that rushed from his leg to his groin, and instead rummaged through his satchel until he found the wineskin. He pulled out the cork and held the skin out to her. "Wine?"

Mariana nodded and took the skin. She'd guzzled the water he previously gave her, but with the wine she sipped daintily, though somehow he could tell she wished to gulp.

"Very good," she murmured.

"Have some more."

"I'd not want to drink all of your wine, my laird."

Brandon shrugged. "I'd simply get more from one of my men."

"I'd not want to take their drink."

"Any of them would offer it to ye."

She gazed up at him coyly, her lips poised to smile. "You'll not allow me to win, will you?"

Brandon chuckled, charmed by her intuitiveness. "Nay."

"Then I shall have some more." She took a longer pull this time, closed her eyes as she savored each drop.

"Which wine is better—mine or Barclay's?"

Mariana gave him the skin back and playfully batted his arm. "A lady never kisses and tells."

Jealousy reared its head, making his skin prickle. He leaned closer, whispering into her ear, "Did ye kiss Barclay?"

Mariana gasped and touched her hand to her chest. Brandon wished to peel back the many layers of fabric she wore to see the suppleness of her figure. He'd felt it. Knew she was curvy in all the right places, but as of yet, he'd only seen her in her overlarge cloak—not even a hint of what lay beneath from the well placed dip in her gown. Hell, he couldn't tell if she was wearing a gown.

And that had his heart pounding and blood surging to his cock. In his wildest imaginings, Mariana wore nothing beneath her cloak.

Ballocks! There his mind went again…

Brandon shoved his hand into his pack again and came out with two bannock cakes, offering Mariana one. She took it with a whispered thanks, biting into the food like a nervous mouse.

Brandon bit into his cake, the dry oat flour quickly siphoning the moisture from his mouth. He took a long draw from the wine, gazed at Mariana and asked, "Do ye like nuts, lass?"

Chapter Three

Mariana bit the inside of her cheek to keep her mouth from dropping open—and to keep in the burst of unladylike laughter threatening to spill.

"Nuts?" she asked, her lips quivering with the need to laugh. "*Oui*, I adore nuts."

Laird Sinclair, having no idea about her position within the French and English court, would not expect a lady to take his reference to an actual food item as sexual. But, indeed, Mariana was no usual lady—had laid witness on more than enough occasions of men's bawdy banter. And she enjoyed playing with Laird Sinclair's mind tremendously.

The man's face reddened a little, perhaps he realized what he'd said. He swiped a hand through his untamed hair and then reached into his bag, pulled out a little pouch.

"Sugared almonds," he said, his voice gruff. "I canna leave on a journey without them."

"Truly?" She stuck her hand into the little pouch and pulled out a few of the nuts, popping one in her mouth. They were covered with crunchy sweetness and spice. "Mmm." It'd been a while since she'd had the sugared treat.

The laird's eyes were riveted to her mouth as she chewed. A spark of interest in his gaze. Mariana's belly did a little flip, then tightened. She swallowed, feeling suddenly parched.

"Aye, lass. I find I am quite addicted to sweet things."

"Like pie?" she asked.

He shook his head. "Nay, I dinna enjoy pie or tarts too much, but marzipan and sugared nuts I canna live without."

Mariana smiled. "I too like marzipan. The sweetness of it melts on my tongue."

At the mention of her tongue, the laird returned his gaze to her mouth, but this time he flicked his tongue over his lower lip, and Mariana had to resist the urge to run her thumb over his moistened mouth.

"Aye, mine too," he muttered, then glanced away.

Mariana studied the camp, pulling Laird Sinclair's cloak tighter around her. Her lungs still burned and the heat of the fire had long since dissipated, leaving her chilled to the bone. But it was more than being physically cold. She was also frightened. What would happen now? How would she get back to King Edward? Not that she wanted to go back to him, but what other choice did she have? Whether or not she wanted to, she belonged with the English court and when they no longer had use for her, she would be sent back to France.

Scouts stood watch in a circle around the camp and a half-dozen more took rounds in the woods beyond. Flashes of sun-glinted metal were the only indicators they were there. They might be a bit away from the village, but they were still in danger if Ross' new following decided to pursue them.

Ronan and Julianna joined them at the fire, speaking in hushed tones as they ate. Mariana dared not flinch when Julianna's gaze met hers. Would the woman confront her now?

Demand to know why she was at Kinterloch or issue her death warrant in the name of her powerful brother?

The chill that seeped into her bones deepened. Julianna was a formidable woman—but Mariana could be just as formidable. Couldn't she?

She jutted her chin forward and returned Julianna's gaze until the other woman glanced away, distracted by her lover. Good, at least Mariana wasn't the one to turn away first. That would have been a sign of weakness, and she had a feeling that any signs of weakness would be dissected and taken advantage of by these Highlanders.

She jerked her gaze around the camp, looking for Wallace. He would surely be questioning her soon. Asking her the questions she did not want to answer. *Mon dieu*, what could she say? Not the truth. Not to him.

"Lass, what is it?" Laird Sinclair interrupted her frantic search.

Mariana turned her gaze back to him, wanting to melt into his arms, and stare into his eyes forever. She could trust him. He would keep her safe. And maybe, just maybe, she wouldn't have to speak with Wallace if she satisfied their curiosity now, by telling Laird Sinclair.

"May I call you Brandon?" she asked, using a low, soft, throaty voice that many a man had fallen over to hear.

Brandon was no different. He reached out, grasped her hand and nodded. An instant jab of guilt centered in her gut. She shouldn't be using feminine wiles to win him over. He was a good man, one she could trust, and yet… She was going to do it anyway.

"Wallace frightens me," she said meekly.

Brandon squeezed her hand, rubbing his thumb over her palm. She tried to resist the shivers his touch brought, but that was even harder than manipulating him.

"Dinna be afraid, lass. He is all bark."

He didn't add in no bite, as the saying went, and she knew that was because, Wallace was in fact a biter. The man truly did scare the stockings off her.

She shook her head, curled her toes inside her riding boots. "I don't want to speak with him, Brandon. Could I not simply speak with you? My throat still hurts..."

Brandon was quick to hand her the wineskin, only letting go of her hand briefly to grasp the skin before taking hold again.

She sipped with her free hand, needing the extra boost the wine gave her. And, to be honest, her throat really did hurt.

"Ye can share with me, lass. I'll speak with Wallace for ye."

Relief flooded through her. And with it, more guilt. She didn't want to use Brandon. He was too sweet for that, and there was an edge to him that said if he were betrayed, there would be hell to pay. In the end, Mariana had to protect herself. Though Brandon had sworn to do so, the only one she could really count on was herself.

Mariana closed her eyes briefly, took another gulp of wine and then turned her gaze toward Brandon, taking in his chiseled features—square jaw, high cheekbones, arched brows. A day's growth of dark stubble covered his cheeks and chin and she wanted so badly to scrape her palm over it. Blowing out a breath, she flicked her gaze toward her cold-numbed toes.

She made a vow not to lie to Brandon. Half-truths and a few missing facts weren't considered lying. *Oui,* it was omitting, but not blatantly changing the truth of things.

"The English king sent me to Ross with a message." She paused, uncertain of what she should say, how much was too much. "He knew where Ross was, and an escort brought me to Kinterloch."

"Did he say how he and Ross communicated?" Brandon stared at her intensely and she guessed he was trying to see how much of what she said was the truth.

Mariana shook her head. "Nay, he didn't tell me that."

"What was your message?"

Chewing on her lip, she delayed having to say anything further. How could she tell him the English king sent orders for Wallace to be executed?

"King Edward sent word of his coming invasion. He also sent orders for…" She blinked away the dryness of her eyes from having stared unblinking at the ground.

"For Ross to put us down?"

Mariana's head flew up, her eyes wide with trepidation as she stared at Brandon. "How did you know?"

He laughed, but the merriment didn't quite reach his eyes. Why did she get the feeling he knew a lot more about Ross' plans than she was led to believe? What all had occurred in the Highlands before she arrived?

"Ross has been hell bent on destroying us for months. Longshanks despises us. 'Tis not hard to put two and two together."

Mariana offered a weak smile. Indeed, she should have known how clever this man was. He would read between the lines of what she said, or fill in the blanks with the things she didn't say. 'Twould appear Kinterloch was not the first casualty of this war for power.

A breeze rustled through the trees, making her already unkempt hair flutter into her face. Brandon brushed the errant waves from her forehead, his fingertips lingering on her cheek. His hand was warm, branding a circle where each of his fingers touched. Mariana swallowed, the lump in her throat suddenly the size of a boulder.

She curled her hands into fists within the soft fabric of her borrowed cloak to keep from reaching up and pressing his hand all the way to her face, if only to feel some connection. A linking on a human, emotional level that she'd never been allowed to explore. Her week with Ross, the months with King Edward, her marriage, none of it was about affection, love. Never did she feel cherished. Only used.

Tears stung the backs of her eyes, but she quickly willed them away. She would not cry or let what Fate had dealt her mar this moment, or Brandon's opinion of her. So, instead, she turned her face away, shunning her needs as she so often did. What reward had she gained for such sacrifice? That was an answer she'd yet to come across. Perhaps life. She was a pawn in a dangerous game. Completely expendable. If she didn't do their bidding, or betrayed them in any way, those with power over her would take away her breath. Snuff her out without a second thought. There was no reward. She did what she must to survive.

"Ross has over two-hundred men with him. He bade me stay at Kinterloch so I could report back to him when you arrived and succumbed to his trap."

"Trap?"

"The fire."

Brandon raised a sardonic brow. "Did he not think we could see it?"

Mariana bit her lip, resisting the urge to laugh bitterly. "I'm not entirely sure he thinks much at all. Perhaps he thought that his armies might catch you by the burn where they waited, but upon seeing Ronan and Julianna, they may have assumed Wallace was not with you. Or they moved too slow to find out for sure. I suppose he assumed you would rush into the village to save the people, and perhaps hoped that your men would succumb as the innocent did." Her voice quieted as she once again heard the numerous screams of the people trapped and burning within their homes. Many had fled when news of Ross' plans were heard. Others were used as bait. One thing was certain, more died than needed. One life lost for King Edward's cause was too many. Shame filled her, for she was essentially involved in his path of destruction.

"May I assume that Ross is no friend of yours?"

Mariana gazed deeply into Brandon's eyes. There was strength there. A strength that resonated deep within her. Brandon was a man who could be trusted. A man she would love to fall asleep with and wake beside each morning. He had more character than all the men she'd had in her life put together—and this she knew from having only met him a few hours before. She also knew, for her, he was only a fantasy. "*Oui*, my laird, he is no friend of mine."

Brandon studied Mariana as she struggled to answer him. Her eyes darted over his face, settling on him with an intensity he felt deep within his bones. There was such pain in her eyes. He wanted to know all that had happened, and to take away the aches of injustice that must have been heaped upon her. How else would she have ended up in this predicament?

"Lady Mariana..." He raked a hand through his hair. Already he'd let her believe him to be soft-hearted. There was nothing more he could do. Nothing more for him to say. Every word he wanted to utter would only make him seem weak. To tell her he wished to take away her pain, she'd think he only wished to bed her. Brandon swallowed hard. Truth was, he had no idea what she would think. He only knew what he would assume if he heard another man say such things.

"What is it?" she whispered, her French accent muted somewhat by her breathy tone.

"Ye are safe here," he said with extra gruffness, even puffed out his chest, though he felt like a complete arse.

Mariana studied his face, a small quirk to her lips. Now he felt like a complete imbecile. She'd found him out, and thought it amusing.

"I know. You told me already."

Curse it! Brandon nodded. "Well, then, ye've told me about Ross and King Edward. Is there anything else I should relay to Wallace?"

Mariana's brow crinkled, and she gazed off in the distance, then slowly nodded.

"I must return to King Edward."

Brandon did his best not to show his surprise. He frowned and leaned closer, trying to look intimidating. Most men would have been cowed by his stern gaze alone, but his attempt to scare her with his size and proximity didn't work. Mariana stared at him as though he were nothing more than a flower she wished to pluck.

"Why?" he asked.

She shrugged. "He is expecting my return. Ross expected me to relay word of Wallace's arrival to Kinterloch. If I don't return, they will become suspicious."

Brandon nodded slowly. What she said made sense, but he still wouldn't allow it.

"We will let them think you perished in the fire."

Her throat bobbed as she swallowed, drawing his attention. His cock tightened with need, but his mind whirled with what that small hint of body language could mean. Was she lying? 'Haps she only said these things to trick him. Did she want to return to the king?

A sudden thought made him feel like he'd been punched in the gut. What if Mariana was a lot closer to Ross and King Edward than he thought? A lover perhaps? Why else would a French woman of noble birth be visiting a Scot who betrayed his country—*and* one sent by the English king?

Ballocks!

The thought had not occurred to him before and now he felt like a complete moron. This woman had tricked him. Played him for a fool. She may have succeeded this go around, but there wouldn't be a next time. He would play her game, and see just where it led. And he'd keep the information to himself.

Mariana spoke, interrupting his revelation. "Do you think such a ploy will work?"

"It seems to me that any ploy can work with the right amount of believable deceit."

Mariana raised a brow, perhaps wondering if he was referring to her current deception. Then again, he had no proof as of yet.

"Very well." She bowed her head. "I would be pleased to accept your protection."

Now it was Brandon's turn to raise a brow. He *had* offered to keep her safe... But to what extent did she think his offer of protection went? To some, protection was an offer of marriage. That was the last bloody thing Brandon was offering, even if the wedding night would bring to fruition her naked length beneath him. Desire fired in his blood, making him feel as though his skin were afire. Her lips were so plush, red, kissable.

He gritted his teeth. Marriage was *not* on the table. Now was no time to be thinking about kissing or bedding the woman. She was most likely his enemy, and he wasn't about to put himself in a compromising and vulnerable position, even if his cock was telling him otherwise.

"Verra well, my lady, consider yourself under my protection." He pressed his lips together before he offered for her to be under him completely.

Brandon hurried to stand, shifting his sporran from the side of his hip over his cock to hide his current state. Her eyes were like pools of seduction. A simple glance and he was ready to drop to his knees and yank her to the ground beneath him.

She reached out, her sleeve falling back to reveal her arm, long and slender, as she handed him his flask of wine. A wee bit lighter than when he'd passed it to her. Or was it? He was having trouble thinking straight. Lady Mariana was most likely going to be a thorn in his arse until the day they parted ways.

"Many thanks, Laird Sinclair. I promise you won't regret it." She batted her eyelashes, and quirked a seductive smile.

He grunted. Regret was something he was most certain he'd feel when this was all said and done.

Chapter Four

Mariana watched Brandon retreat from her presence. He looked disturbed, and she could guess at several reasons why—he felt the attraction that burned a path through her veins, had guessed she was the English king's mistress, or most likely, he sensed their enemy's approach.

His gait was strong, confident, a swagger to his hips that gave character to his powerful form. Broad of shoulder and back, narrow at the hip, Brandon was all brawn. Mariana could do nothing more than stare after him. The wicked thought of seducing him more than just a niggle in her mind. How would she go about it? Sneak into his tent tonight when it appeared all others had fallen sleep? Wait until they arrived at the castle, and then climb naked between his sheets to wait until he came to his bed chamber? Both were bad ideas—she could very well end up in the wrong man's bed.

What was she thinking? Seducing Laird Sinclair was not an option. In truth, she had to figure out a way to return to King Edward's camp, or at the very least locate Ross. She wouldn't tell them the truth. The fact that she'd met both Sinclair and Wallace would forever remain a secret, trapped forever on her lips. Mariana didn't have a cruel or evil bone in her body. This was not *her* war. She might make something up to throw the English and that Scots bastard off their trail. But Edward prized her companionship—he'd not let her simply disappear. Had he not requested her for his mistress upon seeing her in France? Nearly got into a duel over her gracing his bed, too. In fact, the entire debacle had been an embarrassment she'd never live down. In the end, she'd been pleased to leave France so she wouldn't have to face those who'd witnessed her shame.

Becoming a mistress to powerful men had never been her choice. She was merely a pawn stuck in a game of chess she'd never be free of. Indeed, King Edward would never let her go. Her charred remains would be searched out, and he knew how resourceful she could be. Mariana was certain that in his gut, Edward would know she'd run away.

The price of her freedom would not be more Scottish lives. She wouldn't allow it. Perhaps the life she'd been given was a test of her fortitude or penance for coveting the life of her sister. They'd not been close growing up, which made Mariana's sting of jealousy all the more painful. Margot had been offered for *after* Mariana became the French king's mistress. She had a handsome, wealthy, noble husband. They had beautiful children. Love. Happiness. A family. All things Mariana wished for, but did not have, and most likely never would. She was barren. Never in the last eight years had life quickened within her womb.

Without a husband, and with a soiled reputation. Love was out of the question. Who could love someone with such a tarnished past? It was time to face facts, she would never know true happiness. The only way she would ever marry is if she were given to someone as gift from the king. The idea of being someone's compensation made her tremble.

With a hard swallow, Mariana turned her attention away from her bitter thoughts and focused on the camp. She again took note of the guards, ever alert. Brandon had joined Wallace and Ronan. Julianna, too, was with them and kept throwing Mariana suspicious glances.

There seemed to be no chance of escape just yet. But the sun was dimming, turning the area within their camp grey. Darkness would be upon them soon enough, then perhaps her chance to disappear within the forest would surface.

Until then, she'd have to settle in and wait. Several tents had been erected, but she'd not been given one. Would they make her sleep outdoors? She prayed not. 'Twas nearing spring, but the temperature still bespoke of winter, and with the sun's weak warmth gone, the night was sure to be close to freezing.

Mariana shuddered and burrowed deeper within her cloak and Brandon's. The wool of his garment was soft, inviting and smelled of him—woodsy, smoky and a tang of masculine spice. She closed her eyes for a moment, breathing his scent in deeply. Her entire body tingled from it. Odd that a man's scent could have that effect on her, like a potent tonic, the intent to intoxicate and draw in a victim. Mariana was that victim, totally beholden to this man's fragrance.

Oh, mon dieu!

There was something wrong with her.

Mariana pushed from the log, every muscle screaming as she slowly stood. Her movements caught the attention of half the camp. Some of the men gawked and the only other woman—Julianna—frowned. Mariana was sure the men's reaction was due to the soot covering her face and hair.

A cursory glance told her there wasn't water nearby, but she desperately wanted to wash her face. She slid her hands from within the confines of her cloak. They were dirty with soot, her nails black. The sight made her stomach churn. Mariana couldn't stand having dirty hands. A pet peeve of hers.

No one in her service, nor any man she entertained, was allowed to touch her without clean hands.

She tried to think about Brandon's hands. Were they clean? Odd, but she couldn't recall. They must have been, for she wouldn't have let a dirty man hold her in his arms.

Granted, she wasn't exactly being held in his arms. He rescued her, and she pretended to faint so she wouldn't have to talk to anyone. Keeping her eyes closed, exhaustion had overtaken her and she had truly fallen asleep. She frowned, realizing at the last minute that her unseeing gaze had settled on Julianna. Luckily, the woman had turned away and not taken note of her.

With a deep sigh, she made a mental note to be more aware of her facial expressions and surroundings. At court, her face hurt from the constant demure smile or flat affect. When she wasn't surrounded by such formality, she tended to fall into a comfortableness with herself and wasn't on edge. Not entirely bad, except for right now she was within a camp filled with people who would consider her their enemy if they knew the truth.

Fear clawed at her spine.

"Can I get ye something?" One of the guards stepped from his post to speak to her. His form was tense, stiff, as though he thought she might strike him.

Mariana gifted him with one of her flirtatious smiles—the one she used when King Edward was ranting about the Scots. "Thank you, *monsieur*, but I only wanted to find a creek to wash my hands and face." She held out her hands, showing the soot, and hoping to gain his pity.

He nodded. "Just a dozen or so yards that way." He pointed behind her.

Before the man could change his mind, she dipped him a curtsy and rushed into the trees. Two yards in, she was tripping over the copious amount of fabric that was Brandon's cloak. A disgruntled growl left her lips as she yanked it from beneath her feet, and then from a branch it had caught on—and a loud tearing sound rent the air.

"*Mon dieu*!" she snapped.

Mariana carefully pulled the fabric from the branch and examined the damage. A jagged three inch tear. She exhaled, annoyed that her clumsiness had ruined his cloak. Well, she'd have to apologize and then promptly ask for needle and thread. Though she wasn't the best at sewing, a tear this size couldn't be too hard to repair.

Gathering the billowing fabric in her arms, she trudged forward in search of the stream the guard mentioned. She could hear water trickling and knew she was getting close. She quickened her pace, but an odd feeling had her stopping mid-stride.

The hair raised on the back of her neck and gooseflesh covered her arms. Her breath quickened. She sensed she was being watched, but the feeling was menacing, as if she were going to be pounced on.

Trying to breathe evenly, and not succeeding, she glanced around several trees. There was nothing untoward in sight. But Mariana wasn't stupid enough to think that an enemy who intended her harm would simply show themselves. That would be as unwise as her undressing and standing nude in front of a bunch of lusty warriors. Nay, the feeling skating uneasily along her limbs was that of prey being stalked by an animal of higher power.

Soot be damned, she was going back to camp. Perhaps Brandon had returned from his chat with Wallace and would escort her back to the water.

Brandon stood in a tight circle with Wallace, Ronan and Julianna, the latter of whom kept tossing suspicious glances behind him to the spot where he'd left Mariana. It took all of his willpower not to look. Irritation bit at the edges of his nerves, but truthfully he couldn't blame Julianna. The warrior-woman was usually right. She had great instincts and wouldn't be the Bruce's personal guard if she wasn't. And as much as he hated to admit it, Brandon was beginning to believe there was something not quite right about Mariana's situation. But, he wanted to be the one who handled it—not Julianna. Best to catch the woman off guard. He'd found Mariana and he would get to the bottom of her secrets...and possibly steal a kiss or four in the process.

Clearing his throat, Brandon glanced at Wallace who nodded. "She's spoken of Ross," Brandon told the small group. They'd moved out of hearing distance from anyone else, but even still he glanced over their shoulders to make certain no one had tried to sneak closer—namely Mariana. The lass knew he was going to speak to them about her situation, but he'd rather she not hear it. "She reported that Ross has gone. He fled after setting the fire, with instructions for her to remain behind and report back to him, as well as an army in the eastern woods and the bait ye found by the burn."

"And no others?" Ronan asked skeptically.

Brandon narrowed his brows, pressed his lips together. "There were others, she said. But they perished in the fires. She was trying to help, but eventually ran, and that's when we found her."

"Who is she?" Ronan crossed his arms over his chest, the way he did when trying to determine a puzzle.

"I dinna know yet, but I do believe her," Brandon said, glad his voice did not belie his true feelings. He believed most of what she said, that many had perished, and that she'd been left behind by Ross. But there was so much left unanswered—that was where he doubted her, in the shades of gray she left smudged and filled with mystery.

Ronan frowned and Julianna continued her hard stares in Mariana's direction. Lord how he wanted to turn, to see if Mariana was cowering or glaring back.

Ronan said, "Did she tell you why she's turned against Longshanks? Obviously she was close to him, if he chose her to relay his message."

Brandon shook his head, frown deepening. "She did not go into more detail than to say she could no longer do his bidding in good conscience. I *trust* that she's turned a new leaf." He emphasized trust. Mariana may have told half-truths, but she wasn't dangerous. Not as long as she was with them. The danger from Mariana wasn't physical, but more what she might whisper into the wrong ear.

Julianna was quick to respond. "But how can ye trust her? Ye barely know her." Her voice held an edge of suspicion. "Ye want her," she muttered under her breath, so Brandon just barely caught it.

"'Tis a fact, ye are correct that we only just met"—he wasn't going to let her know how much he wanted Mariana—"but there is something in her eyes. She's no danger to us here."

Julianna raised a skeptical brow.

"There is no one better than Brandon at reading people," Ronan said, grasping his shoulder. Brandon was pleased to have his cousin's confidence. "If ye say we can trust her, then I believe ye."

Brandon nodded, receiving a nod in turn from Ronan. From the corner of his eye, he watched Julianna. She stared them down, and he knew in her mind she was assessing the entire situation. The lass was shrewd, and one hell of a fighter, he'd give her that. More power to Ronan for being able to handle her spirit.

"What of the army? Did she give ye numbers?" Julianna asked.

Brandon unclenched his fist, not realizing he'd held it so tight. Relief flung through his blood. Damn, he hadn't recognized how much Julianna's acceptance meant to him. Why was he so hell bent on protecting a woman he barely knew? Aye, 'twas true he desired her, but there was more to it than that. There was something about her, the way her blue eyes enchanted him, made him feel as though she could see his soul and that her spirit melded with his. Ballocks, he hated getting all poetic. He needed more whisky. "Aye, she said there are over two-hundred of them."

"Will they disband or join us?" Wallace asked.

Brandon rubbed his hands together and cracked his knuckles, eager for a fight. Bashing heads and knocking bodies was an excellent way to relieve stress and some of the internal emotions that stirred since meeting the lass. "I dinna know; she didna say."

"Ask her," Wallace ordered.

Brandon hid a grimace. While he wanted desperately to sit beside Mariana again, at the same time he didn't want too. Being close to her only made him want to pull her into his arms and sample the lips she often bit. He had a dozen excuses as to why he should argue the order—how would she know the Ross army's intent? Why would Ross share such intimate details? Could he trust her answer?

But in the end, he didn't give them voice. In truth, he desired nothing more than to sit beside her again, even if it meant speaking about his enemy. As long as he could hear her silky voice, imagine her warm breath on his lips.

Ballocks! His cock pushed against the fabric of his plaid, and he was grateful that earlier he'd shifted his sporran to the front. Brandon nodded at his small group and turned to do their leader's bidding.

But Mariana was gone.

Panic seized him. His stomach tightened, heart ceased beating, breath caught. Immediately, his hand was on his sword, ready to battle whoever had taken her.

"Where is Lady Mariana?" he growled to the nearest guard.

The man shrugged. Brandon turned in a stiff circle, studying everybody, every boulder, every tree. No dark-haired beauty with soot smudged across her nose. No petite figure within his billowing cloak. No seductive eyes, and coy smile.

God's teeth, where the hell was she?

He wanted to shout out her name, but that would only draw Wallace, Ronan and Julianna's attention. They'd not listen to him, then they'd go off of gut instinct that she was up to no good.

He raised his chin to another guard, "Where is Lady Mariana?"

"I dinna know, my laird, but I saw Jared speaking with her."

Brandon nodded and marched toward Jared who examined the forest.

"Where is Lady Mariana?"

Jared jumped, his face pale. Even the red of his hair seemed a shade lighter. "My laird."

Brandon waited a split-second for the novice warrior to regain his senses, about ready to pummel him, when he finally spoke.

"She wanted to wash her face and hands."

"And?" Brandon bit out, irritation making his eye twitch.

"I told her the burn was through the trees."

Fire lit Brandon's blood. "Ye didna offer to escort her?" Brandon spoke through clenched teeth, every muscle in his body seizing.

Jared shook his head. "I figured she'd be fine."

"Ye figured wrong, ye horse's arse. Which way?"

Jared pointed with a shaky finger. Brandon took off at a jog through the trees, holding his arm up to ward off branches that snapped, ready to slice his skin. Almost like the forest didn't want him to find her, wanted to make his life more miserable. Brandon let out a string of curses and swore he'd take Mariana over his knee, spank her bare arse until her cheeks were pink—but that only made his cock hard. He'd barely made it a few dozen yards before he heard a sheer whistle pierce the air.

Chapter Five

Brandon turned toward the sound of the whistle, unsure if it was one of his own men or the enemy. Dusk was setting fast upon them and a wicked breeze ruffled his hair, winding its way down his shirt. Ordinarily, he might have missed his cloak, but rather than the whistle sending his blood to chill, it made him hot with the need to wage war with his enemies.

Had Ross and his men so easily descended upon them? *Ballocks!* He had to find Mariana first, make sure she was safe, before he discovered who was behind the whistle. Turning back toward the burn, he picked up his pace, and bolted to the edge of the water.

Not a soul in sight. No Mariana.

"Damn," he muttered, looking up and down the bank. The water trickled peacefully, completely in contradiction to the way his blood seethed through his veins. Rushes and horsetails grew tall to the edge in places and trampled down in others. He brushed a few aside to make sure he didn't miss her crouching down in the water. No slender fingers dipping into the cool burn, only a few sparlings, plucking at the algae covered rocks visible just beneath the water's surface.

Where was she? Had she already been captured?

"Mariana?" he risked calling out. Several birds took flight at the sound of his voice, their wings rustling.

There was no reply. Not even a whisper of human sound. He could have been all alone in the wilderness. Except—what was that? He tilted his head, fearing the truth of what he heard. A distant clang of metal. A battle.

Mo creach! He couldn't stand here. Praying that Mariana had made it safely back to camp, he rushed toward the sounds of the melee. God only knew how many were descending upon them—and he prayed it wasn't the two hundred Mariana had spoken of.

Brandon broke through a copse of trees at the same time as Wallace, a dozen more of their men and a mass of enemy warriors. Ross stood in the middle facing off with Ronan and Julianna. The forest air filled with the clang of metal, the crash of bodies, shouts of victory and grunts of pain.

Blood rushed to his ears and all thoughts but that of fighting for his country—and winning—left him.

He wasted no time jumping into the fray. Yanking his claymore from the scabbard on his back, he swung it in an arc bringing it down on the closest enemy, droplets of warm blood spraying his face. Brandon turned off the sensation, making his mind blank to everything save the task at hand. He ducked the blow from a new opponent, pulling his *sgian dubh* from his boot and slicing into the back of the man's knees. His foe fell to the ground, howling in pain, briefly clutching his leg, before coming to his senses and blocking Brandon's next swipe of his sword. The man, incapacitated, could no longer harm anyone. Brandon leapt from his range of attack and pummeled the next man to the ground, head-butting him to knock him out.

The battle raged around him. Ronan went head to head with two warriors while Laird Ross hung back, the bastard. His eyes blazed with evil, lips peeled back, baring yellowed and crooked teeth. He half expected to see horns sprouting from Ross' weathered-looking head. But there were none—not that he could see anyway. Brandon sprang forward, catching Ross off guard, but not for long. The old warrior parried like a vicious bear, growls and all, but before Brandon could land a significant blow, two Ross men attacked him from behind—one landing a solid blow to the back of Brandon's shoulder. He hissed in pain, feeling the heat of his own blood seep over his skin.

In the instant he turned from Ross to end the lives of his attackers, the bastard disappeared. And with him Julianna. Ronan called out to her, panic in his tone, and Brandon felt his pain, having had to push off his search for Mariana in an effort to aid his men.

But there was no time to think on it. Several more warriors pushed through the trees, their battle cries making Brandon want to rip out their throats. He moved swiftly toward them, fury burning a heightened energy through his muscles. He let his anger and worry over Mariana out in a heated storm.

At last, most of their enemy fell. The few remaining rushed back toward where they came from, perhaps looking for their leader. Not nearly two hundred had attacked, which meant there were far more of them somewhere close by. They had to move or risk another attack.

Ronan rushed toward them, sweat slickening his face. He glanced at Brandon, his eyes scrunched in alarm. "Julianna! Have ye seen her?"

Brandon shook his head, as did the other warriors with him. There was no sight of her within the copse of trees. She'd simply vanished.

"He's taken her!" Ronan shouted, face stricken.

Was it possible? Brandon wasn't certain when Ross had disappeared. He thought back, long and hard. Julianna had disappeared around that time—he'd seen her, but been pulled back into battle. Damn, he should have warned Ronan then, but there'd been no time.

"I do recall seeing her disappear around the same time as Ross," Brandon offered, but Ronan wasn't listening. He frantically lifted the limp bodies, tossing them aside, 'haps looking for a clue.

Brandon glanced back toward their camp, itching to run through it to see if Mariana was there. If the bastard had taken Julianna, it was entirely possibly he'd grabbed Mariana, too.

Ronan took off running toward where many of Laird Ross' men had escaped, calling out for Julianna. Brandon swallowed hard, and turned back toward camp. He had to reassure himself with the presence of Mariana's face—and dispel the thoughts crowding into his mind. What if she'd escaped to the burn—told Ross where to find Julianna?

Part of him knew that had to be impossible. There was no way she would have known where they were going to set up camp, nor did she have the opportunity to get word to Ross. Unless... Unless what? It was impossible. He had to stop making assumptions.

He looked up through the trees and stared at the sky just now turning grey with nightfall. Bending to the ground, he wiped his weapons on the grass and sheathed them. Muscles tingly from battle, he walked back to camp, mumbling one word answers to his men who were still riled up over the battle. He'd never let any of them know how worried he was about Mariana.

She'd better be sitting pretty on the log where he'd left her.

The camp was in chaos as men ran hither and yon to pack up supplies, sew up injuries, snap shoulders and put other joints back into place, wrap wounds, and drown their pain with swigs of whisky. Brandon narrowed his eyes, until they came to rest on a pale, shaken Mariana—on the bench where he'd left her, an ashen Jared by her side.

A rush of relief so acute, it nearly buckled his knees, pummeled him. She was safe.

He'd not let himself feel the full force of his worry, was too ensconced in trying to win the battle. And now that he saw her, all of the feelings he'd kept at bay rushed him like a pack of wild animals on their prey. He swiped a hand over his face, scrubbed it through his hair.

Brandon took his time studying her. Her cheeks were flushed and smudged with dirt. Dark tresses, wild and unkempt. Eyes wide and frantically searching. She wrung her tiny hands, lips were pursed. Then her gaze met his from across the way and he felt as if time stood still. The sounds of the men packing up camp dissipated, and the only thing he seemed to be aware of was Mariana.

She jumped to her feet at the same time he stepped toward her. A swirl of Highland mist crept in from around the edges of camp. His stomach tightened, chest clenched. Brandon wanted to run to her, to pull her into his arms and tell her never to leave his sight again. To yell at her for having scared him. To take comfort in her warmth, let the rush of battle be soothed by her stroking hands upon his shoulders, through his hair. To kiss her, to slide his tongue between her lips and make love to her with his mouth.

Brandon shoved past a few warriors in his need to reach her, to touch her. Why he felt this uncontrollable urge, he had no clue, didn't want to think about that. Mariana too took a step forward, and he wanted to pummel Jared when his fingers clutched at her cloak stopping her. She turned to yank free, and Brandon growled, intent on issuing the recruit a rebuke when Jared saw his approach. The lad raised his hands in surrender and took a step back. Mariana followed Jared's line of vision, her eyes locking on Brandon's and pink coloring her cheeks. Her lashes closed over her eyes as she glanced down at the ground, an attempt to look meek, but the triumphant smile curling her lips was anything but.

"I…" she started, but trailed off, her voice raspy like she needed to catch her breath. "I saw the other warriors return, but hadn't seen you, my laird. I was…"

Brandon stopped inches from her, forcing his hands to remain by his sides. "Did ye fear for me lass?"

She looked up, eyes wide open then and while her lips played with his mind, her eyes spoke the truth. She nodded.

"I am here. Where were ye?"

"I wanted to wash my face," she said softly, reaching up to touch her chin.

"Ye did not do a good job." This time he gave in to his urge to touch her, his thumb brushing over a streak of black on her cheek.

Mariana leaned into his touch. "*Oui,* 'tis the truth I never got the chance."

"Why is that?"

"Battle broke out, scared me half to death."

"And have ye recovered?"

"*Oui,* my laird."

God's teeth, he loved the way she spoke. Mariana flicked her tongue over her lips, took his hand from her face and held it in her grasp. Her fingers were cold.

"'Tis the truth I am glad you're safe," she whispered. "I feared…"

Brandon shook his head, his smile full of confidence. Without thinking, he took both her hands in his and rubbed some warmth into them. He looked down at their clasped hands and promptly dropped them. "There is no need to ever fear for me, lass. I am invincible."

"My laird, ye're bleeding." Jared pointed to his back, the lad's freckles fading. His mouth flopped open like a fish out of water.

Mariana gasped. "Is it bad?"

"Ah, well, not completely invincible." He chuckled. In his haste to see to Mariana's safety, he'd forgotten about his wound. "Send Hamish over to sew me up then, lad."

Jared nodded, his face another shade paler, and ran to do Brandon's bidding.

"Let me see," Mariana said. She walked around behind him, her gentle fingers probing at the slice in his linen shirt. "Does it pain you?"

He shook his head. "Nay, lass." He dragged in a heavy breath. "Ye have a healing touch."

And he wasn't completely lying. He did like the feel of her hands on him, it made him forget the ache of the slice in his shoulder.

"'Tis not too deep," she said. "But you have lost a lot of blood. Come sit."

Brandon allowed her to lead him to the log where she'd been sitting. Bracing her hands on his uninjured shoulder, she pushed him down. Now, he was at eye level with her breasts. How he wished he could push aside the copious amounts of fabric covering her, so he could bury his face in their ample plushness. Aye, he recalled just how they felt on his arm. Soft mounds. His cock twitched and he groaned.

"Oh, it must pain you so."

Brandon bit his cheek. If the lass only knew why he was groaning… It surely wasn't the pain in his shoulder. That he could handle, but the urge to touch her breasts, that might slay him yet.

He leaned his head forward, an inch from her. "I am feeling weak," he muttered, knowing all the while he'd have hell to pay if she found out about his little white lie.

Immediately, her hands came up around his head and pulled him toward her.

Ah, saints! His forehead fell to her warm body as she cradled him, cooing words for him to remain strong. The tops of her breasts rested on his head, her flat stomach beneath his cheek. Lord, this was heaven. He breathed in her scent, wished to put the front of his face flush against her, kiss her, lick her, taste her.

Damn, he was a cad.

He should pull away, not allow her to think him so weak, when in all reality he was a licentious arse. But she felt too good for him to move. Her warmth seeped into him, sparked a sizzling path straight to his groin. He wrapped his arms around her hips, taking in the way they swelled—not a soft swell like most ladies preferred, this was the type of curve a man wanted, ripe and delicious. Grasping her waist, he took in another breath, certain she would push him away.

"Off the lady now, lad, let me get a look at ye." The brusque voice of Hamish, Wallace's own surgeon, broke through Brandon's sensual haze.

He opened his eyes a little to see Hamish's weathered face, complete with a frown. Brandon gave a slow smile and a wink, knowing the man had every idea of what he was doing. Hamish had been around the Highlands since Brandon was a boy, serving his father for a time, and wiping up a few of his scrapes. The man was a wanderer, never staying too long in one place, although there always seemed to be an angry woman in his wake, which made Brandon wonder if females were the reason behind his frequent change in living arrangements.

"Hamish, excellent timing," he said a little too cheerfully.

The old man grunted.

Mariana pushed him away, crossed her arms and gave him a skeptical look. He winked at her, loving the way her cheeks quickly flamed.

"Rogue," she muttered with a huff.

Brandon chuckled, and went to push himself up off the log, but the pinch of pain in his shoulder made his elbow buckle.

"Stay where ye are," Hamish said gruffly. The old man marched behind the log and with rough hands ripped open, exposing his shoulder. "Lass, if ye could get Laird Sinclair a new shirt, 'twould be most kind of ye." The old goat's voice softened when he spoke to Mariana.

Brandon glanced up, seeing her eyes riveted to his bared skin. 'Haps he affected her just as much as she did him. That thought only made him smile even wider. Mariana rolled her eyes.

"There's an extra in my bag on Checkmate," Brandon told her. "Thank ye kindly, lass."

"I'd not have you thank me any other way," she said, a bit of feisty bite in her tone.

Brandon grinned wickedly, loving the way her blush flowed down her neck, and dammit that cloak once again hid her breasts, which he was sure had also colored a pretty pink. "A matter I'd be most happy to discuss with ye."

"I doubt you will get the chance." She raised her chin a notch and went in search of his horse, her hips swaying a mite more than usual.

Brandon ground his teeth to keep from pushing Hamish away and running after her to kiss her senseless.

"Best be careful with that lass, lad," Hamish said.

He grunted. "Why?"

"Drink this." Hamish handed him a skin of whisky—stronger than his own stuff and with a nasty aftertaste. Brandon winced, his throat burning, and then howled when Hamish poured it onto his shoulder. "Never seen ye so keen on one."

"Keen on what?" Brandon hissed through his teeth as the needle pierced his skin and Hamish went to work sewing.

"A lass. Ye seem taken."

"I'm not taken." Dammit, had everyone noticed how much he wanted her?

The feel of the thread snaking through his skin made Brandon's flesh crawl. He hated the sensation, and though he'd felt the initial prick, the wound was quickly growing numb, as was his tongue.

"Whisky's strong," he mumbled, taking another swig when Hamish offered.

"Aye, 'tis a special blend."

"Shpeshal?" Why the hell was he slurring his words?

Hamish chuckled and took the skin of whisky back. "Aye. No more or ye willna be able to sit your horse when we leave afore long."

Brandon nodded, his head heavy. Just a few sips of whisky… He felt like he'd drunk an entire jug.

"All done, and just in time." Hamish slapped his back. Brandon jerked forward, his bearings all off, but Hamish hastily righted him.

Mariana approached, a clean shirt folded in her arms. Brandon tried to stand, and stumbled, only coming to his feet with Hamish's help.

"I think the lad's going to need your help, lass. Gave him a nip of my special brew."

Mariana raised a brow, but nodded. Brandon glanced down at his torn and bloody shirt, trying to figure out how he could take it off. Before he could remember how to remove his pin that held his plaid over his uninjured shoulder, Mariana grasped it and yanked it free.

"Mind if I help you to undress?" she asked.

"I thought ye'd never ask," Brandon said, trying for seductive, but *ask* came out like *ashk.* He frowned, hating to be so loose with his tongue. Mariana giggled. *Damn.*

She ran her hands over his chest, untying the laces and then tugging the shirt over his head. He didn't even feel the sting in his arm when he moved it. A wisp of her hair tickled his skin, as did her breath, she was so close. His flesh prickled—and his cock rose on end. Damn… There he stood, bare-chested, ready to crush her to him, but unable to work his fingers properly in order to grasp her. Mariana gazed at his chest, a finger tracing slowly and gently over a jagged scar that went from his left shoulder clear down to his ribs on the opposite side.

"Does it hurt?"

He shook his head. "From long ago." A wound he'd never forget. A horrendous wound that had physically healed, but remained open and weeping on the inside.

"I mean your shoulder."

He shook his head again. "I hardly remember it with ye touching my chest."

She wrenched her hand away like she'd been burned. But Brandon somehow regained his motor skills and pulled her hand back, flattening it over his heart. "I like it when ye touch me."

Her gaze lifted, connecting with his. "I fear 'tis a pleasure we can never have."

The word *pleasure,* said in her breathy French accent made his blood run hot. Brandon loved a challenge. Reveled in a triumph. "Never say never, lass."

Chapter Six

He was going to kiss her.

Mariana was sure of it, wetted her lips in anticipation, even tilted her chin. 'Twould be completely inappropriate for him to do so, the entire camp laying witness to such a display, but for some reason, she didn't care. She desperately wanted him to. Her fingers burned where she splayed them on his chest, the crisp hair tickling her fingertips and the muscles beneath sending frissons of longing deep into her center. Her nipples hardened, and she thanked God for the thick set of cloaks covering her.

Mon dieu, what on earth was happening?

These illicit feelings were not something she was allowed to have. And if she did, they were supposed to be for the man whose company she was ordered to keep—not a Highland laird who took her breath away and made her shiver all with a glance from his clear blue eyes.

However, knowing all of that, it didn't matter. Brandon was so close the heat of him washed over her, making her skin prickle. She stepped closer, decreasing the gap between them.

Her fingers itched to tug him closer. Brandon lowered his head inch by torturous inch. His breath fanned warm over her face, the spicy scent of whisky and desire with it. Mariana sucked in her breath, closing her eyes, every inch of her on fire, waiting, reaching out for his lips to touch hers.

"We ride!" Wallace bellowed the order, breaking the sensual spell.

Mariana jumped, as much from being startled as from what she was about to do. Brandon, too, looked disturbed. His eyes were narrowed, mouth in a firm line. Well, could she blame the man?

He hardly knew her at all and yet they'd been about to kiss right out in the open, it was all but branding her his—and oh, how she wanted to be branded.

"Best get that shirt on," she mumbled. Mariana bent to pick up the fabric she'd absently dropped when her thoughts, mind, had been abducted by Brandon's powerful aura.

The laird bent at the same time, and their heads clunked together. Not hard, but enough to unsettle her balance and Mariana went tumbling backward. In his haste to grasp her, Brandon put his weight on his injured arm and he, too, fell forward—on top of her. His weight—a heavenly burden—pressed her into the ground. The rock hard length of his shaft pressed against her thigh. Mariana moaned and Brandon grunted.

"Get off me," she said through her teeth. Well, if a kiss was going to brand her, what in blazes would everyone think of him lying on top of her?

"Sinclair, I hardly think now is the time to bed down with the lass, do ye?" Wallace's jovial barb set Mariana's face to burning hotter than the flames at Kinterloch.

Brandon grumbled something under his breath, which she suspected was an expletive used to describe Wallace's keen sense of humor. She swallowed hard, forced herself not to cover her heated face with her palms, and willed her cheeks to cease their flaming. There was nothing she should be embarrassed about. They'd tripped. Nothing more. Nothing less.

Except it was so much more.

As if to prove that point, Brandon winked at her. She bit her lip, not allowing herself to smile at him, or drag him down for the kiss she'd so wanted him to bestow on her.

Oh, for saint's sake, why couldn't she get the thought of kissing him from her mind?

Because he stirs things inside me I'd long thought dormant.

Using the strength in his uninjured arm, Brandon pushed himself up, followed by a very graceful leap to his feet. Mariana didn't know what made her hotter, his body pressed full force onto hers, or the delicious display of his power. She suspected it was a good mix of both.

"Lass." He held his hand out, and while she'd rather lie upon the moss and pine needle covered ground, she lifted her arm and took his grasp. His overlarge hand was warm and firm as he effortlessly pulled her to her feet.

Mariana cleared her throat and swiped at the debris clinging to the fabric of Brandon's borrowed cloak. "My thanks, *monsieur*," she said quietly. When she looked up, he was intently staring at her. She couldn't guess what he was thinking, didn't want to either, as the hunger in his eyes had yet to dissipate.

"Shall we get on with it, my lady?" His voice came out in a husky whisper, skimming deliciously along her insides.

Mariana was half tempted to ask him if he was talking about the kiss, but knew he couldn't be. Still, her gaze lingered on his lips—quirked into a seductive, roguish smile. His hair was disheveled making him look all the more wicked and appealing. A foray into the forbidden. That would be what it was like to be with Brandon. Endless, glorious, sinful splendor.

"*Oui*." Heaving a sigh, she made a move to walk around him toward his mount, but he stilled her with a tug on her hand.

"Wait, lass." Again his voice was soft, made her think of how gentle he could be, even still possessing the power to make her fall to her knees.

When she glanced back at him, he smiled and put a hand to her hair. What was he about? Surely, he wouldn't try to kiss her here.

But oh, what sweet sin it would be if he did.

Brandon pulled a large leaf from her hair and held it before her eyes, a smile curving his lips. "I know this has been a day filled with wonder, but I dinna think ye need to take souvenirs with ye."

Mariana laughed. "Indeed, my laird, I'd no intention of a keepsake." Save maybe the memory of his body pressed to hers, the heat of his chest beneath her fingertips.

Brandon seemed to read her thoughts, his eyes traveling to her mouth. 'Twould seem she was right and he was wrong—*never* was the case with them. There was no doubt in her mind, 'twas better this way. She'd not entangle herself in something she wasn't sure she could handle. Nor would she risk a broken heart. For men sought only one thing from a woman—and they'd use her to get it. A cunny was worth a lot in this world, especially hers.

With that dark thought in mind, Mariana frowned and turned away. She didn't want to look at Brandon, knowing that all the wondrous feelings she'd experienced since meeting him, could only ever be one sided.

Night was coming, and complete dark would blacken the skies within the hour. The air had cooled and puffs of it breezed through her parted lips. Within the forest, it was hard to decipher if the sky was filled with stars or clouds. The men finished packing up the camp and at least half of them were already mounted. Mariana searched for a horse with an unclaimed rider, but there seemed to be none.

"Ye'll ride with me," Brandon stated.

Mariana nodded. With little choice but to ride with him or be left behind—which she knew wouldn't truly be an option—she followed Brandon to his intimidating warhorse. The animal looked at her with wide, maniacal, black eyes that seemed to take in her very soul. Eyes that indeed earned him his name—Checkmate. If she made one wrong move, she was certain the animal would snuff the life from her with one hoof. A most welcome fact for Brandon in battle, that his horse could be used for defense, but with her…it was only frightening.

Mariana suppressed a shiver. Propping his foot in the stirrup, Brandon hoisted himself into the saddle—showing off a wicked display of male muscle—then held out his hand for her. She gritted her teeth, anticipating the spark that jolted her when their skin touched. He lifted her up, but rather than settling her in his lap, he swung her behind so she straddled his back. He tucked a plaid blanket behind his saddle for a cushion, but she wished he'd put it between them. If anything, the heat of his body between her thighs was more of a torment than before.

Taking a moment to shift about the cloaks she wore, she also sucked in a few calming breaths, hoping to ease her heightened awareness of the fierce Highlander who'd rescued her.

The ride to Eilean Donan Castle was proving more treacherous than she'd ever foreseen. And it wasn't because they were in constant danger from Ross and his crew. Indeed, 'twas her own soul that was under attack, and from one very charming warrior.

A yawn caught her unawares, and she tried to stifle it, but even still, her breath puffed out as did a little noise.

"I promise ye, as soon as we arrive at the castle, I'll personally see to it that ye're given a bedchamber, a bath, and whatever else ye desire to keep ye rested." Brandon spoke the words over his shoulder, and she was touched by his concern.

"There will be no need to pamper me, Laird Sinclair." As much as his concern moved her, she had to put some distance between them. Had to concentrate on how she would get away from these warriors and return to the man she'd been pledged to—King Edward. The thought was thoroughly abhorrent, but what else could she do? She'd been disgraced in France, and had prayed that when the king tired of her, he'd make her a match that was at least somewhat agreeable. But beyond that, she couldn't stay with these people. Couldn't witness the slaying of more innocents, for surely Ross and the king would come after her.

But wasn't it true that they were coming after Wallace and his comrades anyway? Indeed it was. Precisely why she had to return—to mislead them. She'd give them false direction. There was no consequence in that. The king and Ross had been on Wallace's trail for so long, constantly being evaded, so they wouldn't second guess her. At least, she prayed they wouldn't.

The rest of the group mounted up, Julianna and Ronan seemed particularly close. Julianna appeared weak, yet relieved, but Ronan looked as though he'd seen a ghost. Mayhap she'd had a close call during the battle. There had been no signs of her at camp when Mariana returned from hiding in the woods.

Brandon issued a command to his horse, his thighs squeezed around the animal's middle—his buttocks tightening between her legs. *Mon dieu*, how was she going to survive such sweet torture? Checkmate followed his master's command, following the line of warriors as they made their way out of the camp. Mariana grasped the blanket beneath her with both hands. She dared not put her arms around him, even though she'd moved to clutch him several times already. Riding behind him without holding on was a tricky business. But one she'd best get used too. Touching him was too dangerous. Made her feel things she shouldn't. She wanted more than anything to wrap her arms around his waist, and breathe in his woodsy male scent. That, however, wouldn't do. Already, she tread on a thin line.

She gasped again and stopped herself from grabbing onto Brandon's back. Her thighs were tightly clamped to the horse's middle, and she could tell by the way he stomped his feet and made irritating snorts that the animal was annoyed with her and Brandon's differing commands.

"I know for propriety's sake, ye may be trying hard not to put your hands on me, or maybe ye simply find me repulsive, but for the love of all that's holy, grab hold, lass, else Checkmate tosses us both." Brandon's tone was filled with humor.

If the situation had been different, and Mariana in a humorous mood, she may have teased him back, but the simple fact was, she was ready to toss herself from the horse into the nearest loch. They'd only been riding nigh on a quarter hour and her body was steaming hot. There wasn't a sensible thought in her head, and every nerve ending bristled. Had she caught a fever? Because surely, Brandon couldn't be the only reason her body was reacting this way. Men didn't have this effect on her. She had this effect *on them*. It must be a fever. There was no other reasonable answer for how she was feeling. She was completely at a loss as to how to react. She knew the consequences of becoming embroiled with Brandon. Knew them to the core of her being. And yet, she was willing to risk much in order to have just one taste.

One delicious memory forever engrained in the recesses of her mind. A recollection she could pull out whenever another man touched her. A fantasy to dream about when she lay awake at night wondering what might have been.

An herbal tisane. That was what she needed. Something to soothe her nerves and calm her feverish state.

Groaning in frustration, she slowly touched her fingertips to his waist, ignoring the spark that shot up her arms to tingle in her breasts. Never had a man spurred such a reaction from her.

"Ye'll have to hold on tighter than that. I fear ye'll fall with the slightest breeze."

A shift in the wind caused cool air to whip over her cheeks and stir her hair. But she didn't wobble.

"Well, if not the wind, then a faster pace," Brandon conceded. He gripped her right hand and tugged it around his middle, placing it palm-flat on his rock hard middle. Ridges of sinew met her fingertips and she bit the inside of her cheek to keep from making an appreciative noise. Most of the men she'd been made to entertain were soft about the middle, not gloriously built of muscle. He pulled her left hand about him, forcing her to pin her chest to his back, her already pebbled nipples scraping against yet more muscle.

Dear Lord, this was going to be a most sensually painful trip.

"There ye have it, lass. Better?"

"*Oui, monsieur.*"

'Twas much improved—if she wanted to melt into a trembling mass of desire. Immeasurably better if she wanted to make a fool of herself by appearing upon the steps of Eilean Donan thoroughly flushed and ready to strip herself bare just so she could beg Brandon to put an end to her quivering center. As if to torment her all the more, his buttocks flexed again as he urged the horse into a faster gait, but this time, with her pressed even closer, she felt the movement of his rock solid form down *there.*

A whimper escaped her lips.

"Are ye all right, lass?"

Mariana coughed. "Mmm-hmm." Riding a horse had never been so sensual, and she was afraid she'd never be able to ride one again without her body bursting into flames.

Brandon gritted his teeth—an action repeated so often since first laying eyes on Mariana, that his jaw muscles grew sore.

The lass was plastered to his back, and no amount of layers kept him from feeling her breasts, pressed hotly on either side of his spine. He stiffened his back, urged Checkmate to go faster, but it didn't help. If anything, he felt the plush globes more keenly. The more he tried to pretend she wasn't riding with him, her legs spread wide around his body, the more he was conscious of her.

Mariana cleared her throat, the action vibrating her chest. Brandon suppressed another groan.

"How long until we reach Eilean Donan?" Her voice was tight, as though she suffered and could not wait out the hours.

His thoughts exactly.

"Not long. Within the next two hours."

"Why then, did we stop to camp?"

"It was nearing dark, and many were tired."

Thinking back on it, they should have ridden the entire way, exhaustion be damned. If they had, the attack would never have taken place, because they would have been safe behind the walls of the island castle. Archers could have taken out the Ross warriors one by one as they crossed the bridge in hopes of gaining access to the heavily fortified castle.

"I see. Is the ride dangerous…in the dark?"

"Aye, lass, but ye will be safe. Rest."

Mariana seemed to take his command to heart, no longer speaking, her cheek pressed against his back. The wind was harsh, whipping in gusts, and he suspected she was glad to have him as a shield. Thunder cracked overhead. Rain. The last thing they needed. 'Twould slow them down, but not make them stop. Even if the rain turned to snow, Wallace would push them. And with good reason.

A cold drop splashed onto his forehead. Brandon reached behind to pull his cloak over his head, but found nothing save the lasses hair.

Damn. He'd forgotten that he'd give her his cloak.

"Cover your head, lass. Appears we will have a storm."

She shifted behind him, one of her arms pulling free from his middle, then returning as she did his bidding.

"What about you, Brandon?"

Lord, he loved hearing his name on her lips.

"I will be fine." And he would. If anything, getting soaked by freezing rain gave him the opportunity to warm himself when they arrived at the castle, and what better way to be warmed than by a woman?

Och, aye, he wanted that lass to be Mariana, but he knew better than to pull her between his sheets. He still had yet to figure out who she was and what her purpose in Scotland might be. 'Twas far wiser to bed down with one of the willing castle wenches. They seemed to have grown in number since the men had inhabited the castle. How sorely disappointed the lasses would be when they shifted camp in the next two weeks and were forced to return to their homes.

He'd found a few of them appealing before tonight, been as satisfied as a man could be with a woman he used strictly for pleasure. Though, every time he rutted with a woman it left him feeling less than whole, but he suspected that had to do with his own tortuous past, not with the woman.

If he were to bed down with Mariana—which he wouldn't—he'd hate to walk away feeling empty. That scared him more than the possibility of being stabbed in the back by a hidden blade. But the thing of it was, when he'd nearly kissed her…when he'd fallen on top of her…there'd been an extreme, intense need. A desire so potent he'd forgotten where he was, who he was, only the yearning to claim her had been present.

'Haps that was most dangerous of all.

Chapter Seven

Darkness consumed them as they descended the mountain through the trees. Mariana was impressed with the skill and silence with which the warriors and their mounts crept through the darkened woods. Clouds covered most of the light the moon and stars would have provided, and cold rain drenched them with no signs of ceasing.

Her fingers had long since gone numb, even with the heat of Brandon's abdomen to warm her. They'd gone from cold to painfully icy and finally no feeling at all. She kept her eyes closed, dreaming of the nice hot bath Brandon promised. Rain slid over her head, freezing onto her eye lashes. She feared opening them, but they functioned just fine.

"Not much longer, lass," Brandon said. His voice was gruff, tired sounding.

He had to be freezing, though he didn't shiver. They shared heat through his back, but without a cloak to cover him from the elements he'd surely catch his death. He refused to let her give him back his cloak earlier, swore it wasn't because she'd damaged it. Perhaps now, she could offer it another way.

Taking a moment to unclasp the loophole at her throat, she yanked open the cloak and wrapped her arms around him.

"I know you won't take the cloak for yourself, but at least let us share it."

Brandon grunted, but did not refuse. He took hold of the cloak so she could slide her arms back around his waist. Within minutes, her fingers started to tingle back to life, and Brandon's rigid body began to relax.

"I would never have asked," he said.

"I know, which is why I took the matter into my own hands."

"A warrior can handle a harsh rain." His tone had taken on a hard edge.

Mariana had no cause to wound his pride. She smiled against his back and used the wit and charm she'd been known for at court.

"Indeed, you are quite right, Laird Sinclair. Not only have you mastered a tempestuous storm, but you did so with a lady strapped to your back. Most men would regard you as some type of hero."

Brandon chuckled. "Master of the elements."

"Has a nice ring to it."

"Aye, a verra nice ring."

"What will happen when we arrive at the castle?"

Brandon's warm arm pressed against hers and for a moment as he adjusted his hold on the cloak, his hand brushed hers sending fiery tingles up her arm.

"A room will be prepared for ye, along with a bath and a platter of food."

"And wine?"

"If ye so desire."

"I do." She paused a moment, biting her lip. Would he take a respite then once again be on his way? Her mind begged the question of whether she'd see him again. He was after all a warrior—and a laird far from his own home. Would he leave her in the care of Scotland's future king and fare-thee-well? "Shall you be joining me?"

Brandon tensed a moment, before he chuckled. "I hardly think the Bruce would allow me to bathe with a noble born lady—might ruin my reputation."

Mariana chuckled. "Your reputation? Is it so sterling?"

"Och, aye, ye have no idea how pristine."

"Somehow I think you find yourself rather amusing."

"The question is, do ye find me amusing?" His voice went low, deep and sensual.

Oh, indeed she did find him amusing. Arousing. Tempting. But she couldn't very well tell him all those things.

"Perhaps," she said.

When he laughed, the soft rumble in his chest vibrated against her cheek. Mariana squeezed her eyes shut, savoring the moment, for once she felt safe, despite traveling through treacherous territory in the dead of night. The sense of calm that filled her since meeting Brandon was shocking, and wonderful, but it instilled in her a fear she didn't care to explore.

"Look there, Mariana." The way he said her name sent a chill of longing up her spine. Pulling her head from against his back, she looked on. "Ye see the torches through the trees?"

"*Oui.*"

Light twinkled all over, glowing in the darkness like stars falling from the skies.

"What is it?" she asked.

"'Tis the castle."

A rush of relief filled her. Soon she'd be warm and behind thick walls without the threat of Ross at their backs. "'Tis beautiful."

"Aye."

"Is your own home like this?"

"Nay, lass. Castle Girnigoe is on the east coast of Caithness, in the far north. Built on a cliff and surrounded by water on two sides. Not on an island like Eilean Donan."

"Sounds mysterious. Did you play in the water often as a child?"

"Aye." He flashed her a smile. "I still do sometimes."

Mariana laughed. "I would like to see you frolic in the sea."

"Och, a warrior never frolics."

Mariana tried to hide her smile at the images floating in her mind, but it was hard to do.

They broke through the trees, a bridge loomed ahead, and she could see that the lights from the castle reflected in the water, making it sparkle all the more. "*C'est magnifique*!"

"I dinna speak French, my lady, but I take it from your enthusiasm, ye like what ye see."

Mariana smiled, and with her best Scottish brogue whispered, "Och, aye, my laird. 'Tis verra pleasing to the eye."

Brandon let out a hearty laugh that drew the attention of several others. "Mariana, ye give me pleasure with your Scots Frenchie words."

Mariana joined his laughter, noticing with acute awareness that he'd gripped her hand, encompassing her in his massive grip.

"Know this, lass, if ye ever need anything, ye need only ask."

Did he realize what he implied with his invitation? There *was* something she needed. Wanted. Longed for. Oh, how simple it would be to request his presence in her bedchamber, sans weapons and clothes, to let her worship him the whole night through. That she now knew that the years she'd spent pleasuring other men, only led to this moment where she could choose who she pleasured and dared hope for a bit of pleasure in return. Instead, she ceased chewing her tongue and said, "I thank you. 'Tis the truth, however, that you saved me, and so I am in your debt."

"Ye will never be in my debt, Mariana. I could never in good conscience have seen ye harmed."

Was it only his conscience that drove him? Was it possible, in her desperate need for an emotional connection, she'd conjured up the attraction she'd felt simmering between them?

"Let your conscience be clear then, my laird. You owe me nothing." Why did her words have to come out sounding so bitter? They left a sour taste upon her tongue, when what she wished for was the sweet spice of his kiss. She hastened to add, "Apologies, I don't mean to sound ungrateful."

"Mariana, there is no need to apologize. I dinna blame ye for your ire, nor do I think ye're ungrateful." He squeezed her hands gently. "Ye are tired. Ye've been through hell. Let your mind rest."

Brandon's edict was easier said than done. Her mind was anything but restful. She imagined a life that was impossible. Was well aware that the two of them would never be more than they were at this very moment, no matter how much she wished otherwise. Even if they acted on their desires, in the end it could amount to nothing. She had a place and it was not at Brandon's side. Yet, all she could think of was him, and how she was going to save all of the Highlands from King Edward's wrath.

They approached the main gate before the bridge. A whistle pattern blown and returned in kind was the only signal between the men and the gatekeepers. The portcullis was drawn up and the men urged their mounts forward. The horses clopped over the bridge, an eerie sound that broke the silence of the night. The wind picked up, seeming to come from the black water's depths. This time Brandon's back did not protect her. The fierce gusts blew water into her face, whipped the cloak from her head and swirled her hair up into the air. She sank deeper against him and closed her eyes to keep the rain from pecking them out.

"We're back!" Mariana recognized the booming voice of William Wallace.

"As well ye should be," came a response from someone she didn't recognize.

She opened her eyes and peered around Brandon's back to see a large warrior passing through another gate leading into the courtyard. He clapped arms with Wallace and Ronan, pressed a kiss to Julianna's hand and then came around to Brandon.

"Who is this?" he asked, peering toward Mariana. The man was handsome, even looked a bit like Brandon.

Brandon sat taller, his spine stiffening. "Lady Mariana."

"Welcome, my lady. I trust your journey was not overly rough."

"Laird Sinclair did his best to make me comfortable."

The man sent Brandon a roguish smile. "I bet he did."

Brandon punched the man's shoulder. "Enough, Cousin. Lady Mariana, might I introduce ye to my cousin, Daniel Murray."

"A pleasure."

"Indeed the pleasure is all mine." The man pressed his lips to her knuckles and winked at her. "If the rascal offends ye, there are plenty of other more civilized men who'd be happy to—"

"Och, away with ye!" Brandon bellowed, and gave his cousin another solid punch to the arm. Daniel backed away laughing and went to rib another warrior.

Brandon turned in the saddle and eyed her warily. "Apologies, lass. My cousins and I tend to have a fondness for jesting with one another—especially if a beautiful lady is present."

He'd called her beautiful. Her face heated, and she was glad that in the torchlight, he wouldn't be able to see such a reaction. She smiled and lifted a brow.

"I found the interaction to be rather…tender." Her lips quivered with the need to laugh.

"I see ye are in good company then since ye have a tendency to tease as well."

With a tilt to her lips, she said, "The company will do."

"I hate to ask whether ye mean *for now*, or until someone better comes along."

"Oh, *monsieur*, you wound me. A lady would never explain her meaning."

Brandon's lips curved into a delicious smile. He opened his mouth to reply, but Wallace approached them, interrupting whatever he was about to say.

"Will ye stay in the rain all night?"

Brandon faced his leader. "Nay, of course not. 'Twas just telling the lady she'd have a nice bath and a hot meal."

Wallace nodded, his fierce eyes studying Mariana, making her want to sink into the mount's coat.

"Come then, we'll need to brief the Bruce." Wallace nodded toward her. "My lady."

When Wallace left, Brandon dismounted, and lifted Mariana, his strong hands sliding around her waist, sending a shiver of awareness through her. "Let us get ye warm."

How she wished he was indeed the one who'd be warming her. Disappointment threatened, but she held it at bay. It was unrealistic to think Brandon might come to her room. She was, after all, a lady, and ladies didn't entertain bachelors in their rooms, by themselves. 'Twas an odd revelation that—no one here knew what type of lady she *truly* was. If they knew the truth, they would look at her differently, treat her with disdain.

That was how many of the nobles in France and England treated her. Each of them whispering behind their jeweled fingers about how she entertained their sovereign, and wondering if she also entertained other men. Ladies gripped their husbands' arms tight when she strolled by, afraid she might ravish their men on the great hall floor. Ninnies, all of them. Not one had tried to befriend her. Not one ever sought to see into her past, her plight.

Mariana was a fallen woman. The only reason the king's servants treated her with any respect was because the threat of angering the king weighed heavily on their minds. Not because she held any true power.

The power Mariana held was her charm. She could will a man into doing her bidding—through smiles, witty conversation, the perfect dip of her shoulder, and the curve of her lips. More often than not, men thought with their cocks, allowing their fantasies to rule their decisions, rather than their minds.

Brandon's hands spread over her waist as he helped her down. For a brief moment, their bodies collided and frissons of need sparked a path from the top of her head to the tips of her toes. Had he felt it? He took a quick step back, and she liked to think the reason was because he had.

He offered her his elbow and she took it, lifting the copious amounts of fabric from their cloak. They slogged through the muddy courtyard, through the thick, iron-studded wood door and up a curved stone staircase. They entered through another door into a room filled with warriors dispatching their wet garments.

Mariana gasped, her eyes widening for only a second before she averted her gaze.

"Och, lads, ye could have waited," Brandon growled. He steered her quickly through the throng of half nude warriors and up another flight of stairs, where they entered into what appeared to be the great hall, though it was empty. "Sorry ye had to witness that."

Mariana giggled. "'Tis not anything I've not seen before." Her hand flew to her mouth, she'd not meant to say that.

Brandon swiveled his head toward her, stopped in his tracks and raised a brow. "Ye've been in a room full of naked men afore tonight?"

Now, Mariana laughed in full, her hand to her chest. "Nay, nay." Oh, how was she going to get herself out of this? "I meant naught but that I've seen a nude man before."

"Ye have?"

Her face heated, indeed her neck and chest and entire body seemed to burn. Mariana swallowed. Nodded.

"I was married once," she said, choosing to leave out what the nature of her survival was now.

"Were ye?" He studied her, as if seeing her in a new light.

Mariana nodded. "Not for long."

"What happened?"

She shrugged, not really wanting to go into much detail. "He was much older."

Brandon nodded. "Happens to a lot of lasses. An alliance?"

"*Oui.*" Sold to the highest bidder like a sheep for its wool. Too bad she'd proven to be a defected purchase—no babes ever graced her womb.

"I offer ye my condolences. How long ago?"

"A few years ago." Tears touched the back of her eyes, not for the loss of her husband who she hardly knew, but for the loss of her freedom. The loss of her hopes and dreams. She blinked and glanced down toward the floor.

Brandon cleared his throat. "Let me find the housekeeper. She can show ye to your room."

"Thank you, my laird."

"'Tis the least I can do after ye suffered at the hands of Ross."

Mariana made an attempt to tame her tresses which from her peripheral vision appeared to be shooting out at every angle like Medusa. She stopped when she realized Brandon was staring at her. Their gazes locked. His crystal blue eyes flickered with emotion she couldn't decipher in the dimness of the candle-lit room. Lips pressed together in a firm line, Brandon reached up and threaded a hand gently through her hair, tucking errant strands behind her ear. His eyes never left hers, instead, tempted her with what his actions might mean.

"You've more than made up for it," Mariana said softly. "I'm safe."

"Mmm-hmm." Brandon took a step closer, his boots nudging into hers. His heavily lidded gaze caressed her features. "For now. But ye mentioned having to return."

She nodded, every nerve tingling with anticipation of his touch. Just one taste, that was all she wanted. "I did."

"I'm not certain I can let ye leave."

Lord, his words had so many different meanings. Dare she think he meant the one she wished for?

Mariana chewed her lip, pressed her hands to her belly and asked, "What reason have I to stay?"

"A good question." Brandon touched lightly on her elbow.

Never had there been a more sensual caress. An elbow no less. Delicious tendrils of sensation flowed from the spot to every other sensitive area of her being. Mariana drew in a breath, swallowed hard, refused to move her arm in case he took it as a rejection. With unhurried ease, he slid his fingers up her arm to her shoulder. She glanced down at his hand. Strong, long fingers, a few scattered scars, clean nails. A hand she would gladly let glide over her entire being. A hand she'd hold, kiss, never let go of.

Brandon slipped two fingers below her chin and gently turned her to face him, but by the time she glanced up to meet his gaze, his lips were on hers. She scarce had time to take a breath before he stole it.

His lips were warm, soft, yet firm, and utterly wondrous. Mariana sighed into him, grasping delicately onto his shirt, so as not to show how much the touch of his lips made her weak in the knees.

The world seemed to tilt as he snaked his arms around her waist, a hand splayed wide on the small of her back. The heat of his touch seared through her many layers, as though she wore nothing at all.

Brandon didn't force his kiss upon her. It was light, decadent, a trial as he measured the width and breadth of her mouth. His essence surrounded her. She let her fingers curl into his shirt as she breathed deeply of his scent—horse, outside and a spicy, heady fragrance that was all Brandon.

His wasn't the kiss of most men—he didn't shove his tongue down her throat or lick at her lips like she was going to melt away. He applied a slight pressure before he flicked his tongue over her lower lip. One swipe and she swallowed down a moan. His tongue was hot, wet and had her squeezing her thighs together like her life depended on it.

Mariana answered the dart of his tongue with one of her own. Their tongues collided and they both paused. Where did they go from here? Neither was sure. Brandon breathed in deeply, as though he'd take all the air from her lungs, but when he exhaled she took it all in, as though they breathed as one.

Brandon's teeth grazed her lower lip, the same spot he'd tasted moments before. He licked along the crease of her parted lips before sliding his tongue in to completely possess her mouth.

Dear Lord, she'd never shared a kiss like this…never wanted it to end.

His hand, pressed to her back, tucked her in closer, her pelvis pushing hotly against his. A shock rippled through her at the feel of his rigid length fitting smoothly to the apex of her thighs as though he belonged there. How much she desired him. Their surroundings had long since dissolved. All she knew was the man holding her within his arms, laying claim to her.

"Oh, pardon me." The startled voice of an older woman made Mariana jump as though she'd been caught doing…well, exactly what she'd been doing.

Chapter Eight

Brandon cleared his throat, backing away from Mariana enough to be appropriate.

"Helen, would ye show Lady Mariana to her room? She's to be given a warm bath and a hearty meal."

Helen nodded, her face cleared of any reaction to what she'd just witnessed. "Aye, my laird. Right this way, my lady."

Mariana, head held high, followed the housekeeper through the arched doorway that led to the stairs. She didn't look back, and he didn't know whether or not he was disappointed that she didn't. What he was aware of was how his mouth still burned from her kiss. How he'd never been kissed by a lass like he'd just been kissed by Mariana. Hers was completely different. A woman who knew how to pleasure, but whose reaction was so raw and genuine as to be the first time. Had she kissed her elderly husband like that? Or was there another lover?

Brandon growled, raked a hand through his hair and looked up at the oak rafters. A few old birds' nests threatened to fall on his head, but the birds were no longer there. Had flown somewhere else for the winter, though they'd be back soon. He needed to head back to his Girnigoe too, but he was avoiding his dwelling as though it were filled with victims of the plague. No victims there, only memories that plagued his mind. Dark memories.

Memories that pushed him to want to stay within the Bruce's camp. Aye, he wanted to serve his country and future king, no doubt. Aye, even if life at Castle Girnigoe were the stuff made of fairy tales, he'd still be here. Brandon had made it his life's mission to help the Bruce and he wasn't going to back down now. He preferred to be like a bird that flitted from place to place, making his home in one castle, only to fly away with the changing of the season.

He frowned, his hands on his hips. Maybe he was a lot more like a bird than he thought. Hell, he was here wasn't he? Flew the coup the moment the opportunity arose.

"What are ye brooding about?" Ronan entered the great hall, his boisterous voice a welcome interruption.

"Birds."

"They're all gone."

"Aye."

Ronan glanced up at the nests. "Such makes ye sad?"

Brandon shook his head. "I dinna give a damn about the bloody birds."

Ronan raised a brow. "'Haps ye give a damn about a dram."

"Aye."

He followed his cousin back down to the cellar where the men disrobed. The room erupted into bawdy jokes, the slamming of mugs and general rowdiness. Those returning regaled any who'd stayed with stories of their mission.

"We hear ye rescued a lass!" one of the retainers called to him.

Jared, the new recruit who'd sent Mariana unattended into the woods, looked like a deer staring into the face of an arrow, and his face lit like a torch—obviously the one to have filled everyone in on that part.

"Aye, a lady," Brandon said, clearing his throat.

"Is she pretty?" one of the men asked.

"Aye."

"And round?" Angus, an older warrior, hopped to his feet, made a gesture with his hands in the silhouette of a woman and then pumped his hips forward.

"Och, ye buffoon, how the hell would I know?" Brandon hooted. "She might be as flat as this wall," he lied, pressing his groin to the wall, knowing full well the crux of her thighs had been the exact opposite of the rigid, coolness of the stone.

"That she's not, and Sinclair well knows it!" Hamish said vociferously. Why hadn't the old man found a lass to bed down with yet? He'd certainly not waited this long before.

Brandon rolled his eyes. "To the devil with ye, all of ye."

The men erupted into laughter, clinked mugs, just as someone thrust a filled mug into Brandon's hand.

He took a hearty draw of the ale mixed with whisky. "Lads, another!" His empty mug was replaced within moments.

Someone picked up the fiddle, and Angus started a jig, sloshing ale onto the floor and falling with dramatic aplomb.

An hour or so later, Brandon's head grew foggy. The whisky had dulled his senses. Momentarily made him forget about the luscious beauty who bathed above stairs. But sooner than he hoped his memory returned and with it, came visions of her delicious body soaking in steamy water. Soap bubbles floating on top, but not enough to cover what hid beneath.

Hell and damnation.

"Sinclair, what say ye?" Hamish called out.

He lifted his head, eyeing the old warrior he'd known since boyhood.

"To what?"

"Ronan says ye'll have the lass seduced within a sennight. Daniel says a fortnight. Angus says tonight."

Dammit. Why did they have to bring her up—his head was already filled with *her*.

"Never, ye sac sucking maggots."

The men laughed and another round of ale was passed.

"Then I issue ye a challenge," Ronan said. Everyone turned in his cousin's direction.

"I love a challenge," Brandon replied.

"Take one of the maids to bed tonight."

That was not a challenge he wanted to address. Ever. "I've had too much ale. Afraid the equipment's not quite up to it."

"Och, it's not the ale!" Angus shouted.

Ronan stood, a smile of glee splitting his face. "I agree. When I fell in love, no other woman but her would do."

Brandon leapt to his feet, upsetting the stool he'd lounged on. "What the devil are ye implying?"

"That ye're in love."

"Love is for fools."

"My brother Magnus said the same thing. Hell, so did I."

"That means nothing to me."

"Then take the challenge."

"Fine." Brandon puffed his chest. "Ye pick the lass. Send her up."

Ronan's smile widened. "I look forward to the results."

Brandon didn't reply. He turned on his heel and stomped from the room, grabbing a jug of whisky on his way out. *Ballocks*! What the hell was he going to do?

There wasn't a chance in hell that he would sleep or attempt to sleep with one of the maids. Aye, he'd thought about it on his way here. Was sure that was the only way to cure himself of his seeming obsession with Lady Mariana, but now that the opportunity was within reach, he couldn't—wouldn't—go through with it.

The stairs were dark, a single torch lit at the top. The winding staircase made him dizzy. Why had he drunk so much? Mariana. That was why.

He trudged up the stairs, his legs heavy, opened his chamber door and kicked it shut. Not bothering to light a candle, he slumped into the heavy wooden chair by the dark hearth. The room was cold, but he was too ill with unease to light the fire.

When the maid came through the door, he was going to have to convince her to go. Or maybe not. Maybe Ronan was right. He needed to get Mariana from his mind. A life with her was impossible—unsafe.

An image of his mother, bruised, beaten by the hand of his father came to mind. Aye, unsafe.

A night of fornication with one of the maids was all it would take to wipe her from his mind. And keep her safe.

As the maids cleaned up her bath, Mariana sat on the thick, wool carpet, brushing her hair before the roaring fire. The room was dim, with the only light coming from the fire and a single lit candle. The housekeeper presented her with an inviting guest chamber—a decent size four-poster bed with dark wood posts. There was a table with one chair, a sturdy wooden table beside the bed which held the candle and a basin of water. The armoire, however, was what bothered her most. It held a few linens inside of it, but the thing that made her most uncomfortable about the piece was the fact that she had nothing to put into it. The modest piece of furniture stood starkly empty for a guest with an unlimited stay—even if she herself knew her sojourn at Eilean Donan wouldn't be too long.

Her toes and fingers had blessedly regained feeling. The soft shift the maids produced for her was a welcome comfort. Ultra-feminine, the garment was made of expensive, silky-feeling linen. Light pink ribbons were woven in a crisscross pattern just above her navel and ending a bow at her throat.

Setting down the brush, she leaned back on her hands, stretched out her legs and wiggled her toes before the flames. Her eyes felt heavy. In fact, everything felt rather heavy, even the hair upon her head, which had thankfully mostly dried.

"My lady, will ye let us braid your hair?"

Mariana nodded, her eyes slipping closed as they threaded their fingers through her thick locks and began to weave. The maids talked in low tones to each other, their voices lulling her into near slumber. She was certain as soon as her head hit the pillow, sleep would consume her.

But something about the giddy change in tone of the maids chatter made her tilt an ear to listen.

"Laird Sinclair? Truly?"

Silence met the question, to which Mariana could only assume meant a head nod was the answer.

"Oh, my… He's so…big."

They laughed and tugged slightly harder on Mariana's hair.

"Och, indeed he is."

Mariana scrunched up her nose at the particularly naughty tone the maid used in answer. She had to bite the inside of her cheek to keep from snapping at them.

"So, tonight?"

"Aye."

"Did he say exactly when?"

Mariana couldn't believe what she was hearing. Were the maids truly speaking about a tryst with Brandon? Her throat tightened. What did she care? He was free to bed any woman he chose. It mattered not. So, why then did it make her heart flip in a painful squeeze?

"Aye, as soon as we're finished here."

A nervous laugh. "Oh, my... I wish we could both go, 'twould make the deciding so much easier."

"I know, but Ronan said only one of us was to serve the laird."

Ronan? Was he Brandon's go-between for arranging brazen liaisons? The whole debacle did not sit well with her. She *should* simply ignore it. But she couldn't. The feelings she'd had for him, the spark of interest, none of it meant anything if he was willing to allow another into his bed.

"For the *entire* night."

"Aye."

"I will do the whole of your chores tomorrow if ye let it be me."

"Well, I've been wanting in his bed since he rode over the bridge some weeks ago. Besides, ye've already had him, now 'tis my turn."

Mariana's eyes popped open, her mouth forming an O of shock, but she kept silent, hoping the maids would keep talking. Brandon was a rascal. Not wholly unlike any other unmarried man. And she was a fool.

There was a disappointed huff from the maid who was going to miss out this time around. "I suppose 'twould only be fair... But I get to have him next, then."

"If he'll have ye after a taste of me."

Another gasp. "My aren't ye just—"

"Shh!" interrupted the other maid.

Much to Mariana's disappointment the maids stopped talking about Brandon. They finished two braids, and then twisted them into a long rope down her back. The crackle of the fire no longer soothed her, given the way her mind whirled with the unabashed conversation. She kept conjuring up visions of Brandon with two women draped over him, under him, pressing him between them. What little she'd eaten quickly soured in her stomach.

"A pink ribbon to match your shift, my lady." The maid placed the thick, braided twist over her shoulder to show her the matching pink. "Pardon my saying so, but ye are so verra pretty, and any man who could see ye right now would be on their knees begging for your hand."

Mariana pursed her lips. She didn't want just *any* man bending down on his knee for her. There was only one—and these two tramps were fighting over who was going to traipse through his door and into his bed. A place she most certainly wanted to be. She wanted to scratch their eyes out for simply thinking about it.

"Thank you for the compliment." Mariana stood, turned around and faced the two maids. Chin high, she looked one in the eye and then the other.

It was time to take control of this situation. This was her only chance to savor a memory, to spend the night in the arms of a man she could pretend had feelings for her—feelings she herself was beginning to become painfully aware of.

Afterward, she would make her escape from this place. From him. From a broken heart. She told herself it was to keep innocent people safe, but that was only a small part of it. Mariana wanted to keep herself safe too—safe from the feelings Brandon pulled forth.

"You will not be visiting Laird Sinclair this evening," Mariana managed to say with authority, although her hands shook. She placed them on her hips to keep their tremble from showing.

Both maids looked at her with question, their brows knitted together, lips pursed.

"Let me be more clear." Mariana walked to where her purse had been set down. She'd been lucky to keep it tied around her waist beneath her gown, else she'd be penniless. She took out two silver coins and pressed one into each of their palms. "You will be quiet about this. You will tell Ronan one of you visited if he asks. But tonight, Laird Sinclair is mine."

Chapter Nine

The pounding staccato bouncing off the darkened stone walls of the corridor was heard by none other than Mariana. It was in her ears, all around her, consuming her. Her heart beat so fast, booming within her, she was sure it was going to burst right through her ribs and bounce on the floor, mocking her.

But despite that, she didn't still her pace, didn't run back to her room. She kept going toward what she deemed to be the right place. The right decision.

Brandon's chamber was on the level beneath hers. Or so she prayed. The maids had pouted when giving her directions and then with another coin, did as she bid and stayed in her chamber in case anyone happened by. She'd given them strict instructions to tell whomever it was that she was sick and could not be disturbed.

Mariana paused outside the door, barely able to make out the grooves in the wood with only one torch lit several paces away. The iron handle drew her gaze. Once she stepped foot inside his chamber, there would be no turning back. No light escaped beneath the door, but that didn't mean it was completely pitch black inside. Oh, but how she found herself praying it was. She could always run out unnoticed, if the fear burning its way up her throat choked her.

"Just open it," she whispered.

Reaching out to grasp the handle, she barely brushed her fingertips on the cool metal when voices coming from the direction of the stairs, jarred her. Mariana jumped back, whirled in a circle, looking for a place to hide. An alcove near an arrow slit dipped darkly into the wall. Trying to remain silent, and with hurried steps, she leapt into the alcove, pressing herself against the wall, hoping the shadows covered her. To keep silent, she held her breath, too afraid her fearful pants would be heard by those who drew near.

The laughter grew louder. Two or maybe three guards, it was hard to decipher between the guffaws. But then there was a pause and some whispering. Were they listening outside the laird's door? Nay, they couldn't be. Was it possible? Were they all aware of Ronan's duty to find the laird a woman to bed? Were women nothing but a mere conquest? That was almost enough to make Mariana go back to her room. Almost. But not quite enough.

Suppressing a disgusted groan at herself, she waited for the men to finally saunter off, and then she waited a little longer just to be safe. Peeking around the corner, she looked up and down the corridor to make certain it was completely empty. Confident she was alone, she slid with her back against the wall all the way to Brandon's door. This time, without hesitation, she turned the handle and pushed it open.

The room was black, not even a faint orange glow of embers in the hearth. Mariana was thankful for the darkness, and quietly closed the door behind her. Darkness meant she could escape. Darkness meant he might not even be there, and this harebrained idea could be completely forgotten as she went back to her own bedchamber.

"Took ye long enough," he grumbled. The man hardly sounded like one about to be entertained by a female.

In fact, he sounded downright ornery. Mariana tried not to be taken aback. The thought had never occurred to her that Brandon might not enjoy pleasures of the flesh, with or without women. There had been a man the French king offered her to, who was thoroughly against the notion. He made her moan loudly while bouncing on the bed as he wrote letters at his desk, in order to trick anyone who listened outside the door.

Heat infused her face and she backed away, prepared to leave. If he didn't want any woman here, her own presence would only blacken any future moments they might have together.

"Well, lass, will ye stand by the door all night?" Wood scraped across the floor, followed by the sound of his booted footsteps. She felt the faint breeze of his movements and an expectant chill skated over her skin.

Brandon was growing closer. Her buttocks hit the door, and she reached back to grasp the handle, opening it just an inch before he pressed the door closed with his hand which must have lingered just above her head. They were mere inches apart. His breath fanned her cheek, smelling like ale and spice. Was he drunk? She suddenly prayed he was good and in his cups.

"Ye're not going anywhere. The men think I need ye, and I've a mind to see if I do."

For a moment she thought he might know it was her, that they shared such an intense bond he could sense her even though he couldn't see her. But then reality came back to slap her hard. He didn't know who she was at all. Brandon only knew that Ronan was sending in a maid to ease whatever ache the men seemed to think he had. 'Haps they thought—

"Has been too long since I had a woman." His hand pressed hotly against her hip. "And I'll never have the woman I want."

Her heart skipped a beat. He loved another. And was using her, or whoever he thought she was, to ease his heartache. Mariana knew a bit about that. Knew the pain she was experiencing now at hearing his words.

Brandon's lips skimmed along the line of her jaw. "Ye smell like lemons." His teeth grazed her lower lip, his warm whisky-laced breath mingling with her own rapid, but quiet, exhalations. "Why are ye so nervous?"

His voice had turned soft, coaxing. The moment she spoke, he would know who she was, and while he thought her someone else, anyone else, the draw of his sensual magic kept her rooted in place, unable to move as he nibbled at the column of her throat.

She shook her head again.

"Not nervous?"

Again she shook her head. His hand slid over her hip to her buttocks, gripping one cheek in his hand, massaging the muscle until she thought she was going to fall to the floor.

"What about now?" he asked.

"Nay," she whispered, hoping a lowered voice would disguise her accent. She waited for him to shout about her being an imposter, but he didn't.

In fact, he pressed his warm lips to hers. Took possession of her mouth just like he had the first time they kissed. His velvet-soft tongue swept inside to melt against hers, to swirl and tease, to conquer. With one hand still above her head and the other on her behind, he swayed into her, while pulling her closer. Their pelvises collided and sparks of intense need jolted from her groin outward, down her legs to her toes, through her arms to her fingertips. The hardness of his shaft found a welcome home in the crux of her thighs. She cradled that hardness, pressed her own firing nub against him, wanting more, demanding that he continue to entice her with such intense pleasure. Her nipples were hard, achingly so, and she desperately wanted him to touch them, suckle them. The thought shocked her, but only a little, as it was not something she'd previously cared for, but Brandon brought out a side of her she'd never known existed. Made her feel things she'd never dared explore.

And for tonight, he would be hers.

A soft moan escaped her, quickly swallowed by Brandon's kiss and answering growl.

Tentatively, she touched his waist, slowly circling her palm around the small of his back. His skin warmed the soft linen of his shirt. Beneath the fabric, taut muscles bunched beneath her fingertips. She pressed against his spine, running her fingers up and down the length, massaging him.

Mariana was by no means a woman of virtue, or an innocent. More men than she cared to remember had planted themselves inside her. But the differences between those experiences and this one, were keen.

Choice.

Mariana had made the choice to come to Brandon. Chose to offer herself up to him. Wanted him. Longed for him. Desire coursed through her, filled her, made her knees weak and every inch of her skin tingle. Her heart kept doing little flutters, breath catching and stomach twisting. This was new to her. She was coming to Brandon in fresh form, new to a world where passion could be something she chose to enjoy rather than something she endured.

She eagerly kissed him back, rocked her hips in time with the sway of his. This was passion. Utterly unrestrained.

"Och, lass…" he whispered against her kiss-swollen lips. "Ye are so filled with passion. Ye remind me of…"

Brandon trailed off, kissing her with all the more vigor. Removing his hand from the door he pressed it to her other hip, massaging as he worked his fingers against her nightrail, slowly lifting the fabric, exposing her legs to the chill air. When he touched the bare skin of her thigh, her gown bunched up around her hips, Mariana sucked in a hard breath. He slid his hands over the naked expanse of her buttocks, trailing a path of kisses down her neck.

"Ye have such soft skin and your arse… Lord, lass, I want to feast off it."

He lifted her into the air, and she wrapped her legs around his waist. She felt weightless in his embrace. Circling her arms around his neck, she threaded her fingers through his hair.

Pitched in darkness, she could be herself, who she truly wanted to be—and with a man she'd grown so fond of. Brandon didn't appear to be holding anything back, and Mariana wasn't going to either. She pressed her lips to the column of his neck, trailed her tongue over his salty flesh down to the crook of his shoulder. He shuddered at her touch, a low moan in the back of his throat.

"What's your name, lass?" he asked.

She couldn't give him that. Couldn't give him a fake one either. At an impasse, she pressed her lips back to his throat, gave a little nip and then trailed her mouth up to his chin.

"Tell me," he said, pressing her back against the wall.

Passion ignited within her. Never had she been held like this. Not once had she been pressed up against a wall by a man seemingly desperate for her—or at least she could pretend he was. His shaft arched up against her sex, sending spirals of pleasure galloping throughout her body.

"I want to know who I'm touching, kissing… Whose arse is so soft and full."

Oh, Lord help her… His words were sweet sin, made her want to shout out her name, beg him to take her up against the wall like a man driven wild with his passion for her.

Of all the words she'd heard during a liaison, his were the most potent. No wonder the maids were arguing over who graced his bed. Mariana might have to jump into that fray.

"Shh..." She licked a teasing path to his ear and lightly nipped the lobe. She kept her voice low, disguising her accent. "Tonight my name is Desire."

Brandon stiffened a moment, pulled away, but in the darkness, she couldn't see his face. Panic swelled around her heart. Had he recognized her? The stillness in the room grew into a palpable tension. This was a mistake.

"I'm going to make love to ye, Desire." His voice was low, tight and throaty as though he were filled to the brim with need for her.

Mariana nodded, then realized he couldn't see her. She whispered, "Aye," using the Scottish tongue.

Brandon pulled her away from the wall and carried her through the dark. She wondered if he could see through the blackness, because he didn't run into any furniture nor trip on a rug or discarded object. He made straight for the bed, and sat her down upon it. His mattress was firm yet soft, and she sank back against it.

"Wait, lass, not yet." Brandon slid his fingers down her arms to her hands, and gently pulled her to stand. "I want to make love to ye naked."

Mariana's breath caught. He wasn't going to simply toss up her skirts and have his way with her. The image of their flesh pressed hotly together only increased her desire. Her nipples were hard aching buds and between her thighs was slick with dew. No man had ever made her feel like this. Wanted, needed, and considerate of her response. Brandon expected her to find as much pleasure in their union as he did.

Thick, coarse fingers trailed along the neckline of her gown, skimming over the ribbons, and then taking hold. Brandon tugged lightly, letting the knot slip undone.

"Ye came to me dressed so prim and proper... In your nightrail, lass. Did ye think to do that for me?"

What could she say? He was right—a maid would have arrived in the gown she'd worn that day.

"Did my cousin wrench ye from bed to come and please me?"

She shook her head, realized he couldn't see her, then whispered, "Nay."

He touched the dip in her throat. "Your heart beats fast." He slid his fingers down her chest, between her breasts, pulling at the ribbons, until he touched right above her navel. Gooseflesh followed in his wake. "Your skin is so soft." He pressed a hot kiss to her collarbone.

Mariana's breaths came quicker.

"And ye taste like heaven itself."

He slid his mouth to the center of her chest, and then traveled down between her breasts, sliding her gown open to expose her breasts and puckered nipples to the chill air. Her mouth went dry. Jumbled thoughts filled her head. Brandon's thumbs brushed over her nipples and she moaned, jumped a little.

"Mmm," he said. "I like the way ye respond to me." Again he brushed over her nipples and saints preserve her, she thrust her chest forward, wanting more.

She bit her lip to keep from begging him, feeling more and more out of control, she didn't trust herself not to speak in her French tongue.

Brandon's lips branded a path from the valley of her breasts to the undersides, feather-light in his teasing quest to drive her mad. He licked, kissed, suckled at nearly every part of her breast save the peaks that wanted him most. Mariana threaded her fingers through his hair and tugged in an effort to move him where she wanted, but he only chuckled, mocking her desire.

"Ye're an eager, lass." He gripped her hand and dragged it from his hair, down the thick muscles of his chest to the hardness beneath his plaid. "Do ye feel that? I'm eager for ye too."

His cock was long, thick, and stood as though waiting for her for an eternity. Mariana stroked a path upward, listening to his guttural moan. And that appeared to be the key, for his mouth fell over her nipple and drew it into the velvet, heated, cavern.

Mariana welcomed his touch, craved it. For the first time she would be with a man of her own choosing, and how glorious that she was truly enjoying it thus far. Her head fell back, mouth open on a moan. His cock jumped as if impatient to be inside her. She gave him a little squeeze, and Brandon growled, teething a warning over her nipple. Shivers made her skin tingly.

Brandon pushed her gown off her shoulders and with nothing to hold it up, the fabric slid to a puddle at her feet. Gooseflesh covered her, partly from the chill of his room and partly from anticipation and a little fear.

"I want to see ye," Brandon said. He skimmed his hands over her bare shoulders, breasts, her belly and hips.

"Nay," she whispered. If he lit a flint, this night would be over. "The mystery…fills me with—"

"Desire," he finished.

Mariana didn't answer, simply pulled the pin at his shoulder to free his plaid, reached for his belt, loosening it, and smiled hearing the pop of the clasp. The pleasure of undressing a Highlander had never been hers. She dropped the belt on the floor, the clunk louder than she expected. Like her nightrail, with nothing to hold it up, his plaid, fell around his feet.

"Ye're no timid, lass," he said, but his words came out sounding like a question.

Mariana wondered if he'd figured it out. Figured her out. But that was absurd, for if he knew she would be back in her room. Unless making love to her haunted his thoughts the way it did hers. There was nothing she wanted more. Nothing she wouldn't do to have him. Was it possible that he felt the same way? Was he willing to do anything to have her? It could be that they both realized this, dark, secret coupling, was the only way. Or, mayhap, just wishful thinking on her part.

She resisted the urge to shake her head nay. Brandon was a man of honor. If he'd guessed it was her, he must have discarded the notion, else she would no longer be there.

To prove just how bold she was, Mariana reached forward and clasped his length against her palm once more. His skin was satin soft, firm. He was heavy in her palm, and when she stroked upward over the tip, Brandon let out a low guttural moan, his forehead falling against hers.

"Ye do that too well for a virgin."

Mariana laughed softly, brushed her thumb over the tip.

"Ye're no virgin, are ye?"

With one hand on his shaft, and the other on his cheek, she whispered, "Nay," then ran her tongue along the shell of his ear.

"Och, I am in trouble then." His voice held a teasing glint. He ran his hand over her naked behind, massaging her buttocks. Against her, she felt his breath quicken.

She laughed again. "Mayhap."

"Ye've bewitched me," he whispered back. Both hands now stroked her behind, then one came forward on her hip, slid over her belly and down toward the thatch of hair covering her sex. "I want to bewitch ye." He slid a finger between her slick folds, finding the throbbing nub of her desire with no problem.

Mariana moaned, bit her lip to keep from crying out. Her entire body quivered with need.

"I'm afraid you already have," she murmured.

Chapter Ten

If God were to strike him dead now, Brandon would die a happy man.

In his arms he held a woman of great mystique, beauty, and passion. Mystical, because she spoke in whispers and preferred to go by Desire rather than her given name. Beauty, because her skin was so soft, her curves supple and he knew that her cheek would dimple slightly when she smile or laughed. Passion because of her response, her desire, the fevered way her tongue stroked over his and her hands clasped in his hair.

Mariana might have tried to disguise herself—but even in pitch black, with her softly spoken words and a barrel of whisky in his system, he'd always known it was her.

When she'd first entered the room, her face had been outlined by the dimly lit corridor, the shape of her jaw, cheek and nose, a torturous reminder of what he wanted so desperately and couldn't have. She'd stood there, quiet, waiting, and he'd given her an out, pretended she was one of the maids. But she'd not taken it.

'Twas wrong, utterly immoral for him to take her offer, but he couldn't help himself. He was powerless to her kiss, her touch. Brandon couldn't even blame the drink because he knew full well if she came to him like this when he was sober, he'd still lay her on the bed and cherish her from head to toe. Under the guise of being strangers in the dark, it seemed possible that they could share this moment, however fleeting it would be. He'd let her pretend to be someone else, all while he truly made love to her. Mariana, in his chamber, in his arms. He had to keep from shaking his head and pinching himself.

Was this what he'd wanted all along? When he saw her lying on the ground, covered in soot? He'd seen the beauty shine from behind the layer of grime, but he'd also perceived her passion and fierce nature within those glorious eyes when she held his gaze.

"We shall both remember tonight for days to come," he said.

Mariana shivered, her skin trembling beneath his touch. Her sex was hot, wet, and dammit if he didn't want to press her backward and sink all the way to the hilt. But he couldn't. He was serious about tonight being memorable, and though his cock was hard as stone, he wasn't going to burst now, not when there was the whole night to savor her.

Her silky palm stroked him into oblivion, his eyes rolling with pleasure.

"Stop," he said, although he could have lain back and let her do her worst for the next sixty seconds before he exploded.

Mariana pulled her hand away, and he could practically hear the questions running through her mind, the stillness speaking volumes.

"Dinna fash, lass, 'tis simply that it felt so good," he murmured in her ear, skimming his tongue along the edge of her sensitive lobe. "I nearly came undone and I want to last much longer for ye."

Mariana sighed, slid her hands up over his chest to his shoulders and then circled his neck. Her soft, warm body pressed against his, almost a shock at the difference between the two of them. His cock probed against the junction of her thighs, a mind of its own. But he couldn't pull away, the combination of heat, the tickle of her hair and the dew that wetted the tip were enough to make a man get down on his knees and beg for entry.

"Och, lass," he ground out.

Her nipples were hard, and scraped tantalizingly against his chest. He'd teased about her bewitching him, but now he feared 'twas the truth. Burying his face against her neck, he kissed her bare flesh, breathed in the scent of her clean skin. Brandon seared a path from her neck to her breasts and this time didn't tease her, but laved at her nipples in earnest. Her breaths quickened, and he swore he could hear her heartbeat pick up the pace, his own lurching into motion to match her steady cadence.

"Oh," she moaned, tilting her hips forward, his cock sliding along the slickened folds of her center.

If she kept that up, he'd lift her off her feet and bury himself inside her in mid-air. As much as it pained him, Brandon pulled his cock back, the cold air in direct opposition to the warmth he'd just been cradled in. But it helped to calm his charging libido.

Brandon replaced his length with the pads of his fingers, making sure to rub softly, teasingly over her nub. He stroked until her soft moans and gasps of pleasure were cries of bliss. He captured her mouth with his as her body quivered and pulsed against him. Mariana's response, her climax, they were almost more than a man could take.

Lifting her in the air, an arm beneath her knees and another behind her back, he carried her to the bed and placed her upon his coverlet.

"Are ye cold?" he asked.

A shifting sounded on the fabric. "Nay," she said.

When he stroked a hand up her thigh, her skin was covered in gooseflesh. His chamber was exceptionally chilly.

"Let me light a fire." *I know who ye are*, he almost added.

"Nay," she said even softer.

"Then I shall warm ye with my body."

"Aye, please," she murmured.

Brandon longed to hear her say something in French, but he knew if he broke the spell of her mystery, Mariana would leave. He didn't want that. Never wanted either of them to leave this room again.

But that was unrealistic. There was a war going on. One he'd dedicated his life to. And then there were his lands. His duties.

"Come," Mariana whispered. She reached for him, her hand sliding around his upper arm. She tugged.

Brandon could do nothing but obey, for he wanted nothing more than to be with her.

Lying down lengthwise beside her, he explored every inch of her skin with his fingers and mouth. From the curve in the arch of her foot, to the ticklish spot on her inner thigh, he cherished her, tasted her. When he slid his hand between her thighs, she was so slick and ready. *For him*. She undulated her hips, and then broke apart once more. It was enough to make him come undone. Brandon had never taken his time with a woman, never savored the moment, like he did with Mariana. Aye, he'd left them all satisfied, but never sought to them bring them to release time and again. But that's what he wanted with Mariana. To see her thoroughly spent. Wanted her to remember this night for eternity. When she lay in another man's arms, he wanted her to think of him.

And there lay the truth. If he couldn't be the one to take her night after night, he wanted to be the one she dreamed of doing so.

His. All his.

"Och, M—lass…" he trailed off, catching himself before he uttered her true name.

"I want you," she murmured.

"I canna wait."

"Don't."

He rolled onto his back pulling her atop him, her thighs straddling his hips. Lord how he wished he could see her face, how desire would make her eyes hazy and lips plump and wet. The heat of her cunny hovered near his cock, an act of torture to his aroused state.

"I want to be inside ye, Desire," he murmured.

Mariana didn't respond with words, instead she reached between them, her slim fingers wrapping around his shaft. Lifting slightly, she guided the tip of his erection to her sweet opening. Brandon ground his teeth, guttural moans on the brink of becoming shouts.

He slipped in an inch, and then she imbedded him fully by thrusting her hips downward. Both of them cried out, Brandon gripping her hips and Mariana clutching at his chest. She began to rock, transfixing Brandon wholly.

He tried to ignore the easy cadence she found, the smooth and eager rhythm that meant she knew how to meet her end. Surely a lass who'd only been married to an elderly man wouldn't be able to ride him like one accustomed to making love. Or would she?

Brandon thrust the thought aside, refusing to let a little thing like Mariana knowing how to give and receive pleasure ruin the moment. If anything, he should be more than pleased that she knew what she was doing. And then a fleeting thought had him nearly tossing her from the bed and lighting the nearest candle—what if this wasn't Mariana?

What if in his need for her, his desire to fall heavily into her arms, he'd fantasized the whole thing, and only a stranger straddled him?

The thought made him sick to his stomach, and he nearly lost his edge.

"Brandon…" she moaned, her French accent heavily lacing her call.

No fantasy, this was the real deal.

"Love," he answered back, still afraid to use her name. "Ye feel so good."

She moaned, her hands stretching over his chest to his arms. Her pace quickened, hips swiveling in a circle and then bobbing up and down. Brandon tried to keep pace but it was hard to concentrate on her pleasure when she pushed him so close to his own.

Mariana slowed down, a painful surrendering of his pleasure.

"Dinna stop, lass," he growled. "Please."

Brandon had never begged before. Not even when he'd lost his virginity to the shepherd's daughter in a pile of freshly shorn wool. This was a first for him, and it rocked him to the core. 'Twas too much, too soon. He didn't understand it. Didn't like the change taking place within him.

As if she could hear his thoughts, Mariana slowed even more, her breathing ragged. But Brandon refused to beg. In fact, he needed to take control.

Gripping her around the waist, he flipped her onto her back, without dislodging himself from her warm center.

"Ye tease me too much, lass." He skimmed his teeth along her neck.

Mariana's nails found anchor in his back, clinging to him as he plunged deep and then pulled nearly the rest of the way out.

He was relentless in his pursuit to see to her climax, and he didn't have to wait long. Lithe legs clenched tight to his hips. The image within his mind of her toes curling spurred him further. Just as she was about to find her end, he stilled.

A long, tortured sigh escaped her.

"Tell me, lass." He wanted to hear her beg, as he had moments before.

"Please," she gasped.

That was enough for him. Brandon drove deep inside her, connecting their bodies with such ferocity the bed shook and hit the stone wall in a rhythm that could only be associated with love making. He couldn't stop, not even knowing that half the castle could wake from the noise they made.

Beneath him, Mariana bucked and writhed. She called out, little mewls mixed with frenzied cries. And then she shuddered, nails raking down his back, every inch of her trembling. Her cunny clenched tight then tighter around him, fluttering in a feverish beat. He was no match for her climax.

"Och!" he groaned, letting his peak take over his senses as a pulsing pleasure captured him. He pulled out at the last second, letting his seed spill over her quivering belly.

With a corner of the sheet, Brandon wiped her clean, then pulled her into his arms. Their legs entwined, she rested her hand on his shoulder, and he absently stroked over her back.

"That was…" Words escaped him. "I've never…"

"Shh…" She swiped at the sweat at his temple and then kissed him there.

Brandon clenched his jaw. She was right; he was about to share more than he should with a woman he knew little about but had become enamored with. He'd been enamored with the shepherd's daughter as well. But this was different. That was a lad's first taste of what love was. He refused to think it was a man's taste now.

Shaking his head, Brandon stood from the bed, rifled around for his shirt and threw it on. His skin was blazing despite the cool temperature of the room. Hands on his hips, he faced the bed, fingers itching to light a flint. In the pitch black he imagined Mariana lying on the bed, a knee bent up, breasts prominently displayed with her hands behind her head as she gazed at him.

The closing of the door was his only warning that she'd left the bed—in fact left the chamber.

"Mariana?" he asked, disbelieving that she actually left.

There was no reply. No whisper of sound. How silently she'd crept to gather her nightrail before slipping out. Brandon couldn't help feeling slighted. A lass had never sneaked from his chamber before now. In fact, he was the one slipping silently from a lover's bed time and again. Was the slight pain in his gut hurt feelings? That thought was disturbing. Why should he care? He should be glad that she'd crept out without telling him. There'd be no awkward goodbye or empty promises neither of them could keep. He sat heavily on the edge of the bed where moments before he'd been locked in an erotic embrace with the most enchanting woman.

Brandon scrubbed a hand down his face, rubbed his temples. Aye, his reaction was indeed disturbing.

More disturbing was how his senses had been dulled and he'd not heard her. She'd dulled his senses, made him weak, vulnerable.

Anger surged within his chest. He hurried as quick as he could to wrap his plaid around his hips, belted it, but didn't bother with his boots. Barefoot, he rushed from the room in search of her, trying his best to remember the way to the guest quarters. Up a flight of stairs, down the hall. He stood before her door, quiet voices slipping through the wood.

Who was in her room?

Brandon didn't bother knocking. Whether it was his injured pride at her having seduced him and then slipping away without a word, or anger at how she made him feel, he didn't know. He burst into the room, surprised to see her standing with her back to him between two maids, their mouths forming surprised O's.

"My laird," Mariana gasped. Her brow wrinkled in irritation as she turned around fully to face him.

Addressing the two maids he said, "Leave," between clenched teeth.

The maids lowered their heads, curtsied and then scurried from the room, closing the door behind them.

"What the hell was that?" Brandon asked, swinging his arm behind him, hopefully in the direction of his chamber.

Mariana raised a brow at him. "I was unaware that a lady was not allowed to speak with her maids." Her tone was haughty, her stance rigid.

Brandon let out a brusque laugh. "That is nay what I'm talking about and ye well know it."

Slowly, she shook her head. "On the contrary, my laird, I've not an inkling as to what you refer."

Ah, so she would play games with him. "Mayhap this will jog your memory."

He stalked toward her, slid his fingers over the curve of her cheeks and behind her head, then kissed her senseless.

Chapter Eleven

"I knew it was ye."

Mariana nodded, the gruff tone in Brandon's voice sending a chill across her skin. Her heart raced from him barging into her room. Their heated exchange. Moments later, her lips tingled from his kiss. She could still taste him on her tongue. With them pressed so closely together, his breath mingled with hers, his heartbeat pounded just as fiercely as her own. Candlelight flickered in his eyes, showing off the blue of his irises like a prism. Every angle and cut of him was magnificent, intoxicating. She could stare into the crystal of his eyes for hours on end and never grow bored. Let him kiss her, touch her.

She'd guessed while they made love, that he knew it was her, and she had cause to hope he wouldn't come after her. As they'd laid there entwined in each other's arms, panic took hold. Lying with someone, stroking them as she had—her fingers making whirls over his chest hair—'twas too intimate. Certainly she'd pretended such intimacy before, but she'd never actually felt it. With Brandon she'd felt exposed—not physically, but emotionally. Open, and vulnerable.

Brandon had climbed from the bed and she took her opportunity to escape. To run away. She was a coward. Afraid to go down a road she had no control over. A road that would most certainly end in doom. And she prayed he wouldn't come after her.

But here he was, darkening her door just as he darkened every corner of her mind. She wondered if the maids had told anyone and everyone who would listen that Laird Sinclair stormed into Lady Mariana's room. Or would they show the shiny coins she'd paid them to allow her the pleasure of climbing into his bed?

"Why did ye leave?" Brandon's tone revealed nothing of his feelings. His eyelids were lowered as though to shield himself from her.

"I couldn't stay," she said quietly, making no effort to disengage herself from his embrace and deny it was her in his chamber. His warmth surrounded her. However unrealistic it was, she couldn't pull away. Whether he did so or not consciously, he rubbed a circle against her hip with his thumb.

"Why?"

Swallowing hard, she said, "We both know why, Brandon."

She hated how condescending she sounded, how pessimistic, but before they fell into bed once more—which it appeared they were close to doing—Mariana had to bring them back to reality. Disappointing Brandon went against everything she'd ever been taught, a complete contrast to the way she'd lived for half a decade. It left a foul taste in her mouth. But even worse than that, it went against what her heart was screaming, too.

Brandon let out an expletive under his breath and pushed away from her. Mariana took a step back, relying on every ounce of training she'd ever had to keep from reacting to him. He was in a right state. She needed to be gentle and passive so as not to incite him further. 'Twas obvious he was agitated, and she could guess why. So, while he raked a hand through his hair and paced the room, she took a moment to breathe deeply, make her face serene and fold her hands in front of her. She couldn't react based on emotion or she would be in trouble. More emotional turmoil than she could even imagine. But how was she supposed to turn off her feelings? This was new territory for her, and she didn't like it one bit. Staying away from Brandon, avoiding his kiss, touch, and penetrating gaze was the only answer. So why did it seem near impossible?

Brandon continued to pace back and forth three times, before stopping, hands resting on his narrow hips. Mariana watched him closely. Shadows and light flickered over the angles of his face, but still he refused to look at her. His face was turned to the side as though he found something deep and meaningful in the way the wall met the floor. Mariana raked her gaze hungrily over him, partly because she liked the way he looked, as well as to count his weapons. None. He'd been in such a hurry to see her that he'd not even bothered to put on his shoes.

"Who are ye really?" Brandon asked, turning back to gaze at her, his eyes narrowed.

"I am who I've said I was." She kept her tone low, even. Who she was and what she was, were two different things and she wasn't about to sully the memory of what they'd experienced with her exceedingly inglorious background. Her past was her past. He didn't need to know that she'd served as mistress to as many men as she had fingers on her hand. That the men she served, ordered her to bed down with their friends. That she'd been ill-used by many and loved by none. Mariana was a pawn, and well she knew it. But that didn't mean she wanted him to know. The shame of it heated her cheeks.

Brandon shook his head, disappointment flickering briefly over his features. "All right, ye'll not tell me all. I've not gained your trust, I understand that. But I'm not some shallow arse who'd let ye rut him and then walk out without a word. Ye have to give me more credit than that."

Mariana's eyes widened only slightly. She struggled to keep her emotions in check. Never in her wildest imaginings would she have guessed walking out would cause so much trouble. Most men were glad when she quietly slipped away. No awkward moments. No trying to explain when they'd see each other again. No need for her to pretend she'd enjoyed it—however this latter notion held no ground with Brandon. She'd thoroughly relished their lovemaking. Her gaze fell to her bed and then back to him. How very much she would enjoy making love with him again. She swallowed, hoping her voice wouldn't come out a croak.

Mariana locked eyes on Brandon. "I don't think you are shallow. And I didn't do what I did for any reason other than…" But her voice trailed off. She couldn't tell him the truth. How would she explain why she sought a moment that would forever be ingrained in her memory?

Brandon stiffened. His jaw muscles tightening to the point she could see them flex again and again. "Dinna tell me." His voice was filled with anger and he turned abruptly toward the door.

Regret made her belly twist sharply. He'd taken her silence to mean something different. She turned around, forcing herself to stare into the small fire in the hearth. This was for the better. She curled her toes into the carpet. If he left now in anger, there'd be no heartache. Like a splinter, the quicker it was torn out, the faster it healed. Brandon wasn't a splinter—but the feelings she was starting to have were like a thousand thistles embedded beneath her skin. Uncomfortable. Maddening.

The door closed, and yet she still faced the hearth. Watched the tiny orange flames lick half-heartedly at the burning embers. When her eyes started to sting from lack of blinking, she rubbed at them, half hoping to see Brandon still standing beside the closed door.

"You're a fool," she muttered to herself.

She'd wounded him in more ways than one. He wouldn't stick around for more. Wouldn't allow her to add insult to injury. Brandon had pride, she could tell that much. Even if he did harbor strong feelings for her—which she was certain he did not—his pride would have bade him to leave her standing there.

Mariana ambled to the bed. The maids had already pulled the coverlet aside for her. She slipped between the soft sheets, grateful for them. Her sheets were not always of the finest fabrics. Heated rocks were nestled at the base of the bed, warming her toes. Had they known she'd be freezing upon her return from Brandon's chamber?

One of them had admitted to bedding him before. She'd probably known firsthand how cold it was leaving the warmth of his embrace. A spark of jealousy singed her blood. To think he'd shared such intimacy with another woman. The envy of anyone who'd had the pleasure made her crazy.

So much for escaping the castle tonight. Not only was she exhausted, but Mariana felt more trapped now than ever. The walls being erected didn't necessarily trap her inside the building as they did inside her own mind.

On the morrow, she'd wake and observe the comings and goings of the people. 'Haps her two maids would be willing to make extra coin and help her get across the bridge unseen.

Mariana flopped onto her back, pressing the heels of her palms against her eyes.

Why of all the Highland warriors, did Brandon have to catch her from falling outside Kinterloch?

Before the break of dawn, Brandon gathered with William Wallace and the Bruce within their future king's chambers. Only a single candle lit the room. The shutters were closed tight and a plaid rolled against the bottom of the chamber door kept any light from filtering out. They didn't want anyone to know they met in secrecy.

"And ye know this for sure?" Wallace asked. His dark hair was mussed, clothes wrinkled, from having hastily risen from his own chamber to join them. Even still, Wallace looked every bit the Guardian of Scotland. Weapons were strapped to every available inch of his body. Fierce brows slashed his forehead and yet wrinkles creased around his eyes and mouth proved that he did in fact laugh.

The Bruce stood beside Wallace, his skin pale, having just recovered from another bout of ague. A wrap made of red squirrel fur was placed around his shoulders and despite having been ill, the man was in a robust spirit, and looked well-rested.

Brandon nodded. Damn him to hell for what he was about to do. He'd taken the time to go back to his chamber after leaving Mariana, to put on his boots and weapons, even though he'd wanted to rush back to her, grab her by the shoulders and shake some sense into her.

A dirk dug into each forearm as he flexed his hands, a reminder of all that was at stake. At home, he wore weapons only if they were under threat of attack or for training. Here, he was armed at all times. An enemy could attack at any moment—even from within.

Ballocks, his ego was bruised after the night he'd had, but he dared not think about it more than that. Mariana was nobody to him. At least that was what he was trying to convince himself. He'd been caught up in a fantasy. One that had no place in his life. She'd made that clear in her chamber when she turned her on him.

He'd given his life to the Scottish cause, and he would never allow a woman to come between that dedication and himself.

Brandon cleared his throat. "She told me herself that Ross and King Edward expected her return. That she was to report back to them all she'd seen—including who. She alluded to the fact that they would come looking for her."

"Do ye think she's a spy?" Wallace asked.

Brandon shrugged. "I canna say." But he wouldn't be surprised. 'Haps she'd hoped to gain his cooperation through intimacy and had been planning on pulling information from him when he was weakest. Not a bad move, but not one he'd fall for. And though he had his suspicions, something held him back from telling his leaders what they were.

"Though ye may not know for certain, what does your gut say?" Wallace pressed.

Normally one to act on instinct, not giving a clear answer was at odds with Brandon's usual input. Hell... His gut was telling him to keep her safe. "Nay. I dinna believe she is."

Wallace nodded, but the Bruce narrowed his eyes. "Why the sudden change of heart?"

Brandon shrugged, brushing aside the question. He pointed at the map spread upon the table. "We'll head out at first light. The journey should take us two, possibly three days at most. We're guessing that we'll meet Ross upon the road here, or at the point where Lady Mariana was to rendezvous."

"And where was that?" Wallace asked.

"That I dinna know."

"Ye want me to send the men into the wild Highlands, blind?" The Bruce spread out his arms, irritation glinting in his eyes. A subtle hint that he might not be one-hundred percent well. Another clue was the absence of Julianna who never left her brother's side and whose advice he was never short of hearing. Then again, she and Ronan may have been up late into the night.

Straightening his spine, Brandon prepared for a fight with his future king. "They are Highlanders, hardly unaccustomed to the *wild* Highlands."

The Bruce snorted. "Aye, but Ross plays dirty. And ye forget, he may be in league with the English, but he was trained as a Highlander just as ye were."

"I'm aware of that, and I dinna underestimate the strength of my men."

Wallace stepped forward. "No one is misjudging the strength of your men, Sinclair. The Bruce is merely stating his concerns."

Brandon took a deep breath, the fight gone from him. He nodded. "As he should. Apologies, my lord."

The Bruce shook his head, waved his hand. "'Tis nothing. I've a feeling this is a trap. That ye were seduced into this plot."

Brandon blew out a breath and looked up to the ceiling before speaking, afraid he'd start shouting again. "There was no seduction."

"Ye willingly believed her, then?" The Bruce winged a skeptical brow.

"Nay!" Brandon held out his arms in agitation. "I didna discuss this plan at all with the lass. She has no idea that we're going to take her."

The Bruce scowled, but Wallace leaned against a wall, a smile on his face. He liked it when he wasn't the one arguing with their future king.

"If I were to call her to this chamber right now, she would have no inkling of what we speak?" Robert asked.

"Aye. None."

"And ye did not feel the need to warn her of our plans?"

Brandon ground his teeth. "Why would I? We dinna need her permission to carry out our mission."

"Huh." The Bruce crossed his arms over his chest. "Yesterday ye weren't willing to let the lass out of your sight. Today ye are using her as bait."

Yesterday she wasn't using him. Yesterday she wasn't conniving. He'd still not figured out exactly why she'd seduced him. When he'd confronted her, she wasn't able to answer. Couldn't even finish her sentence. He wasn't going to wait around to find out why. She wanted to go back to Ross and King Edward—that much was clear—and he was going to hand deliver her.

Brandon pressed his lips together, gave each of the men a straightforward glance. "I think ye've misread my actions and intentions. The lass is nothing more than a pawn. I gained her trust in order to do what must be done to take down our enemy—Scotland's enemy."

The men stared at him, assessing him, and Brandon prayed they wouldn't see through his pretense. Truth was, he'd been duped by a beautiful woman and while he wasn't the first man to have been deceived, he certainly didn't want his leaders to see him as a fool. To see him as weak.

Swallowing back the foul taste in his mouth, he forced himself not to grimace and planted his hands on the table. The wood was cool, sturdy, beneath his palms, helping to steady him. "If ye lasses are through with your gossip, we've a mission to plan."

Wallace and the Bruce chuckled.

"I ought to have ye whipped for a comment like that," Robert said. "But instead, I'll settle for sending ye into the vipers nest with your ballocks tucked tight against your arse."

Brandon laughed then, a true laugh. "I'll drink to that." He walked over to the sideboard, poured three small cups of whisky and carried them back. As much as they had been through together, seeing each other bleed, keeping each other alive, they deserved a moment of ease.

Scotland was at war with known enemies, and those too cowardly to step from the shadows.

Lord, pray Mariana had not betrayed him regarding the war, though she'd done so with his heart.

Chapter Twelve

"My lady, time to wake."

Mariana blinked open her eyes, unaware of exactly when she'd finally fallen asleep, but fully aware that it hadn't been too long ago. Her head pounded, eyes felt heavy and dry. She blinked, tried to rub away the sting of not getting enough sleep. Every muscle protested as she stretched out her limbs.

The shutters weren't open but several candles were lit around the room. A different maid than the ones who'd served her the night before placed a linen cloth beside her wash basin.

"Open the shutters," Mariana said, her voice gravelly even to her own ears. Though she was accustomed to warmer air, she was also used to getting more sleep. Fresh cool air would help to wake her. "'Haps the sun will help motivate me to rise."

"I canna, my lady. 'Tis too cold, and still dark."

Sure enough, a glance at the closed shutters showed not a lick of light filtering through. "Why did you wake me then?"

"The Bruce's orders, my lady."

That brought her fully awake. Mayhap Brandon's words with Robert the Bruce hadn't been enough and now he wanted to speak with her personally. Mariana sat straight up in bed, a chill covering her skin in gooseflesh. Her stomach did a flip and her throat tightened.

"Why?" she asked.

The maid shrugged. "Said ye needed to be roused and dressed and ready to leave."

"Leave?" They would cast her out in the middle of the night? Was Brandon that angry with her? She'd never imagined he'd be so cruel, even with a bruised ego. King Edward had oft lamented that the Scots were barbarians and the Highlanders the worst of them all, but she'd never thought of Brandon that way, nor any of those she'd met thus far.

Would he prove to her that they were indeed heathens?

Well, she wouldn't give him the satisfaction of seeing her bothered by it. She'd leave this place with her head held high and never look back. Those moments of bliss within his bedchamber were bittersweet memories now. A portrait of a man that didn't exist.

"Aye, my lady. I can have a fruit pastry sent up from Cook. There's enough sugar in one to keep ye awake for nigh on three days."

"Nay, I don't like fruit tarts." That was a lie, but with the way her stomach was clenching so tight any food was surely to retreat the way it came. She pulled herself, regrettably, from the warmth of the bed, her toes stinging against the cold planks of the floor. "Hurry up, then," Mariana snapped, feeling instantly bad for taking her irritation out on the girl. "I'll be glad to leave this place," she muttered.

"Och, we're not so bad." The maid lifted Mariana's feet, slipping warm, soft wool hose over her toes, halfway up her thigh where she tied them with a ribbon.

Mariana kept her mouth closed, held out her arms and allowed the maid to dress her in her own gown, which someone had attempted to clean and repair. Darker smudges could still be seen within the green where soot and dirt had made its home, and lines of tightly knit threads dotted the once jagged tears. Not the best of work, but it would do, and she was grateful not to have to wear it in the condition it had been in before.

"Who repaired my gown?" she asked. "I wish to thank them."

The maid smoothed out the wrinkles with her hands and then placed Mariana's silver looped belt around her hips—a gift from her mother on the day of her fifteenth summer. An apology or a bribe, no doubt. Where it hooked was a shiny onyx stone. Not the most feminine of gifts, but one she cherished all the same—not for what it represented, but because it was the only piece she had left of home. She fitted the small eating knife within its sheath into one of the loops.

"Cook, my lady."

"Cook is also a seamstress?"

"And a surgeon when need be. This is a war camp after all. We all have many duties."

The maid's voice was matter of fact, not condescending, but instructing all the same. Mariana wondered what other duties were this maid's—and thought prior to her stint here she might have been in charge of children somewhere, perhaps even her own.

Mariana nodded, not realizing until that moment that not only did the warriors suffer the ravages of this war, but everyone else as well. She'd been so buried in courtly intrigue and her own misery, that she hardly noticed those around her suffering.

"What is your name?" she asked.

"Jean, my lady." Jean glanced up at her, an odd expression on her face.

Mariana wondered if anyone had bothered to ask before. Stepping away from Jean, she reached under her pillow and pulled out her coin pouch.

"Please," she said, pulling out two silver coins. "Take these."

Jean shook her head. "Nay, my lady, I couldna."

"Please, you must. For your suffering."

Jean frowned, her wary gaze meeting Mariana's. "I've not suffered overmuch. I have work here, and I'm safe behind the walls. If I may, my lady, please dinna assume that because the English have tried to ravage us that they have already won."

Mariana absorbed Jean's words, wishing she could somehow rid the country of its unwanted guests. "These coins were given to me by the English king. Consider it a just reward for his intrusion. Keep it in case the day comes, God forbid it, that you are no longer safe here." Mariana thrust the coins into Jean's hands. "Go now. I will walk myself down to the great hall." She turned away from the maid, unable to look at her. Unintentionally, she'd offended this woman. But what was worse, by being rescued by Brandon, Mariana had almost certainly led the English here, for they most assuredly followed at a distance.

Jean thought herself safe because she was behind closed walls, but the woman had no idea the extent to which Laird Ross and King Edward would go to see that their will was done. Mariana was a prime example, left behind for the sole purpose of leading them to Wallace and the Bruce. If she'd believed in their cause, if she'd had a cruel heart, she'd not be standing here, willingly leaving. Truth was, Mariana didn't have a cruel bone in her body. Somehow, despite what she'd been through, she maintained a warm heart.

Tears welled in her eyes. In the privacy of her chamber she let them drip down her cheeks, weaving warm tracks on her cool skin. Her dreams as a child had never foreseen a life such as this. *Mais oui,* she had clean, beautiful clothes, food to eat and coins to spare, alas, she had no true pleasure save the moments she stole for herself.

Pressing her hands to her belly, she blinked up at the ceiling, let out a long shuddering breath. "Why?" she asked no one.

There would be no answer. There never was. In the past she took comfort in the knowledge that this must be the path God chose for her. Now, that comfort ebbed with each passing day. If she were to find her own happiness, wouldn't that be something God wished for her, too? Perhaps she could when other people's lives weren't dependent on her choices.

Cloak in hand, Mariana took one last look around the room. She pulled her dagger from beneath her pillow, and attached it to her thigh. Her coin purse jangled against her hip, beneath her gown. Nothing left of her here. She blew out the candles, the smoke curling up in white tendrils before dissipating into the air. Much like she would do. Here for a moment, gone the next. Darkness surrounded her. She felt her way along the floor with each step, until she pressed her hand to the doorknob.

It was time to go. Time to leave Eilean Donan, Robert the Bruce's camp—Brandon—and whatever hopes she'd had with it.

Mariana stepped into the hallway, lit only by a few torches spaced a dozen feet apart. The corridor was empty of people but full of shadows. From the distance she heard a dog barking, another howling. But there were no other sounds. How early in the morning was it?

She flung her cloak around her shoulders and rushed to the stairs, her gown swishing around her ankles the only sound. As she reached the last stair, she took a moment to rearrange her expression to one of serenity, hoping she revealed nothing to the men who would see her die. For that was what they were doing by tossing her into the night in a place teeming with enemies. Guaranteeing her demise. At least she had a dagger strapped above her knee should she have need to use it.

Unwilling to stand in the dark silence another moment, she entered the great hall, surprised to see only Brandon. A small fire crackled in the enormous hearth. No servants slept curled beneath woolen blankets, perhaps finding a place to bed down elsewhere, or already having woken. A single candelabra sat upon the long trestle table, every candle lit.

Brandon stood on the opposite side of the room, staring out one of the arrow-slitted windows. He was fully clothed once more, boots, weapons and all. Her breath held seeing him there, and her heart broke all the more.

He barely looked at her, a simple glance acknowledging her presence, as though she were less than nothing to him. Guilt or shame? She'd seen both on men's faces more times than she could count, but with Brandon it was different. This time it was entirely directed at her, not a himself or a wife he'd left cold in bed.

Clearing her throat, she straightened her shoulders, lifted her chin, prepared to get this ordeal over with. The sooner she was away from here the better. "Will you at least give me a horse?" she asked.

Brandon's head shot up, brows knitted together. His gaze raked over her, giving away for a minute that at least his attraction to her was real, before he too looked serene.

"Ye will have a mount."

Mariana tried not to wince. Just like that—a mount to ride out on. Although she kept a straight face on the outside, inwardly she felt as though she was being ripped apart. How different this man was than the one she'd kissed and let inside her body.

"Would it be too much to ask for a skin of water and perhaps an oatcake or two?"

"It would not." His tone was clipped, cold.

Mariana chewed her lip, unsure if that actually meant that he was going to provide the requested provisions. He could only mean that it wasn't too much to ask, even if he would deny her the luxury of food and water. Bitterness threatened to pull her down into its sour depths, but reason battled on. The man had been so kind to her before now. Even charmed her into believing he felt something for her beyond the contempt he exhibited now. Was there any piece of that man left, or had it all been a charade?

The room grew thick with uncomfortable tension. She could no longer allow herself to be there. A woman could only take so much before she broke down. Mariana was not going to lose control in front of Brandon. She mourned her losses privately.

"*Très bien*. I shall be on my way. *Au revoir*." She spoke quickly, without pause.

She didn't wait for his response, but turned on her heel, intent on making it through the castle the way she'd come, hopefully finding the mount assigned to her outside in the courtyard. Barely through the door, his voice stalled her.

"My lady."

He'd not moved, or at least not much, judging from the distance of his voice. Even still, a shiver caressed her skin as though he stood behind her. Touching her. Mariana squeezed her eyes shut against the invading memoires of the night before. His sensual whisper against her neck. His fingers gliding up her thigh. His hips pressed to hers. "Don't turn around. Don't turn around," she chanted in a whisper to herself. "Keep moving forward." The way she always did—without turning back.

Her wayward feet did not obey her command. They remained rooted to the floor. If she'd not just stepped into the spot she'd have thought one of the maids played a trick on her, nailing her shoes to the floorboards.

"My lady, ye will not have to travel alone."

Brandon was closer now, mayhap four or five feet away. Her body tensed, at war with itself on how to react—desire, fear, anger?

"Will you send an assassin with me?" she asked, keeping her spine stiff and voice stiffer.

"What?" Confusion filled Brandon's voice, but she refused to take it for what it was.

He'd tricked her before, leading her to believe that he cared for her, that the memories she took would be sweet and not tainted with the vile fact that he'd used her.

"Don't play games with me, my laird. I know what your plan is."

As silently as he'd moved before, he was suddenly behind her. His voice like icy steel, cut against her ear. "What do ye know of my plans?"

He was angry. She could practically feel his ire radiating from his body. The heat of him seeped against her back, spreading all the way around her, but still left her cold. Mariana had been in many situations with an angry man. King Edward was one of the angriest. He'd killed a servant at dinner one night when he didn't like the way his wine was poured. He'd said it was because the wine was poisoned, but she'd seen the king berate the poor man the day before on his pouring skills.

But being with a murderer, as terrifying as it was, was nothing like having Brandon's anger sliding over her.

Mariana knew people. Could read them. But with Brandon, she wasn't an outsider deciphering a person's intent and emotions, she was involved and her own feelings were getting in the way of figuring out Brandon's.

"I know you intend for me to leave under the cover of darkness."

"Aye. What else?"

"That you would send me into the wild without a moment's hesitation." She took a deep breath. "To die."

Brandon grunted. "Is that what ye think?"

She nodded. Her mouth was suddenly dry, and she felt light-headed.

Silence greeted her for so long she nearly turned around. If not for his chest pressed to her back, she'd have thought he disappeared. What was he thinking? What would he do? Was she right? Or had she gotten it terribly wrong?

"I'd no idea I left that kind of impression on ye." Brandon's voice was too low for her to sense whether he was angry or not.

"'Tis not an impression, my laird, simply a fact."

Again he grunted. Mariana desperately wanted to turn around, to look into his eyes. To ask him why he'd made her feel so special, only to toss her away like a used rag. But she wouldn't. She had to remain strong, for her own sanity. She had to keep moving forward.

"If you will excuse me, I'm going to find my mount."

Strong fingers gripped her shoulders sending spirals of unwanted, yet alluring, sensation coursing within her.

"I will not excuse ye."

Now it was her turn to be confused. "What?"

"Ye accuse me of being cruel. Of attempting to murder a noble born lady. I will nay allow ye to leave this castle with those foul assumptions. Ye can think anything else of me, but ye will nay strip me of my honor."

Mariana gasped at the vehemence in his voice. His hands held her in place, and good thing, because if she turned around she was bound to melt against him in apology, then slap him for his cruelty.

"I would never try to strip you of your honor, my laird."

"And yet ye have."

She shook her head. "I could not. Never."

"And yet, *ye have*."

Mariana took a step forward, a little surprised when he didn't hold her in place. She used her passive voice, the tone saved for all angry men, and one that helped her shut down, to distance herself from the situation. "Apologies, that was not my intention. I'm not sure what I was thinking."

"Och, dinna take that tone with me, Mariana. I'm not some overlord bent on seeing ye cowed." Air brushed her back as he stepped toward her once more. Sliding his hands over her hips, he pulled her back hard against him. "I made love to ye last night. Let ye play your game, called ye Desire. But the moment ye walked out, I knew that I was the fool. I dinna know what your purpose was in coming here, but I will not be led afoul again."

Mariana's breath caught, his words barely scratching the surface of her fazed mind. Mariana shook her head again, and this time did turn around. Not so she could look into his eyes, but so he could see inside hers. "I would never play you for a fool. I'm not that kind of woman. I know we haven't known each other long, and you have no cause to trust in what I say, but I pray you believe me when I tell you last night was one of the happiest moments of my life. A night I was going to cherish, until you stormed into my chamber and yanked it all away."

Brandon's face was unreadable. His lips in a firm line, his eyes locked on hers. She searched his gaze, wanting some reaction, but he'd not give her any, as though he'd erected a sturdy wall around himself, no longer allowing her to see inside his heart. Lying to him, omitting the truth of who she was…seemed wrong. He had to know the truth, but she didn't want to hurt him either.

She swallowed hard, and the words that blurted from her mouth were furthest from what she'd ever wanted to reveal, "I'm the English king's mistress."

Brandon looked stricken as he searched her gaze. He stumbled back a step, mouth slightly open in surprise. Tension, thick as mountain ice, surrounded them. Mariana's knees grew weak and her stomach leapt into her throat. She wanted to pull her words back, wanted to erase this moment from both of their minds. She wanted to say something, anything to wipe the look of torment from his face. Willing her knees to be still, she pressed them together. Forced her belly to its natural place, and opened her mouth to speak.

But before she had a chance, Brandon spoke, his voice gruff. "Then it would seem Fate has dealt us both a coarse hand."

Chapter Thirteen

Brandon's heart pounded a staccato beat rivaling that of a hundred warhorses drumming a path upon the battlefield.

The English king's mistress? Though he was certain he'd not heard wrong, Brandon wished he had. Longshanks had laid a path between her thighs before himself? He'd never given thought to the previous lovers of women he bedded, but Mariana was different. She wasn't simply a woman he'd lain with. Their coupling had not been about gaining pleasure, but a mutual give and receive. A transferring of something deeper within their souls. The fact that his enemy had been inside her body, kissed her skin, smelled her essence, disturbed him immensely.

He loathed King Edward with a passion that threatened to overwhelm him. Inside, rage clashed with jealousy. If the man stood before him now, there was nothing that would stop Brandon from running him through with his sword. Slitting his throat from ear to ear. Burning his insides as the man still breathed, then scattering his body in pieces from the north, south, east and west.

Before he returned to his seat in the northern Highlands, he wanted to see the bastard hanging from a noose he made himself—but now even more so for having laid claim to a woman that for a few brief moments, Brandon had thought could be his.

His hands clenched at his sides, jaw throbbed from grinding his teeth.

Mariana's eyes were wide as she stared at him. But that was the only discerning set to her face. Her lips were flat, no curve up or down, and her brows were neither furrowed nor raised. She tried hard to hide how she felt, but Brandon could see the regret within her eyes. He just couldn't figure out if she regretted sleeping with him or telling him her secret.

"Say something," she said, her voice husky with held in emotion.

Brandon swallowed and forced himself to speak. "Your horse awaits ye in the courtyard." Not the words he wanted to say. Not the reaction he wanted to have. But what could he do?

She belonged to another man—his enemy.

The words he both longed for and dreaded did not leave her lips. There was no declaration of her loyalty to him. She'd not said she *had been* the king's mistress, but that she *was*.

"I see." Mariana lost face for a single second.

Brandon would have missed it if he blinked. Her lower lip quivered, and she rapidly blinked back tears. Then, as though she'd suddenly recovered, she lifted her skirts with dainty hands and turned away from him. Head held high, she marched to the archway, and disappeared down the stairwell that led toward the courtyard.

His feet remained rooted in place and he was unable to move, unable to speak. He'd watched, disbelieving, until her skirts swished and vanished around a corner. The lass wouldn't get far since they were on an island and the men waiting outside wouldn't leave without Brandon. Even still, the fear that she'd walked out of his life forever made his chest burn.

Longshanks' lover. His enemy's mistress. How many nights had she laid in his arms, laughing, kissing, feeding him almonds and grapes? How many nights would they lay together still, laughing at Brandon for falling for her ruse? The vivid images of her naked form entwined with the wrinkled, rough visage of King Edward made his stomach turn. Running a hand through his hair, he blew out a disgusted breath. He was an arse. The lass had shown she was upset, but that didn't seem to fit with a woman who would run back to her lover. Or was he only seeing what he wanted to see?

Ballocks, but she was messing with his mind!

Mistress be damned. They had a plan in place and she was the bait. 'Haps it was best they'd had this spat and could now go their separate ways. They were obviously not meant to be together and a relationship would only get in the way of his plans. He was grateful for having fallen upon her, because she would now lead them to Ross and the king. He supposed he could think of their night of passion as spoils of war.

An image of her above him, hands pressed hard to his chest, her lips parted on a moan, eyes blazing on his… That hadn't been the look of a woman thinking of another. He'd filled her mind as much as he filled her body.

But she was right. They didn't know each other. And he couldn't guess whether or not he could trust her.

Awareness of everything that stood between them didn't change what he was beginning to feel. A warmth that seized within his chest, directed at Mariana. One that would probably get him captured by the damned Sassenachs—or killed.

"Hell and damnation," he muttered.

"That bad?"

Brandon whipped around to see his cousin Ronan walking down from above.

"Shouldn't ye be with your wife?" Brandon asked.

"She's sleeping like a sated—"

Brandon held up his hand. "Dinna tell me, please."

Ronan laughed. "Och, wait until ye're happily wed to a siren."

"A day that will never come to pass." His words were said heavily and with regret. He glanced at the empty archway, then forced himself to turn away from it. Pushing Mariana from his awareness was for the best.

Ronan frowned. "What's on your mind?"

"The mission," he lied.

"Are ye worried it will not play out?"

Brandon shook his head. It would play out. The problem was, how it played out.

"The woman then?"

He crossed his arms and frowned, silently admitting defeat. There didn't seem to be a way to push her from his thoughts. "Aye."

Ronan studied him, assessing as he always did. "She's beautiful."

Brandon tilted his head from side to side, cracking his neck. The usual welcome relief of tension didn't follow. "That she is."

"Ye dinna want to leave her with Ross and Longshanks?"

Not a question he had the right to ponder. What he had to do, what his duty to Scotland was, were both obvious. His own desires had no place here. Brandon had to think like a warrior. A true leader didn't give concessions to their enemies. Well…not always. Clearing his throat, Brandon said bitterly, "Nay, I dinna mind leaving her. She's made her bed and I shall let her lie in it."

Ronan furrowed his brow. "Heavy words. What does that mean?"

Brandon clenched his jaw, already regretting what he'd said. "Nothing. I will see ye when we return."

He turned around, intent on leaving the great hall, but the sight that greeted him, made him wish he'd never entered it. Mariana stood in the doorway, her face pale, hands clenched together in front of her. How much had she heard? His stomach plummeted to somewhere around his feet and he longed to run toward her, to take her in his arms and tell her he didn't mean what he said. As stoic as she'd been before, she looked absolutely stricken now. Her lips quivered, eyes were glassy with tears. She'd heard most, if not all, of what he'd said. Knew that he didn't mind her going back to Longshanks, in fact probably thought he preferred it.

"I—" She cut herself off and whirled around.

"My lady," he called out, but she didn't stop.

She disappeared the way she'd done before, through the blasted doorway.

"Good luck with that," Ronan said under his breath.

Brandon ignored his cousin and chased after Mariana.

Mariana could hardly catch her breath. She ran down the stairs, sucking air into her lungs, but the air never seemed to get inside. Her throat was tight with unshed tears. Nearly blind, they watered so much, she could see only in blurs. One hand held her skirts up so she wouldn't trip and the other slid over the roughened stone stairwell, stinging as jutted stone scraped her tender flesh. She tripped on the last stair, pitching forward onto the armory floor.

Her hands and knees slapped with cruel measure against the stones, the threadbare rug hardly a barrier. She choked on a sob and prayed that none had witnessed her fall. Through the haze of her tears, she saw that she was indeed alone.

Mariana sat back on her heels and gave over to her tears. Oh, the awful things Brandon had said. The confession she'd made had only put a rift between them. He would blame her for the choices she'd not been able to make. She'd never be able to look another member of this camp in the eye again. They must all know her past. Perhaps Brandon had guessed it long before she told him and that was another reason she was being cast out.

Swiping at the tears falling unabashedly from her stinging eyes, she wiped her hands on her skirts and pushed to rise. She took a few shuddering breaths, trying desperately to calm herself. Steady. Soon, she would be back within the English court and could hopefully beg the king to let her go free. She didn't know where she would go, the church seemed the best place, for she didn't want to go back to France either. If Edward ever got word that she'd lain with Brandon, that she had feelings for him or that he might have even cared for her, he would use it against them both, and never let her go.

The look on Brandon's face… He'd regretted her hearing his words. His condemnation. Probably was embarrassed. Ronan had been the man who sent a lass to his room after all. Most likely knew that Mariana had paid the maids to let her lay with him instead. They obviously shared everything with each other. As if her face didn't burn enough from the tears, now she was inflamed with mortification.

Footsteps hurrying down the stairs caught her attention. Not wanting to wait and find out who it was, she lifted her skirts and ran toward the door leading outside. She slammed it open so hard it bounced against the stone wall. Mariana didn't bother to shut it, but instead ran down the second set of stairs to the main keep door, and burst into the courtyard. Crisp night air washed over her, making the tears still drying on her cheeks freeze in icy streaks. Moonlight shone on the warriors who filled the space, some on horses, some beside. They were all here to witness her shame.

One of the men stepped forward when he saw her, and she automatically took a step back, the heel of her boot catching, knocking her off balance. She reached out, gripping the door frame, and cried out when a splinter sank into the tender flesh between her thumb and forefinger. Yanking her hand away, she stared at the wound, unable to make out how deep and thick the offending splinter was.

"My lady." William Wallace's voice was easily recognizable. "I have your mount."

Mariana swallowed, ignoring the throbbing in her hand. Judging from the many warriors and horses, this was more than simply being tossed into the wild. When Brandon said she wouldn't travel alone, had he meant an entourage?

"What is happening?" she asked, walking up to Wallace and speaking in a low enough voice that she couldn't be overheard. The men surrounding them all pretended to be preoccupied.

"Ye dinna know?" Wallace's face in the dim night was indiscernible, but she could tell by his tone that he was skeptical.

"I thought to be escorted by one," she probed.

"Brandon?" Wallace's question seemed more a statement. He took her hand and pulled out the splinter like he did such all the time.

"I…I suppose," she stammered. The throbbing in her hand dissipated only to be replaced by a throbbing in her head.

"Did he not tell ye his plan?"

"His plan?" Why did that sound so ominous?

"Aye, lass." Now Wallace seemed all business.

She shook her head. Frustration welled within her. What was going on? "Only that I was leaving."

"Ye are leaving, and ye will be returned to Longshanks."

So, Brandon had known all along. She was simply a conquest of his. Her heart squeezed painfully, and she pressed her hands to her belly, hoping her reaction wasn't too noticeable to Wallace.

"Ye would let me go freely?" It was hard to keep the surprise from her voice. Wallace and his men did not seem the types that would let enemies go so easily. Brandon on the other hand seemed all too willing for her to simply disappear.

"Lass, ye are not our enemy, as much as King Edward is. We want to know where his camp is. We want Ross. Ye are the key to getting those things."

She was a pawn. And she'd be handed over to their enemy, a sacrifice in the greater scheme of their war. If she returned to Edward now, he would kill her. She was sure of it. The king would know she betrayed him—and she'd not do any different if given the chance. Not any amount of bribery or torture would make her give away the Scots secrets. And so she was doomed.

"I see." Her voice came out calm, but cold. The hands once pressed to her belly, grew steady, and she folded them in front of her. She'd not let these men see how they affected her, how they pained her. Mariana lifted her chin, pressed her shoulder blades back. She would stand strong, remain in control.

"Dinna be offended. We would have done this to anyone."

"Not a particularly comforting thought," she muttered. How many others had there been, and had Brandon bedded them as well?

Wallace laughed. "If it were not for this war, and for your knowing those we want captured, I would have liked to share a cup of wine with ye. Ye're a lively lass." Wallace's attention flickered behind her. "I see ye've decided to finally join us."

Mariana glanced behind to see Brandon standing tall in the moonlight. Her body did a little jolt as she took him in. Unwelcome as it was, the intrinsic attraction between them was strong. There was no hiding from it, and no trying to control it, she just had to learn to ignore it. He was an impressive warrior. Tall, with shoulders as wide as a door, corded muscle that filled the expanse of his linen shirt. Muscle she'd seen naked, run her fingers over, kissed. His features were chiseled from marble. Perfect, masculine, raw, powerful.

Her cheeks heated with her thoughts, and with her anger. His scent surrounded her, even though he stood several feet away—and she was aware that the scent was but a memory and not the real thing. Despite how he'd shunned her, she still desired him. An overpowering desire that threatened to wreak havoc on her sanity.

Brandon gave a curt nod in their direction and then walked toward his horse. Ignoring her. Giving her a direct cut. Despite having told herself she wouldn't let him get to her, that she had to move on, doing so appeared easier conceived than accomplished.

There was strength in his stride. A fluidness and agility that was mesmerizing. She would have given anything at that moment to know what his true thoughts were, even if they hurt. For she had an idea that he might just be pretending as much as she was. But why should she care? He was an imbecile—and she wasn't exactly flawless either.

She sniffed the air, pretending indifference, and turned back to Wallace. "My horse, sir?"

Wallace chuckled, seeming to read through her bravado. "This way, my lady." He took her hand and placed it on his arm as he led her toward a horse.

In the darkness, the horse looked black, chestnut perhaps. There was no stable hand to help lift her, and the stirrup was higher up than she was used to. But even still, she lifted her leg and propped her foot into the stirrup. Bouncing on her other foot and gripping the saddle, she tried for purchase. With another laugh, Wallace lifted her onto her mount and waited while she adjusted her skirts.

"Dinna take this personally," he said.

For a moment she didn't know what he was talking about—thought maybe he referred to the odd placement of the stirrup, but the seriousness set about his eyes made her realize he spoke of their decision to hand her over to King Edward.

She looked down at the great warrior, connecting her gaze with his, and then looked up, searching for Brandon. "I will not harbor any ill feelings toward *you*, sir."

"Dinna harbor them against any of us," he said softly. He adjusted the straps to her saddle, making sure they were tight. "We all do our duty for Scotland."

"And some of you do more than that." She looked away, wishing Wallace would mind his own business.

Wallace patted her horse on the rear, nodding his head. "Alas, ye are correct. Some men are afraid to…admit their heart leads them in a certain direction."

Mariana jerked her gaze back to the man. "Sir, certainly you aren't suggesting—"

"I am nay speaking of myself, lass." He said no more, and did not wait for her reply, but turned and headed toward his own horse, leaving Mariana with her mouth slightly open in surprise.

What had he meant? Was he speaking of Brandon?

Someone shouted an order and the men all mounted. In the chaos of them readying for departure, Mariana never lost sight of Brandon. He stood out among the rest of the men. There were some who reached his height, and some who matched him in breadth, but none who equaled the power and draw that surrounded him. He sat fierce and proud on his horse, and she instinctively trusted him with her life, though he was thrusting her aside.

The moonlight glinted off his weapons. She could see his gaze was on her, feel it penetrating her. She was powerless to turn away. He held her captivated and she didn't even know whether he looked at her with the raw ferocity she'd seen in him before or with the disdain he'd shown when she'd left the great hall. And it didn't matter. They were leaving this place. Though he wasn't tossing her into the wild, he was willingly giving her back to the English king—his enemy. A fate worse than death, for a man would typically accept death over being controlled by their enemies.

"Move out!" Wallace's voice cut through her thoughts.

The men filed side by side into a pattern they must have made on many occasions. Mariana was unsure where she belonged. She urged her horse forward twice, only to be jostled back by a warrior taking her place.

"Rude," she muttered under her breath. When it happened for the fourth time, she chose to remain rooted in place. They couldn't go ahead with their plan without her, so if they wanted her to come along, someone would have to let her into the line.

"Ye are to ride beside me."

Brandon.

Mariana refused to look at him. Every inch of her skin prickled, sensing his nearness. Her face was hotter than a flame. She was sure he'd seen her scorned by the other warriors and taking pity on her, chose to ride beside her.

Should she even acknowledge him? 'Haps another warrior would take pity on her, saving her from the very man who would push her aside. The chances of that happening were slim, but none the less, she would wait to see.

"Mariana." Brandon's voice was a low growl as he enunciated each syllable in her name. "We've no time for ye to decide your course. It has already been chosen for ye. Now ride."

How true his words were in every aspect of her life. She frowned and whispered to no one in particular, "There will be a day that I choose my own path."

If Brandon heard her, he didn't acknowledge it. His thigh bumped against hers as he urged her mount into the line, and stayed there, burning a hole right through her cloak and gown. She tried to shift away, but he only came closer, and then they were under the gate and on the bridge, riding side by side and the only escape for her was to jump into the loch.

She looked down at the darkened waters, seeing the stars and moon reflected on her depths. When she was a child, a *sennachie* had come to their chateau with one of her mother's cousins, and regaled them with fantastical stories of mermaids, nymphs and fairies. She'd always thought the mystical waters of Scotland to be filled with magic and searching out their depths now, she didn't think any differently.

"The loch is cold still, lass. I promise your suffering would be worse if ye jumped."

Mariana flicked her gaze from the inky depths to the road ahead, hoping to appear as though she weren't as jarred as she was. Why did Brandon have to read her thoughts? Since they'd met, he'd taken up lodging inside her mind with no intent to leave.

"I imagine the water is frigid considering 'tis freezing out," she muttered.

"Spring is nearly upon us."

She hated that he was trying to make small talk, as though nothing had happened between them. "Mmm-hmm."

"Have ye seen a Scottish spring?"

Mariana had not, and wanted to know why he was bothering to ask. But didn't dare ask him. It would only lead to a longing for something she would never have. Instead, she shook her head, kept her gaze straight forward. The sound of horse hooves clopping became quieter with each passing minute as the men moved off the bridge and onto wet earth. Flecks of muck sprayed up from the horses in front, a few landing on her cheeks.

"'Tis beautiful," Brandon said.

"I don't imagine I'll ever see one." Her voice was clipped and she felt bad, but there was no point, in her mind, of small talk or any talk really, especially of a Scottish spring.

"Mariana—"

She cut him off, unable to listen to his voice a moment longer, as it only brought her memories of laughter and sensuality. "My laird, please, I beg you, stop this. You have made your judgment and issued your sentence. If you would give me but one small reprieve, I don't wish to speak."

Brandon's mount slowed, allowing her to gain an inch or two, but only for a moment.

"I dinna understand ye, woman," he mumbled.

"Well, that makes two of us."

"Ye dinna understand yourself?" His voice held a hint of teasing, but she refused to answer.

She saw he meant to torture her along the road to Edward's camp. Brandon didn't say anything else, and the silence heavy with unspoken questions between them. Though she'd asked for that reprieve, she now wished to hear him say something.

Mariana glanced at Brandon from the corner of her eye. His face was outlined in the moonlight, strong and handsome. Features that could have been cut from marble, like the many statues of gods in the garden of Fontainebleau Palace. Her heart constricted.

"I didna mean for ye to hear what I said in the great hall." Brandon flicked his gaze toward hers, and her breath caught.

Mariana sighed. "Whether or not you meant for me to hear does not take away what you said."

"I know."

"Don't feel the need to explain to me, Brandon. You won't be the first to judge me."

"I think ye mistake my words."

Mariana let out a bitter laugh. "There was no mistake on my part."

"Aye, lass, I think there was."

She stared at him, mouth pressed in a hard line. "Explain it to me, then."

They rode into the forest, the dark of pre-dawn made even more gloomy by the slew trees. Mariana breathed in the crisp air, hoping it would help to calm the beating of her heart.

"I'm nay sure I can."

Chapter Fourteen

Struck.

That was the best way to describe how Brandon felt. How could he explain to her what he meant, and would she believe him if he told her? Had she heard the part where he said she was beautiful? Even if she had, she wouldn't know of his internal battle of whether to claim her as his own or push her aside. Or how he was afraid that his anger could hurt her one day.

Brandon had never raised a hand to a woman before, didn't have any intentions of doing so, but his father had laid his fists upon his mother often enough and Brandon lusted over violence when in battle. Didn't that mean that he was susceptible to hurting a woman?

He wasn't willing to find out. According to his mother, his grandfather had been one in the same. A violent streak passed down from one generation to the next. As he'd wiped blood from her lip or brow, she'd made him promise never to treat a woman in such a way. A promise he meant to keep. Only cowards beat on the defenseless. Brandon was no coward. But keeping such a promise meant he couldn't love a woman, or even hold her close. Not when his blood demanded that he do much the same as his forebears.

The darkness of night was beginning to give way to a hazy, misty gray morning. He glanced Mariana's way, wishing it were light already so he could see her face, and glad it wasn't at the same time. He'd seen her lip quiver, known he'd hurt her. The pain etched on her brow wasn't something he wanted to witness again.

Pushing Mariana away was for the best.

Even if he desperately wanted to pull her into his arms and press his lips to hers. To drag her back to his castle in the north where all this strife seemed so far away.

Brandon cleared his throat. He had to get a hold of himself. He'd become a pathetic excuse for a warrior in the past few days. Thinking about love and beauty. What he needed to be doing was concentrate on the war, and the magnitude of what was about to transpire.

"A warrior does not disclose his true thoughts to anyone," Brandon said, his spine straight, hand clenched tight on the reins.

"Your words to Sir Ronan were not your true thoughts?" Mariana's words were smooth, a stroke over his nerves. Her expression guileless.

The minx was trying to trick him. Brandon would not be fooled. "Didna I just explain a warrior does not disclose?"

"But moments ago, you said I was mistaken."

"Aye."

Mariana let out a little exasperated sound, but the slump in her shoulders gave away her defeat. They were both conquered by the world around them. Somehow, they had to rise above, to overcome the things they had no control over. And part of that was not allowing her to needle her way further beneath his skin.

"Ye are Longshanks mistress, my lady. Even knowing that, I will not go back on my promise to protect ye. I've already told Wallace and the Bruce that I dinna believe ye are a spy."

She didn't even flinch, keeping her gaze on the top of her mount's head. Brandon stretched over, briefly touching her hand. A mistake, as he wanted to reach back and entwine their fingers together. Mariana's fingers curled tighter on her reins and her horse shook its head in protest.

"Tell me now, Mariana," he said in a low enough tone that no one could overhear him. "Are ye a spy for Longshanks?"

She licked her lips, the tip of her red tongue darting over her lower lip and then the upper. With a tilt of her head, she looked toward him, her coquettish stance one he hoped was natural and not learned.

"When I was fifteen, my mother gave me this belt." She opened her cloak, pointed to the silver. "She also gave me away to the French king. Told me to do my duty to the family and I would be rewarded with a good marriage."

Brandon swallowed around the anger rising in his throat. At such a tender age she was sacrificed for greed.

"You ask me if I am a spy. You think I've made my bed willingly." She leaned closer, the scent of her hair filling his nostrils. "I ask you, Laird Sinclair, what girl at fifteen chooses to be mistress to a king?"

He wanted to draw his sword and ride all the way to France—his horse running upon the water. He'd call the king out, make him take up his sword and fight. Fight for her honor.

"My lady, I—" He felt like a fool. Didn't even know what he could say to make it better.

"Please don't. The last thing I ever wanted was your pity."

Brandon nodded, understanding her need. "I dinna pity ye, lass," he said softly.

Mariana gave a curt nod.

"But I am sorry that ye had to undergo so much at such a tender age. That ye still are."

Mariana let out a short bitter laugh, looking briefly at him with cool eyes. "*Oui,* I can tell. I shall think of your apology often as I attend King Edward."

Brandon ground his teeth. The only thing he seemed able to do was make an arse of himself. The thought of her attending the Hammer of all Scots, made him physically ill. Rage burned in his belly and he had to resist the urge to bellow his refusal for such to happen.

But the truth was, she belonged to King Edward and if Brandon took her as his own now, he'd only bring the king's wrath down harder on the Scottish people. Mariana was the key to finding and bringing down Ross. To disabling part of the English king's regiment. They had to hit him hard. And that required sending Mariana back, and making her believe he didn't care.

"I'd had hopes ye'd think of me kissing ye."

Mariana gasped. "You're a brute."

"Ye flatter me."

"I am in no way meaning to do such."

Brandon laughed. "Ye've spirit."

"'Tis the only way to survive."

"I'm surprised no one has tried to break it."

Mariana was quiet. He glanced over to see her chewing her lip and strangling her horse with the reins again.

"I..." she trailed off, loosening the reins a bit.

"Aye?" he pressed, overly curious about what she would say.

She looked up at him then, her eyes piercing his. Such strength and resilience in their depths. "I've never let my spirit, as you call it, show with anyone else."

An arrow to the chest. Brandon reached out, then snatched his hand back, aware that he was about to grasp her reins and pull her mount to a stop. He was no better than any of the other men who'd sought to rule over her.

The evening before, he'd willingly bedded her, knowing who she was. Had taken pleasure in her body, and when his own pride was hurt, he'd thrust her aside. Now, he would put her into the midst of a battle. There was no telling if Longshanks would kill her, beat her. No wonder Wallace and the Bruce had second guessed him for choosing to put her in the midst of danger.

"I'm sorry," Brandon said, conviction in his voice as his gaze held hers.

Mariana shook her head. "There is no need for you to apologize."

Brandon didn't hesitate this time when he reached out to grasp her hand. So much smaller than his own, the overwhelming urge to protect her at all costs surged from within. "But there is, lass." He searched for just the right words. "Ye put your life in my hands. I made a pledge to protect ye, yet I'm returning ye to a place that brings ye pain."

A tentative smile touched her lips and she placed her hand over top of his. A bond, that was how it felt, as though they were connected in some way he could not name. "You did protect me. But you also have a duty to your people and your country. I understand that."

He ground his teeth in frustration. "That doesna mean ye have to be tossed into the middle of it."

She shrugged daintily and frowned. "I was already there when you found me."

Brandon wanted to smooth her brow, rub his thumb over her lip and see her smile once more. He leaned closer, enough so her scent was hinted in the air. "I've made a mistake," he said.

In another hour the sun would be shining. Brandon watched as the tip of Mariana's pink tongue slid along the plush line of her lips. A nervous reaction, but one that sent his blood to boiling. He had to fight to keep from stopping his horse, pulling her atop his lap and kissing the past twelve hours away. Brandon found himself leaning closer. She glanced up at him. In her gaze, he read her permission, her need. To hell with the mission, he'd never felt this way about any other woman, never wanted anything in his life as much as he wanted her.

Last night had been proof of that. There was no going back.

Brandon caressed from her hand up toward her elbow, her shoulder, her neck. He touched her cheek, his thumb rubbing over the arch of her cheekbone. A few more inches and their lips would meld as one.

As shrill whistle filled the air. Wallace called for them to pick up speed. Reluctantly, and with great regret, Brandon pulled away. What a spell she'd cast around him. He'd been about to kiss her in broad daylight, in the midst of men.

Mariana's throat bobbed as she swallowed. From relief, regret or fear of the unknown, Brandon had no clue. He preferred to believe she felt as he did, but in all reality, he wasn't privy to that either.

The pounding of the entourage's horses' hooves forced them to quicken their pace, else they be run over by those behind them. Brandon found it physically difficult to pull his eyes away from her, but he did so all the same. Forced himself forward instead of hauling her from her mount and placing her on his lap where they could ride fast and still steal a kiss. Or two.

Galloping made it hard to talk, but he would try all the same. The loss of what ground they'd regained may prove to be the end.

"I dinna want to give ye over to him."

"You don't have a choice, Brandon. And neither do I." There was sadness in her words.

"There is always a choice," he called over the din, convincing himself as much as her.

Mariana smiled briefly, flicking her gaze from him to the parade in front. "Not always. Sometimes duty comes before our preferred choices."

Given what she'd told him, Brandon could see how Mariana had come to such a conclusion. He had much the same opinion. 'Twas a shame. His desire to kiss her only increased. To pull her into his arms so they might share their misery. A sense of togetherness had never revealed itself before meeting her. Someone he could relate to and commiserate with. With Mariana he could find peace and happiness.

"Duty," he ground out. That was where he was torn. Fiercely loyal to his country, his men, his family, his future king, where did Mariana fit? A lover held little claim to a man's life, save for pleasure. But Brandon wanted more than that with Mariana. A future. A bond. Choosing that path was risky.

"When I was young," she started, her voice as bouncy as her horse. "I used to stare at the stars and wonder at the meaning of the word duty."

Brandon had never done that. Duty had been a way of life, no questioning it, only acting on it.

"My mother would say, *'tis your duty, smile and placate those you serve.*"

"Were ye not noble born?" Brandon asked.

She nodded. "Surely you realize the duties of a woman, even noble born, are to serve. She serves God, country, king, father, mother, brother, husband."

Brandon realized. Though, he'd not thought about it often enough without a sister or wife of his own. He frowned. In his mind, women were not placed on earth to serve men. They were here to make the world a better place. A woman's touch had the power to heal. Already Mariana had smoothed over some of the cracks on his heart. Mended his broken soul. He could fall heavily into her arms each night, knowing that when the sun rose, he'd be lighter.

Only those men too cowardly to control their anger, to put it to good use in other ways, thought women were placed on earth to be their living quintains—practice targets for their blows.

His mother was strong on the inside for being able to take his father's abuse, but Brandon often questioned why she allowed it to continue, why she never ran away. 'Haps her own mother, his grandmother, had instructed her much the same as Mariana's mother. Or maybe it had been because she had no other choice, no place to go. And then, he'd also blamed himself. She stayed to protect him from much the same abuse. Rage against his father boiled anew.

If only he'd understood more, had insisted his mother run away, to her family, the church, anywhere. Compelled her to believe there was always a choice better than being abused. He'd have protected her. He'd have stood up to his father and forced the man to let her be. But he hadn't. The few times he had stood between his mother and father, the beatings had been severe, leaving Brandon bloody and swollen, and his mother had paid for it brutally. She'd come to Brandon, insisted he stop, that it only enraged his sire more.

Brandon obeyed his mother, not wanting her to suffer more than she already had.

"I know a woman's duties well enough," he finally answered, his mouth turned down as a bitter taste coated his tongue.

Mariana gave him a quizzical look, her lips parted to ask him a question when a whistle from ahead sent a cold shiver of dread down Brandon's spine. 'Twas not Wallace's call for speed—but something worse. The men all slowed their horses. He gripped the claymore at his back and pulled it free, the metallic zing as he did so a welcome echo.

"Stay close to me," he said to her, reaching with his free hand to grasp her reins and pull her mount tight against his.

Their legs brushed, sending a frisson of desire straight to his groin, but he willed his cock to tame. Now was not the time to be thinking with his ballocks instead of his brain.

Mariana's gaze focused on the road ahead, her hand squeezed his. "I will."

A retainer near the front turned and rode back toward Brandon. As he approached, Brandon recognized him as Luke, one of Wallace's squires. The man stopped beside him, leaned over and said in low tones, "Wallace believes we are being followed."

Brandon's jaw muscle ticked. He drowned out the sounds of the horses and men and honed in on the surrounding area. 'Twas hard to tell if anything were out of place. He'd been so focused on Mariana, he'd not been paying attention. Yet another reason they were bad for each other. He trusted Wallace's instincts, and if he had to stake his life on it, he was certain of who they were being followed by.

"Ross," he said.

"Aye. No English could be so silent."

Brandon agreed. Only a Highlander knew these woods well enough to keep quiet and stalk a hundred ambitious warriors.

"What are Wallace's instructions?" Brandon asked.

"He's sending out scouts now. We are to await their return."

Brandon nodded and grinned, his stomach growling. "I'd enjoy nothing more than taking Ross out before I break my fast."

Chapter Fifteen

From the corner of her eye, Mariana spied an arrow whizzing toward her. It's point slicing through the air straight for her face.

"Mon dieu!"

She ducked just in time, the tip riffling the hair just above her ear before skimming a stinging path on her cheek and finally sinking into the neck of her mount.

Shrieking, she jolted backward as the horse reared up, whinnying its own scream.

Everything happened at once.

Brandon's battle cry pierced the air. His leg brushed over hers. Hand pulled free of her grip. His cry was followed by dozens of others, and answered by men who poured from the trees. A nightmare come to life. Dressed in Highland garb, plaids of various colors, these were no English soldiers, but Scotsmen attacking Scotsmen.

Clashes of metal echoed in the early morning, sparks flashing with each ensuing clang. The hazy gray of predawn was replaced by the orange glow of the rising sun. Shadows danced like fire through the budding trees.

Wallace had been right. They were being followed, and Brandon was dead on. Ross walked from the trees, surveying the chaos around him. She'd recognize him anywhere. Long grey hair, greasy and unkempt. Weathered skin, wrinkled and sallow. Belly round from too much whisky and ale.

His pale eyes locked with hers and a cruel smile curved his lips. She'd known the man was evil when she met him for the first time in Kinterloch. The way he'd laughed and kicked at the servants. How she'd heard a woman's screams from his chamber later that night. At the time, Mariana even planned to return to King Edward to tell him, when she overheard Ross explaining Edward's plans to burn the village and its people, in an effort to lure Wallace from his camp.

Edward had always been harsh himself, but he didn't necessarily like his vassals to be brutal without his explicit directive. A man who took it upon himself to act as God, often forgot his place as servant to the king. Edward's chosen hound would turn on him at any given moment, biting the hand that fed him.

Mariana gripped tight to her mount's reins, her thighs clenched around the animal as she felt herself being pulled backward, Ross no longer in her sights. Turmoil ran rampant all around her. Wallace's crew fought fiercely against those who'd ambushed them. 'Twas hard to tell who was a friend and who was foe. Looked only like Highlander against Highlander.

She scanned frantically about for Brandon as the horse pounded back to earth, only to rise up again, her view of the morning sky clear. He'd been beside her to the right, and she saw that he still was, surrounded by at least four men who sought to take him down from Checkmate.

She watched for only a second as he sliced through one man, blood spraying from the cut in his foe's skull, before her mount once more reared, his forelegs curling and pawing at the sun-kissed morning. Oddly tranquil in this brutal battle.

Blood trickled from the horse's wound. The arrow still protruding six inches below his ear.

"Steady," she called, her voice wavering. The animal could sense her fear as her limbs trembled, only exacerbating its terror.

Even a warhorse would react when wounded, but this was no warhorse and so the wound, the battle, her fear, was only making matters worse. She had to calm the animal.

Swiping at a tickle on her cheek, she noted blood on her knuckles. Just a scratch, she told herself. Nothing more.

Mariana grappled with the reins, taking them into one hand and somehow managed to grasp the arrow. Warm blood on the cool shaft, made it hard to grip. She tried to yank it out, her hand sliding up over the feathered fletching. Cursing under her breath she tried again, but the scared animal reared again, and having only one hand on the reins, she slipped back further on the animal's haunches. He pounded his forelegs back to the ground and she nearly went over his neck. Her thighs burned from clenching tight.

At last she found a good grip on the arrow, and yanked it from the animal's neck. He whinnied in pain again, and this time when he reared up, she was ready, though her body protested every clamped muscle. But, Mariana mastered the animal, just as she did back in France on her family's land. She could break even the most ornery of stallions.

A skill she prided herself on, but not one she often shared.

"*Aller, maintenant!* Go, now!" she shouted.

The horse flared his nostrils, snorted, but beneath her, his muscles bunched tight before he bolted through the throng of battling warriors.

Through the drowning noise, she thought she heard her name called. Then louder still. She turned around, looking to see if it was Brandon, wanting to give him a signal that she was headed for safety, but that brief moment proved to be her undoing.

She caught sight of Brandon, his face contorted into a ferocious frown as he ran toward her. Frozen in fear, she watched his approach. A second arrow hissed past her face slamming into the other side of her horse's neck. The horse bucked, reared, unsettling her first forward and then backward. The animal lurched onward, and Mariana jostled in the saddle, the reins sliding through her fingers and over the horse's neck.

Arms flailing out, her fingers sliding into the horse's mane, she tried to find purchase, but the animal was too bouncy, and all her work to calm him didn't seem to help. They'd already gone too far. Too much fear filled his blood.

Mariana clung to the wounded animal, but the blood flowing from both sides of his neck and his frantic movements, impeded her grip. Her hands and arms slipped with each frantic attempt to hold on. There was no stable anchor. Her thighs screamed in protest. She yanked her feet from the stirrups and hooked them under the pit meeting the horse's forelegs and belly, trying somehow to maintain her seat before she was tossed into the midst of the battle.

"Mariana!" Brandon's bellow sent a chill through her, settling in her gut.

"Brandon." She tried to call loudly, but her voice came out in a gasp as she clung to her horse. "Steady, *mon garcon*," she crooned.

Beneath her bloody fingertips, the horse's withers shivered. The animal tried valiantly to remain calm but the chaos of their surroundings and his pain continued to destroy his reserve.

All around her men fought for their lives, fought to gain control of one another, and someone, whoever was behind the bow that had now shot her horse twice, wanted her dead. If she fell now, she would likely die. Trampled by the horse, or crushed under the feet and swords of those who fought.

Mariana lurched forward once more as her mount leaped over fallen bodies. This time, when her arms slid around his bloody neck, she laced her fingers together and held on for dear life.

Searing pain wrenched through her arm, the backlash of someone's sword. A scream tore through her throat, and it was only after that she realized she'd called out for Brandon.

Her horse stumbled, on what she couldn't see as her eyes had become hazy with tears of pain. Could have been that animal was simply succumbing to his injuries, maybe even shot again by whoever wanted to see her taken down.

When her horse stumbled again, the pain tearing up and down her arm made her fingers tingle with numbness and try as she might, she could no longer hold on. But it didn't seem to matter as the horse pitched forward.

"Mariana, fall backward." Brandon's voice cut through the fog of her fear.

She shook her head. Wrenched around to see where Brandon was. Wanted to hold her arms out to him, to have him catch her from falling for the second time since they'd met. But he wasn't there, and she couldn't see him. And she was falling, but she landed hard on the ground, screaming as her arm bent in the wrong direction. The resounding pop sent shivers up her spine, and made her stomach churn, bile rising up her throat. The ground was cold, wet and vibrated beneath her.

The mount fell hard beside her, his breath puffed violently against her cheek. A whispered prayer of thanksgiving that he hadn't landed on her tumbled from her mouth. She blinked away her tears, meeting the poor animal's eyes. Pain was etched in their depths.

"Hush," she crooned, soothing herself as she calmed him.

Mariana reached her uninjured arm toward the animal, brushing her fingers over his velvet soft muzzle. His hot breath puffed onto her palm.

Suddenly, she was wrenched into the air, and another scream pulled from her throat. A hard arm circled around her belly, fingers digging uncomfortably into her ribs. Her mount took a last breath, his eyes glassing over as she was slammed, belly down, onto someone's lap upon another horse. The man forced her face down toward the ground, his leg covered in blood smearing onto her cheek. The scent of death filling her senses. She grew dizzy as he lurched forward, jostling her. Her arm throbbed, pinned to his smelly, loathsome body.

Mariana was able to peer to the left only enough to see the horse's hind legs working as it ran. Beyond the moving ground she saw a pair of familiar boots running toward her, her name shouted on the wind.

"Brandon," she whimpered.

"The king's been wondering where ye were, bitch," said her captor.

Mariana swallowed back her pain and fear. Just as she had the ability to calm a horse, there was always the chance she could charm a man into keeping her safe. The only thing was, she was not entirely certain whether the man who held her now had been the one shooting at her, and who had ordered her killed. The sour knot in her belly, had fear swelling thick inside her.

If Longshanks wanted her punished, it would not be a pleasant experience.

Her captor kicked his horse hard, his spurs digging into the animals flank and drawing dots of blood against his chestnut fur. Mariana closed her eyes against the horse's pain and her own. There was no escaping this man's hold. The best she could do now was rest, and gather her strength for what was to come, for it would certainly not be enjoyable.

"Bastard!" Brandon bellowed. "Stop! Put her down!"

His feet pounded into the ground as he ran after Mariana. Ross had scooped her up from the ground like she was no heavier than the arrows that felled her horse. His heart felt like it had stopped beating, and he ran until he could no longer breathe. Until Mariana and Ross were no longer in sight.

A whistle sounded, not a signal Brandon recognized. When he turned back toward the fray, Ross' men were retreating back into the forest, leaving in their path a horde of angry warriors, blood soaked earth and no Mariana.

"Brandon." Wallace raised his hand as he approached. The man was covered in blood and muck, his breathing as labored as Brandon's.

"Wallace, I have to go after her." He shoved his sword into the ground, put his hands on his hips, forcing himself to regain his breath. "I canna…"

"'Tis all going according to plan." Wallace seemed convinced.

"What?"

"Is this not what ye planned? To return her?"

Brandon nodded, trying to swallow around the lump of guilt in his throat. "Aye, but not like this. Not a battle. Not with that bastard Ross tossing her over his horse. She's hurt."

Wallace frowned. "We'll get her back."

Brandon scraped his hands through his hair. "If they hurt so much as one inch of her…"

"Ye can send them all to hell." Wallace shouted orders for a few men to remain behind to bury the dead and for the rest of the men to mount up. "His trail is still fresh. Let us follow him. The maggot will lead us straight to his new camp, and if we're lucky, to Longshanks."

"Aye." Brandon sheathed his claymore, feeling its weight comforting on his back.

His horse waited dutifully for his return. Brandon wasted no time grasping the saddle and hoisting himself onto Checkmate's back. Wallace rounded up the men and followed Brandon on the trail through the woods, the divots deep in the ground where Ross had pushed his horse to its full capacity.

The trail zigzagged through the forest, over a burn and onto a road that led up a mountain.

Why would the English hide within the mountains? They had the constitutions of bairns still at the teat—the mountains were harsh, cold, and though he could fare them well, he didn't like to. He imagined Longshanks shivered in his makeshift tent, demanding his many servants to warm the various parts of his body.

As his horse made the ascent over the steep incline, he was aware that it could be a trap. Longshanks may not even be near. In fact, they could reach the top only to find that Ross had led them astray and gone down again, or a pack of traitors waited to ambush them once more.

This time, at least, while he had Mariana on his mind, he was also fully aware of his surroundings, listened for any change in the air, and kept a hand on the sword at his hip in case he needed to pull it quickly from his sheath.

The next rise proved to be just as he suspected. 'Twas a trap.

Not a single person was in sight, and the horse's imprints came to a halt. Brandon and his men stopped, turned in a circle. But there was nothing. Almost like Ross had simply disappeared, his horse lifted into the clouds. A cloud covered the sun overhead, giving the air a sudden chill, and turning everything grey. An ominous wind swept over him in bursts.

Brandon swallowed, his breath coming hard through his nostrils.

"*Mo creach,*" he growled. This entire plot had been a mistake and an innocent woman—his woman—was going to pay for it.

His woman.

Aye, indeed. Mariana was his, and no bastard traitor was going to take her from him.

There was no denying it any more. She was his. And he was going to get her back. Claim her. Hear her say that she was his. Brandon's heart constricted, making his ribs ache. He'd not been able to admit before, beyond desire, what he felt for her. And even now he was apprehensive, but if he were honest with himself… He loved her.

As if hearing his personal confession, the clouds opened up, a beam of sunlight seeping through their grey expanse and shining down onto the rise. Brandon's mouth went dry, his gaze caught by where the sun hit.

A message. A piece of Mariana's green gown nailed to a tree—smeared with blood.

Chapter Sixteen

A swift jolt awakened Mariana. A muffled cry escaped her and she flailed, eyes popping open. Her vision blurred, she made out the white of the sky and a bunch of blobs of black and brown.

A split-second later she landed hard in the dirt on her hip and elbow. The impact was shocking, and jarred her from head to toe. A metallic taste in her mouth and the sting of her cheek told her she'd bit herself. Thank God, she'd managed to twist in time so that her already injured arm wasn't further damaged. In addition to the gash from a wayward sword, she was almost certain it was broken. Her hip and elbow were most assuredly bruised, but at least they were still whole.

A cloud of dust surrounded where she'd landed, filling her lungs. She coughed, sneezed, and willed herself to hold back her sobs. Pain throbbed in her injured arm. She feared moving, not knowing where she was. Nothing about this place looked familiar to her.

"Lady Mariana," a cool, uninterested male voice cooed. "I see you decided to rejoin us. Tell me, how was your visit with the Scots?"

A shiver of fear curled around her spine. Shifting to kneel, she waved away the cloud of dirt, and slowly raised her eyes to see King Edward standing a few feet in front of her. The sun glinted blindingly off of his chainmail. He looked like a glowing king. A purple velvet doublet, trimmed and embroidered with gold thread gave her eyes reprieve from the striking metal. His shoulder-length silver hair was streaked with sweat. His long, chiseled features also glistened. In his arms he held a shiny helmet. She lowered her gaze to stare at the dust upon his boots.

The king looked as though he'd been out fighting. He was not afraid to venture out of his camp. Not afraid to take his sword to another man's throat—though he preferred that his men held that man down while he completed the deed. She prayed whoever he'd been railing against had not suffered overmuch.

"Your Highness," she managed, though her voice came out sounding strangled. "'Twas horrendous."

Her heart lurched when she lied, though she knew it was to protect Brandon as much as herself.

"Horrendous?" King Edward drawled. He stepped closer to her. Knelt before her, and placed a cold, gloved finger on her chin, lifting her face so that she had to look him in the eye. "How so?"

His grey eyes were cruel, indifferent. The man didn't care so much about her answer, as he did that she was here before him. He didn't take kindly to others thieving what belonged to him, and Mariana was well aware that she was as much a pawn to him as any other man. But that didn't matter. He considered her his property.

"Come now, don't be shy. Tell me." His voice, though soft, was etched with malice.

Mariana was more afraid of the king now than she'd ever been. Her stomach tightened and gooseflesh rose on her arms. If he didn't like her answer… Thought her to be lying, there was no telling what his response would be. What cruel punishment he'd have doled out on her.

"They are barbarians," she said through chattering teeth. She clutched at her injured arm, the limb hanging limp by her side, and thankfully the bleeding gash had staunched its flow. Moments of numbness made the pain bearable, but right then a searing agony took hold. Mariana squeezed her eyes shut, ground her teeth.

"Are you injured, my lady?" The king's voice was solicitous, but Mariana knew better than to think he would be kind.

Slowly, she nodded, then opened her eyes, trying to see him through the mist of her tears.

The king scowled over her head, then stood. "I told you to take care of her, not bring her back to me broken."

Mariana's throat grew tight, and she found it hard to breathe. That tone he used… Chills of dread shook her.

"She was already injured when I found her, Your Highness." Ross' voice was confident. Too confident. The man wouldn't last long with King Edward.

"And you didn't think it necessary to tend to her wound? I don't like my property to be damaged."

Mariana put her weight on her uninjured arm and tried to stand. The king, most likely sensing her struggle from the corner of his eye, actually held out a hand to her. She gripped it, the leather of his gloves soft and cold. As he brought her to her feet, she tried to keep in mind that though he was a cruel man, he'd once been kind to her. Took her in, clothed her, fed her. The price had been steep—her dignity, her body—but still, she was alive.

That was the hardest part. Hate him she did, but regretfully, for he'd never beaten her or punished her. He never had to.

Once on her feet, she swayed, feeling light-headed. She held her injured arm close to her, afraid if she let go, whatever bone had been broken would shatter further.

King Edward snapped his fingers. "Will someone take Lady Mariana to a private chamber and see her properly tended?"

Three women, dressed in plain gowns and shoes, hair coiled at the napes of their necks, hurried forward. Mariana recognized the servants from before she'd left. Loyal they were. Odd, but at that moment, their names escaped her. They snaked their arms around her waist as they clucked about her blood soaked gown, her hair, her injury.

Mariana allowed them to take her away, praying first that King Edward beat Ross with a whip—almost wishing to stay behind to witness it—and second that Brandon was able to follow their trail. If he wasn't any good at tracking—or he simply didn't care—then she prayed she succumbed to fever and never breathed again.

Mariana didn't recognize the castle she was being led toward. The air smelled salty. They were near the shore. Surrounding them, the outer wall was high and thick, made of stone, but the interior keep was built of wood, nearly four stories high. The building was sturdy, newer, and terrifying in its raw expression of dominance. A war building, with many thin, arrow slit windows, and great main doors as tall as two men. A thick spiked, deadly iron portcullis hung halfway down the door—as if stilled in time. She feared it would fall, pinning her forever to the ground when they passed through. On the ramparts, dozens of soldiers marched, scanning, ready to fire their notched arrows.

Most likely, they were still in Scotland, but even if they were in France, she wasn't sure she'd have been able to tell where they were. She'd slept for most of the journey here. Had passed out from pain within a few minutes of being captured, and thankfully her body had forced her to remain in such a state until they arrived at King Edward's camp.

Just as they reached the doors to the castle, she heard Edward's voice, filled with disdain, demand, "Get off that horse you bloody fool and bow to your sovereign, before you find your head rolling at your feet."

Mais oui, Ross would be a lucky man to make it through the next few days in Edward's company. The king was in a foul mood. A vengeful mood.

The castle was dark, no candles lit. The women led Mariana up the circular stair, and even with three holding her up she found it difficult to stay steady on her feet. On the second floor, they led her down another dark corridor, opened a door, and bustled her in. Once in a chamber, they laid her on the bed. One lit a few candles, another the fire and the third carefully undressed her down to her chemise, which was thankfully without sleeves. Her arm was misshapen and discolored, dark purple and blue around a bulge that hadn't been there before. The gash, covered in dried blood, didn't look as deep as she'd thought.

Her stomach flipped and rolled. Mariana leaned to the side, gagging. She'd not had any food or drink, which made her convulse instead of forcing out the non-existent contents of her stomach.

"Oh, my lady, look at your arm." A tender hand probed at the wound, only making her more nauseas as the pain pervaded.

One of the other maids wiped a cool cloth on her brow. She was pretty, young, whereas the one who undressed her had been older, withered looking. "We'd best get it set and wrapped, else you damage it further, my lady. Need to get this cut cleaned and treated as well. Could set in with fever too."

"I'll have a tisane made," chimed someone from across the room.

Mariana tried to look, but pain made her eyes squint and seeing was getting harder.

"And an herbed poultice to go within the bandages. Doesn't look like the bone broke through the skin. A knife or sword most likely."

"Who will set it?"

"Get the surgeon."

Their voices all collided and made Mariana dizzier than she already was. As they clucked around her, the room swirled. The walls and ceiling looked like they were moving toward her, ready to suffocate her. The room smelled musty and sweet like herbs. She was close to fainting again. Felt so tired and weak.

A door opened. A door closed.

Footsteps.

More murmuring.

Mariana's head rolled from side to side as she fought to remain conscious.

Someone gripped her arm and yanked. Bone ground against bone. Searing pain stabbed through her limb. Her eyes rolled back in her head, her stomach churned. A shriek sounded from somewhere.

"Oh, my dear, I'm sorry." A woman's voice. She didn't know whether she recognized it or not.

The shriek…it was her own.

"All set now, my dear. The healing can begin."

Healing. Nay, she would never be healed. Mariana moaned, her eyes rolling in her head. "Brandon…"

"Hmm? What did you say, my dear?"

Thankfully, Heaven saw fit to pull her from consciousness before she had the chance to answer.

Sweat poured in an ungodly flood over Brandon's temples, his spine. Even his knees and elbows seemed to perspire. The end of winter chill did nothing to cool his burning blood. He was in a frenzy. A madness consumed him.

The men followed him, Wallace allowing Brandon to take the lead on the mission. On horseback, they'd torn up and down the mountains, over burns and through marshlands, for the past several hours. But they'd found nothing. No one.

He would tear the highlands apart if he had to. Push his horse to the point of dropping if that's what it took. They had to be here. *She* had to be here and he wouldn't stop until he found her. They returned to the site where their enemy seemed to have simply vanished, in hopes of picking up a clue they'd missed. Wallace bellowed, halting Brandon.

"Do ye see this?"

Brandon slid from his horse and ran to where Wallace kneeled, nose to the ground. "Someone covered up their tracks." Wallace pointed. "They pick up once again on the other side." He put a comforting hand on Brandon's shoulder. "We'll find her and Ross."

The bastards had tried to fool them, but they'd not done a very good job.

Urgency permeated his every move. He had to get to Mariana. With each passing minute, the clues to her whereabouts depleted and her safety was a constant, distressing question in his mind.

Was the blood on the torn fabric hers? Had he cut her and smeared it onto the gown? Was she conscious? Where was she? Was she alive? Had she been hit with an arrow? Trying to remain calm, he prayed the blood on the gown was simply left over from her horse, that Ross used it to frighten him—knowing Brandon would automatically assume the blood to be hers. The man hoped to play a game with them.

That only put Mariana in more danger. If Ross knew Brandon and the men would come after her, that the sight of blood would spur their vengeance, then Mariana was in more danger than Brandon previously thought. The king would not stand for her to be in league with Scots.

But they couldn't know. Could they? Would Mariana tell them, lead them all to their deaths? Was she so deceitful that she would risk her own life to put an end to theirs? Brandon shook his head. He couldn't, *wouldn't* believe that.

However violent Ross was, Longshanks was a conniving, vile demon. There was no end to his cruelty and he would surely meet out his anger on Mariana. Flashes of her bloodied and whimpering stormed his mind in a wide-awake nightmare.

They had to get to her. And now. Before Longshanks chose to punish her. Before it was too late. Before Brandon lost the chance to confess his true feelings for her. That he wanted a future with her. That he was willing to change everything if only she would be his wife.

The sea air was stronger now, the salt mixing crisply in the breeze. Brandon leaned back on his horse, sniffing. They were close to shore again. For a moment, Brandon feared they had only followed their own prints back to Eilean Donan. That the mist surrounded castle would loom ahead of them, Robert and the others waving their arms in welcome.

He held up his hand for the men to slow. Through the trees he spied a road ahead. Brandon swirled his hand in arc in the air and four men departed from the group to scout out the road.

"Do ye know where we are?" Wallace said in a low tone, pulling his horse beside his.

Brandon shook his head, eyeing their surroundings and taking in the sparser trees, the road, what appeared to be a castle some distance away.

"'Tis Ion Dubh Castle." Wallace stared straight ahead, his lips pressed together in a disappointed line.

"Ion Dubh?" Brandon asked. He'd never seen the castle before. Nudging his horse closer to the road, he saw that the fortress sat upon a rise overlooking the sea. The sounds of splashing could be heard in the distance as waves crashed upon the cliff.

"Aye. Now that we are here, I'm almost certain King Edward has taken claim of it." Wallace's voice was filled with anger.

Brandon studied his leader, wondering at the complexities of the man, what happened in his youth to make him so rough. "Why?"

"Ion Dubh has remained vacant for the last several years. A fighting ground between the MacLeans and the Ross." He shrugged. "If I remember, the men called a truce some years back that neither would claim the castle until the other was willing to pay its worth in silver. No one dare to come near it, else they face the wrath of two clans coming down on them."

"And neither has been willing to pay each other the silver?"

"I wouldna know, but my guess is, either MacLean paid or Ross simply claimed it in Longshanks' name."

"Mariana is in there." Brandon reached inside his sleeve to feel the folded up cloth of her gown, rubbing his thumb with care over its softness.

"We can only hope." Wallace gave him a glance that said he felt anything but hope.

Not what he'd been looking for in the least. Wallace had to have faith, couldn't put those sorts of doubts in Brandon's mind. Not now, when everything was at stake.

Brandon turned away, studying Ion Dubh. The task at hand seemed more grim by the moment. He could barely make out the outskirts of the castle, only that it was at the top of a steep rise—one that would be difficult to climb and impossible on horseback. There appeared to be plenty of brush along the rocks to hide from archers, but making it to the top alive would be risky. The only other way looked to be a main road, much like that of Eilean Donan—in other words, also impossible. "How do we get in?"

"That is something we'll have to figure out. The place will be crawling with English bastards and traitor Scots alike." Wallace jutted his chin toward the fortress. "Might be able to get in by the water. There's most likely a port of some sort. No use having a castle by the sea if ye dinna use it."

'Twas nearing dusk. Only an hour or so left of sunlight.

"The maggots will be on high alert," Wallace pointed out.

"Aye, as will we."

"No fires tonight."

Brandon slowly nodded his agreement. "'Haps ye and I should go at sunset to look at the water and see if there is a way in?"

"An excellent plan."

By this time tomorrow, Brandon planned to have Mariana in his arms and be well away from Ion Dubh Castle.

Chapter Seventeen

Outside, thunder crashed and rolled, drawn out in long dramatic booms. Lightning sizzled and popped, firing bolts into the trees beyond the road below.

Mariana cracked the shutter against the lone narrow window in her room, and gazed outside. An icy wind burst in gusts into the opening, but she didn't mind the cold. She needed to see outside. If not to gain some idea of where she was, to see if there was any hint of Brandon coming to her rescue.

Rescue.

She belonged to Longshanks. And in his eyes she was home. But this would never be home. There was only one man who could give her that. And it wasn't King Edward. In her heart she was no more than the king's prisoner. While the doors weren't barred and there were no guards, she didn't have the right to make her own choices. Any and all decisions were made for her. He would never let her go. Not willingly. He would kill anyone who tried to take her from him. Or he would kill her. What she wouldn't give to have the right to choose. To fulfill her own destiny, to no longer cow down to those more powerful.

Biting her lip, she realized what she truly longed for—in addition to a draught of liquor to dull the pain in her arm—was for Brandon to steal her away. To charge the castle, like she'd dreamed the barbarian Scots would do.

Oui, since setting foot on Scottish lands, she'd dreamed of the warriors storming the various castles they'd stayed in. They took mercy on her, all while acting out their revenge on the men who made them suffer.

Mariana was kept at court, but that didn't mean she was ignorant to the destruction Edward laid around himself. Kinterloch was not the only village they'd burned—others had been pillaged too. Mariana had never laid witness to the acts, but they'd passed through the villages. Edward always blamed the Scots for the destruction, but now she had serious doubts. He'd been the one to do it.

Tremendous rain drops splattered on the stone casement, ricocheting onto her fingers and face. The sky was a dark grey, the sun trying valiantly to shine through the storm clouds was sorely defeated. Thankfully, the temperature had not dropped overmuch, causing the raindrops to remain liquid rather than ice.

The castle sat high on a ridge, overlooking the sea and the land beyond. From her room, Mariana didn't have a good vantage point of the sea, but she could see the road. The way out. Had Edward chosen this room so she could see her escape just beyond her reach? Most likely.

She frowned down at the grounds, slowly turning from dirt-packed to a sloppy, muddy mess. Mariana had never asked Edward for anything. Had never begged him to let her go. To give her in marriage to another. Never voiced any complaint.

That didn't mean he hadn't read it in her eyes. He had the uncanny ability to see within someone's soul. To read their true heart's desires. And the callousness within his own heart to tear it all away.

Mariana could not underestimate King Edward. She'd best move forward with the knowledge that he did know what she truly wanted—to leave him and this place. And that he may even know she'd fallen in love with another.

Fallen in love?

A gasp escaped her, and her hand fluttered to her chest where her heart suddenly felt like it beat at triple its normal pace.

In love?

"Oh, *mon dieu.*" It was true. She was utterly, unequivocally, in love with Brandon Sinclair.

This was terrible.

Horrible.

A disaster.

She stared hard at the charcoal and white swirls of the storming sky. Why did she have to fall in love? That would make not being with Brandon all the more painful.

For in truth, he wasn't going to come and rescue her. He'd most likely moved on already, 'haps already finding comfort in one of the willing maids' arms.

She slammed the shutters closed, and pinched the tender flesh of her finger in the process. "Ouch!" She stuck her finger in her mouth.

Well, if she wasn't just one pathetic woman. She hobbled toward the chair set before her hearth, her hip covered in bruises from being tossed off Ross' horse. Her injured arm, splinted and held within a sling at her waist—and now a sore finger.

Mariana dropped into the chair, grateful for the cushion against her rear. All she could do now was wait. She felt like a prisoner within the chamber. Edward hadn't specifically given the order for her to be held inside. The door wasn't locked. But if she ventured out, she ran the chance that Ross would accost her, or Edward himself would demand more answers regarding Wallace and Brandon. Answers she couldn't give.

She supposed having the ability to leave was good enough for her, and staying behind the closed door, she had a better chance of staying safe and sane.

The door handle jiggled, making her belly flip up into her throat. She held her breath, bracing for whoever entered.

"Thank God," she muttered when the older maid who'd helped to set her arm entered with a tray of food.

"Morning, my lady. I've brought you something to break your fast."

"My thanks, Mrs. Busby."

The older woman smiled. "So you do remember me."

"How could I forget?"

Mrs. Busby's husband was killed in a freak gardening accident—crushed by a man the king had tossed from an upper window at Westminster Palace. Mariana had been in the garden at the time, and promised the woman she'd find her employment, which she did, but hadn't seen the woman since. At least two years had passed since then.

Mrs. Busby nodded, her eyes solemn. "I am glad to see you up and about. After you eat, I could change you into a gown, though you should be in bed resting."

Mariana smiled. "There is no need." If she dressed in a gown, she might be deemed well enough to accept visitors—which she did not want to do.

"Eat up now. You need your strength." She wagged her finger at Mariana. "And drink that tisane, 'twill help with the healing of your injuries."

Mrs. Busby didn't know the half of it. Mariana needed more than food and tisanes to heal and grow strong. Peace of mind would be a good place to start. Brandon would be another…

She leaned over to study her breakfast. The scent of porridge wafted from the bowl. A little milk and honey had been drizzled over it. A steamy cup of tea and a sliced apple accompanied the meal. Mariana picked up the spoon and swirled it around in the porridge, making a divot in the middle.

"There is some talk of His Majesty traveling to France when this business is done." Mrs. Busby spoke casually as she fluffed Mariana's pillows and straightened her bed sheets.

She set down her spoon and took a gulp of the warm tisane.

"Talk of his marrying Princess Margaret."

"Margaret?" She swallowed past the lump in her throat. She and Margaret had played together as children. Now her childhood friend would marry Edward…

"Aye, did you know her?"

Mariana did a slow blink, praying to God that Edward disposed of her before Margaret ever crossed his threshold. That would be the worst sort of mortification. Mariana would toss herself from an upper window before she faced her childhood friend to tell her she would be sleeping with her husband on the nights her wifely duties were not required.

She managed a stiff smile and bit into a crisp apple slice. "I may have met her once or twice."

"I've heard she is beautiful." Mrs. Busby moved from tending the bed to stoking the fire.

"Any word on when that might be?" Mariana tried to keep her voice casual.

Mrs. Busby shrugged. Not exactly forthcoming with information, but at least Mariana's question hadn't piqued the maid's interest. "No telling. Just a lot of talk right now. You know more than any how negotiations must go." The older woman gasped, pressed a hand to her cheek. "My word, I can't believe I just said that. Please accept my apologies."

The woman's eyes were filled with regret. Mariana pressed her lips into some semblance of a smile. "There is no need to apologize. We all know how I came to be here, and what my place is."

Mrs. Busby swallowed, her throat bobbing with an audible gulp. "All the more reason I should have watched my tongue. This marriage business is bound to distress you."

For reasons Mrs. Busby was obviously taking out of context. Why did everyone believe that Mariana must be in love with the king?

"Indeed, 'tis distressing. Alas, what am I to do about it?" She gave a dainty shrug, allowing the maid to believe what she would. "I am beholden to my king, and I will do whatever it is he asks."

With that said, she turned back to her cooling porridge. The boiled grains felt heavy in her belly as her stomach churned.

"I think I should like to rest." As gracefully as she could manage, Mariana stood and walked slowly to the bed. "If you'd let everyone know I'm not to be disturbed?"

"Aye, my lady. Aye." Mrs. Busby backed out of the room, her head down.

Mariana slid carefully onto the bed. Lying on her back, she stared up at the ceiling, thinking about Brandon, his enchanting eyes and mischievous smile. The easy way he spoke with her. She escaped into the dark night that she and Brandon made love. A memory she'd worried would leave a bitter taste on her tongue, but which in reality saved her from falling apart.

She closed her eyes, and could almost feel Brandon's touch, his lips skimming over hers. At first, the memory of his caresses, the moments of abandon where she felt she lived in a dream comforted Mariana. But as the minutes ticked by, and she longed desperately to see Brandon again, those precious flashes only haunted her. Teasing her with what she couldn't have.

Mariana was grateful when Mrs. Busby's tisane took effect, lulling her into sleep.

"Are ye ready?" Wallace eyed Brandon as though he were preparing to leap off a cliff.

"More than ready." He wasn't going to wait any longer to take control of this situation. To get Mariana back and put Ross down.

"'Twill be dangerous."

Brandon winged a brow at Wallace. "That I am aware of. Where has your confidence gone? Ye're the man whose defeated countless English, rallied the country to join you in the fight for our freedom, our very lives. Ye are our guardian, and yet ye seem to have doubts about this mission."

Wallace clasped his shoulder, studied him, his bushy brows knit together in a frown. "A man is only good with his sword when he is nay compromised."

"I'm nay compromised."

"Aye, but ye are. Ye're consumed with thoughts of the woman. I can tell ye now, from experience, 'twill get someone killed."

Brandon swallowed. He'd heard rumors of Wallace having lost a woman. Knew the man's cousin had been killed a few months prior. Many of his men, long since in their graves. He turned serious eyes on Wallace. "I willna let my feelings for Mariana get in the way of this mission."

"And what is the mission?"

"Extract Ross from Ion Dubh."

Wallace let go of Brandon's shoulder and gave a single, solid nod. "Aye."

Brandon held his breath and waited. Would Wallace give him permission to rescue Mariana? And if he didn't, would he go after her anyway, deal with the consequences after? He'd pledged his loyalty to this man, would he betray him for the likes of one woman? A woman he couldn't truly trust? 'Haps

Wallace was right. He was compromised. Mariana was not the mission. Ross was. But, he could get Ross *and* Mariana out alive. He was certain.

"If ye happen to come across her, or ye happen to get Ross out, and there is still time, I give ye my blessing to find your woman."

The words he'd been waiting for. Brandon's chest tightened. "Gratitude, sir."

"Och, dinna talk to me like I'm so much the better of ye."

"But ye are."

"Ye are a laird, of higher position within your clan."

Brandon shook his head. "But ye are Guardian of Scotland." This time he clapped his hand on Wallace's shoulder. "Let us not get bogged down with names. What is troubling ye?" It had become obvious there was much more going on in Wallace's mind than the task of finding Ross.

Wallace gave a half-smile, a short laugh. "Naught that ye want to hear."

"Try me."

Wallace glanced up at the castle, a crack of thunder rolling overhead. "I've been here afore now."

A shot of lightning streaked through the sky, landing somewhere not too far away. The horses shifted uncomfortably, a few whinnying their disproval.

"Now is the best time for us to go." Wallace frowned. "The watchmen will be huddling under cover, their guard down."

As much as Brandon wanted to refuse so he could hear what Wallace was going to say, he knew the man spoke the truth. Getting inside Ion Dubh was going to prove a feat he'd be lucky to live through.

After the sun had set last eve, he and Wallace had gone to the cliff by the water. There was indeed a port, and a pulley system that would bring a man right to the top. It was loud, and squeaked. With the thunderstorm, the sound of their approach would be dulled.

"Let's go." Wallace rounded up the men.

A half dozen could fit on the platform at a time, with another four yanking on the ropes that lifted the platform into the air.

A cursory look around the quay showed no guardsmen. Brandon gave the sign that it was all clear, and they sneaked closer to the lift.

"Ye go up with the first round," Wallace instructed.

A dozen of them were going to breach the walls, another dozen remaining behind to pull them down when they were done. If the lift was consumed by guards, they would make it out the front, and pray not to get shot in the arse by an arrow.

Rain pelted them in droves. Brandon tore a piece of his shirt and wrapped it around his forehead, stopping some of the rain from falling into his eyes. His men did likewise.

The wood boards of the lift creaked as he stepped onto it. His men followed, a tight fit for six overlarge warriors covered in weapons. He grabbed hold of the wooden railing and nodded to Wallace. The men in charge of the pulley gave their first yank. The screeching sound of the metal contraptions was in fact dulled by a roll of thunder and the crashing of the waves below. Thank the gods.

Salt water sprayed up onto his face, mixing with the rain water. He was soaked through. The cold temperature not quite freezing his clothes in place, but making it uncomfortable nonetheless.

Agonizing minutes later, they were near the top. The men below stopped pulling as they'd been instructed so Brandon could make sure the area was clear.

Damn. One guard, but he was huddled beneath a plaid on the damp stone platform. It appeared this part of the castle as like a man-made cave. Ahead, stone stairs were lit. That would be how they got into the castle.

With a glance down, he drew in a deep breath. 'Twas steep. Deadly. No rail or rope to hold anyone back. How many men had fallen to their deaths here? Brandon held up one finger to the men below, who kept their hold steady. Just one guard they had to get rid of.

"We need to take him out before he sounds the alarm," Brandon said.

The warrior directly in front of him, John, nodded. "I'll do it." He pulled out a long dagger from his sleeve, pulled his arm just to his shoulder and then let the weapon fly.

The guard didn't make a sound, just slumped over.

Brandon signaled the men below who cranked the pulley enough for them to disembark.

"We're in," he said under his breath. The next few minutes were going to be crucial. "Let's get that whoreson."

Chapter Eighteen

They swept like shadows through the halls of the castle, taking out guards as they passed. Servants seemed to have caught a sixth sense and disappeared. Many of the corridors were dark, but the men seemed fueled by a sense of vengeance that gave them vision through the dimly lit spaces.

When they'd reached the center of the castle, just outside the great hall, they stopped.

Loud voices and boisterous laughter sounded through the door. A feast. They were having a feast when his woman was somewhere within these walls. Bastards.

Brandon pointed at his eyes and then at the door, signaling to his men he wanted to look inside the great hall. The men nodded, each standing still with a sword drawn. Most of the castles in Scotland had secret spaces for viewing inside rooms. He just had to figure out where it was. He felt along the wall for a door, a cabinet, anything, but his finger fell into a hole, that was what he was looking for.

Brandon peered through the crack. The great hall was well-lit. Men sat around two long trestle tables, eating and drinking.

Servants lined the walls. So that was where they'd all gone. The only women he spied were servants. No Mariana.

No Longshanks.

No Ross.

"Damn," he said under his breath. Brandon walked back to his men. "Ross and Longshanks are not within."

"We'll find them," John said, his voice filled with confidence.

"I think we should split up." Brandon nodded at the men. "Four groups of three."

The men all paired up, agreeing.

"If ye find Ross, tie him and gag him and take him to the pulley. Lower him. We dinna want to take a chance of losing him. If none of the rest of ye find him within the next quarter hour, ye need to leave all the same. Someone is bound to find their men we've left behind and sound the alarm. We dinna want to be trapped here."

John and Big William—teased for his not so tall stature—followed Brandon up a flight of stairs. They listened at doors for voices, having found none at each they listened to, they still opened the doors to make sure.

One of the doors was locked.

Brandon pulled out his *sgian dubh* and picked the lock. The door creaked open to reveal a study. A banked fire gave off some light, and a fully lit candelabra held candles melted to just an inch tall.

The shutters were tightly closed. A long trestle table took up the middle, surrounded by carved wooden chairs, one at the head with embroidered velvet cushions. Obviously, the king's. Maps and rolled scrolls were everywhere. On the table, covering the various wooden shelves against the wall. Hence the lock. They'd stumbled upon King Edward's war office. And shame on the man for not putting a guard here to make sure no miscreants picked the lock.

Brandon smiled. "A quick look men, for Wallace and the Bruce."

But a quick look ended up being no more than three seconds. *Bloody hell*! A map sprawled out on the table with tiny ships all over it showed a force converging on Eilean Donan Castle.

"*Mo creach*." Brandon grabbed the map, rolled it and stuffed it in his sporran. The Bruce had tarried too long at Eilean Donan. "We need to find Ross and be done with it." *And Mariana too.*

"What of this, my laird?" Big William held up a pouch filled with jangling coins.

"Take it. We'll give it to the villagers we meet along the road. The Sassenach bastard's payment for forcing himself on our people."

Just as they were preparing to leave the room, a light shining through a crack in the wall caught Brandon's attention.

He walked over to the wall and ran his finger along the line. Candlelight definitely flickered through. He was afraid to open the door and see what was on the other side. There was one reason in particular a man would dismiss his guards in favor of a locked door—because he was with a woman.

Brandon's mouth was dry, his throat tight.

Longshanks could be right behind the door—worse still, so could Mariana.

But he had to open it. Was compelled to do so.

He gripped the handle, prepared to lift the latch when John touched his arm. Brandon glanced at the man, saw the subtle shake of his head. He narrowed his eyes.

John pointed to Big William who'd disappeared into a cubbyhole. Brandon walked over, saw Big William crouched low as he peered through a hole made in the wall for guards to keep an eye on the master of the room.

"What do ye see?" Brandon whispered.

In the shadows of that faint light, when Big William looked at him, Brandon felt his stomach turn. The man looked positively frightened. Brandon had to muster all his willpower not to lift Big William and toss him out of the way. He jerked his thumb, and Big William moved back into the study.

When he bent low to gaze through the crack, he wished he hadn't. Wished he'd felt Wallace's fear in the woods and nixed the entire plan.

His heart literally felt like it was being torn from his chest. His cock ripped off. His body felt shredded by a cat-o-nine tails. Was this what heartbreak felt like?

Through the looking hole he had a perfect view of the room. A monumental view of the woman he loved on her knees before Longshanks. The bastard's head was thrown back in passion. His long, gnarled fingers curling through her hair as he pressed her down then yanked her up. Even the sound of her mouth working his pike echoed in the stone cubbyhole.

Her glorious hair was wrapped around the king's wrist. Though he couldn't see her face, her hair gave her away. The heart-shape of her naked arse. Her slender back.

Big William must have recognized her too. Mariana's glorious midnight locks were her signature. He'd never seen another woman with hair like that. Shiny, dark, like sparkling black diamonds.

The woman moaned with pleasure as Longshanks shoved her mouth down harder on his erection. Bile rose in Brandon's throat. He clenched his hands into fists. Only John's hand firmly on his shoulder kept him from charging into that room and lopping the king's head off with one fell swoop.

Lord help him, he wanted to punish her too. The pain of her betrayal was unreal in its intensity. How could he have been such a fool? That he'd allowed himself to fall for her. To love her. To come after her…

A crushing blow. In all the battles he'd been in, no pain had come close to this. Loving her, no matter how good it had felt, had been the wrong course to take. He'd had his doubts, even fought the feelings that cocooned him, but he'd lost. This was a battle where victory went to his opponent. And dammit, why did the opponent have to be the bloody English bastard king?

"Let's go," he said gruffly.

Those two deserved each other.

Mariana paced the length of her room. She kept trying to wring her hands and then remembered that her arm was broken and squeezing her fingers would only bring her pain.

She'd yet to speak to King Edward. Had not seen him since he helped her up in the courtyard. What was taking him so long to summon her?

Marching over to the window, she flung back the shutters. Her gaze caught on a group running into the woods in the distance. They looked to be in a hurry. As though they were running away from something or someone. She rubbed her eyes in attempt to clear any haze and then gazed harder at the group.

Scotsman.

They were most definitely dressed in plaids. Swords strapped to their backs. White strips of something tied to around their foreheads. Brawny Highlanders. Four of the men carried a large sack of something.

Was it possible that Brandon was one of them? Mariana placed her hand on the cold casement and leaned closer to the rain, willing her eyes to see who it was. The movement of the leader, so at ease with his physique, powerful, confident. There was no other man that moved like that. No other man that drew her attention like he did.

Mariana chewed her lip, stopped the call of his name from leaving her mouth. She reached out into the rain, hoping, praying he would turn back. That he'd come back to the castle to get her. But it didn't appear that would ever happen.

He was running away. Leaving her here.

Gasping a sob, she couldn't turn away from the window. Couldn't stop watching him.

Just before the men disappeared into the trees, he turned around. She swore he was looking back at her. His hand came up to his forehead, as though he were trying to block the nonexistent sun, maybe the rain that fell into his eyes.

"Brandon." His name left her lips in a rush of air, and with it, her heart shattered.

When had she fallen so hard? Just that morning she'd realized she loved him. It was as though with that admission, her soul had released and searched for his. Only, he did not return her affections. For a moment she almost believed he did. But now she knew the truth. If he cared for her, he wouldn't leave her here to fend for herself.

'Twas obvious when she wasn't summonsed, and since no one but Mrs. Busby had checked on her, that she'd lost her place within Edward's court. Should she be disappointed? Afraid? She felt relief, though being out of favor didn't bode well for her. Escape was her only option.

The door to her chamber burst open, causing Mariana to jump away from the window and whirl around. Standing in the open doorway was Mrs. Busby, breathing heavily, her hand to her chest.

"My lady!" she screeched.

"What is it?" Mariana rushed forward, her heart pounding.

"The castle is under attack!"

"Attack?" Mariana caught herself slowly turning back to the window, but forced herself to focus on Mrs. Busby, else the woman ask what she'd seen—or worse, tell King Edward she suspected her of seeing something.

"Aye, my lady. I must get you dressed."

"Dressed? Why would you worry over that?" Seemed a trivial thing that she was in her nightgown if the castle was under siege.

"The king has ordered everyone to the great hall."

"Including me? Can you tell him I am still recovering?" The thought of going down into the great hall, seeing everyone, being subjected to the king, and finding out exactly how little she meant in the court was the last thing she wanted to do. Not when she'd just realized that Brandon no longer wanted her.

Her future hung on some invisible thread. She wasn't truly sure there even was a future for her anymore…

"My lady, I cannot. You must let me dress you. If you don't come down to the great hall… The king will be most displeased."

Mariana sighed deeply. If she didn't come down, he would most likely take it out on Mrs. Busby. Having already lost her husband, she couldn't stand to lose her position as a servant to the king and Mariana would never forgive herself if she were the cause. "Very well."

Mrs. Busby breathed an audible sigh. The woman must have been holding her breath, afraid of Mariana's answer and what would happen should she refuse.

"'Tis a good thing I have a gown with loose sleeves so your splint will fit without having to cut it." Mrs. Busby pulled a gown of deep blue from the wardrobe, and along with it, matching slippers.

Mariana stood in place, wincing as Mrs. Busby dressed her, shifting her arm, until finally the gown was in place and she could remain still. The maid tapped her foot to lift it so she could place on her slipper.

"I need to warn you…" The woman cut herself off before finishing.

"What is it?" Mariana glanced down, catching the woman's gaze. "You can tell me."

"You didn't hear it from me."

"I heard it from no one," Mariana answered. Her stomach doubled up in knots and she swallowed hard against the lump in her throat.

"The king has a new mistress."

Mariana nodded, having figured as much.

Mrs. Busby frowned. "She is your spitting image."

Now it was Mariana's turn for her brows to knit. "Me?"

"Aye, my lady. Same glorious hair and feminine figure." She tapped her other foot, slipping on the second slipper. "Not as well-mannered as you are. And English, not French. I suppose if the king's thinking of marrying a French princess, he ought not to be dallying with someone who might be her friend."

Mariana shrugged, pretending indifference. "He would not be the first king."

"This must pain you sorely."

She flashed her maid a wan smile. "'Tis not my place to be pained by it."

And she wasn't. Not that the king had found someone new to warm his bed and accompany him to the feast. No, to Mariana that was all well and good. What made her worry was what the king would do with her now. There'd been no talk of arrangements. She had belonged to him, but now that he was done with her… Dear God, she prayed he hadn't already tied her to another man.

The image of Brandon staring up at her through the rain flaunted itself in her mind. If she'd not been so sure that Brandon was running away from her, she might have welcomed the opportunity to flee to him. To slip from this grim fortress and make her way back to his arms.

"My lady, we must hurry."

Mariana nodded, feeling her head start to pound. She pressed her fingers to one temple, rubbing, wishing she had free use of her other arm.

"My lady…" Mrs. Busby drawled. The woman was positively fretting now, her fingers turning red with the exertion of wringing her gown.

"I am ready."

They encountered only a few guards on the way to the great hall. When she entered, the room fell to a hushed whisper. It appeared everyone had already gathered there. Mariana wanted to hold her head high, to march right into the middle of the room and declare the king set her free. Instead, she lowered her head as was her station, and meekly stepped four feet into the room.

"Lady Mariana. I see you finally chose to join us." The king's voice was drawn out, as though he hoped to set her on edge.

She dipped into a curtsy, but didn't say anything, instead waited for his directive.

"Well, take a seat."

Mariana rose from her curtsy and lifted her chin, her gaze quickly finding the king lounging on the dais with another woman by his side. She did indeed have the same dark hair as Mariana, long and falling in soft waves, but her face was not the same. This woman had a pinched, hungry look about her. In her mind, Mariana wished her luck, for she would need it.

The king studied her intently, watching to see if she was jealous or upset at being replaced. Mariana may have bowed her head, curtsied, and followed all the other rules he implemented, but she wasn't jealous and wouldn't pretend to be. Oh, she could play the part well, but she didn't want to. Not anymore.

The only woman she was jealous of was the next one Brandon fell against.

Mariana turned from the king, and sat down between two nobles. They ignored her, but were not rude.

The game was over.

Chapter Nineteen

It took the stinging slap of a wiry tree branch hitting Brandon in the forehead to realize he was completely insane.

What in bloody hell was he doing?

Blood trickled warm on his forehead, the force of the branch having torn the linen he wore to ward of moisture. He didn't reach up to wipe it away, but felt each minute drop as it made its descent.

Any man in his right mind would continue on, but Brandon thought perhaps his mind hadn't been right to begin with. 'Haps what was right for him was completely different from the norm, but also completely perfect for him.

She was perfect for him. Made him whole in a way he never thought he'd find. Mariana completed him.

The woman was his.

And yet, he was running away from her. Fleeing in the exact opposite direction from whence she was. Like a coward. He should be storming into the castle, tearing her out of the king's arms and demanding she return with him. Stake his claim on her, just as he had the night she called herself Desire.

She was his destiny. His forever. And he'd seen the same in her eyes until he'd rejected her. Forced her into the king's arms. Given her no other choice. Brandon was willing to admit, most of the blame fell on his shoulders. But that didn't mean he couldn't change it now.

He stopped dead in his tracks. Stared ahead at the men as they ran forward a few more feet before sensing his motionless. They turned around, gawked at him.

"We have to go, my laird. Did ye nay hear the alarm raised?" Big William gave him a look that said the man thought he was an absolute imbecile.

"I heard it." He ground his teeth. What he was about to do went into the realms of irrationality. But he'd already deemed himself mad, had he not? "Go on ahead. I'll catch up."

The men gaped at him, slack jawed.

John shook his head vehemently. "Nay, my laird."

Brandon puffed his chest. He'd not change his mind. "Dinna disobey me. I gave ye a direct order."

"My laird…" John hesitated, obviously trying to figure out the right words to change Brandon's mind. "'Tis suicide. I canna let ye go without at least making ye pause for a moment to think on it."

"I've thought long enough already." Brandon didn't hesitate to answer. He knew what he wanted. What he needed—*her*—and he knew exactly how to get it. He thrust the rolled up map showing King Edward's imminent attack toward John. "Tell Wallace to inform the Bruce they must leave the castle. Find a new camp. They are not safe at Eilean Donan any longer. Dinna wait for me. I'll find ye."

The man hesitated. Looked ready to say something, but Brandon shook his head stopping whatever words he'd say. John's face fell. The man was resigned to the fact that he would have to let his laird have his way.

Brandon crossed his arms over his chest and narrowed his eyes. "I'll nay change my mind. Go. Now."

"Move out," John bellowed at the men, his frustration obvious.

Brandon grinned, though it probably looked more like a grimace.

Without a backward glance, he took off at a run toward Ion Dubh Castle—and Mariana.

At least thirty uncomfortable minutes passed in the great hall. Mariana between two overlarge men who stuffed their faces and spoke over her to each other, particles of their meal falling into her hair. Disgusting.

If the castle had in fact been under attack, the king did not seem in the least bit worried over it. And that, actually worried her most.

Finally, he stood at the dais and cleared his throat. Everyone silenced at once. An eerie thing to transpire. But not one of them wanted to end up swinging from the end of a rope, or bleeding from an ear to ear slice to the throat.

Mariana had barely been able to eat a thing. She was able to grab a slice of meat, but once on her trencher, there was no way for her to cut it with the use of only one hand, and she dared not ask one of the men to do so for her, lest they get the wrong idea. She speared the hunk of meat with her eating knife and held it up to her lips, taking a bite. The meat was tough and it took a good bit of gnawing to break a piece off.

She might be sitting between two disgusting oafs, but she wasn't about to become one of them. Besides that, her stomach roiled every time she felt a bit of food land on her head.

Hunger was a far better thing to fair through than vomiting all over the table. The wine on the other hand, was easy to reach, and easy to maneuver. The liquid warmed her insides and took the edge off not only her hunger but her weariness.

When King Edward did finally stand, after her long laborious bout of non-merriment between her dinner partners, she was almost interested in what he had to say.

Edward walked down from the dais, sauntering with all the arrogance he possessed up and down the aisles. The silence in the room was so great, Mariana could hear the clink of the chain mail Edward wore beneath his doublet.

He stopped right behind her. The hair on the back of her neck stood on end. What did he want? Was he trying to make her nervous? If so, he was doing a damn good job of it. Her fingers trembled. She shoved them in her lap. She had to remain calm. In control. The wine she'd drunk didn't make her forget how dangerous he was. Anxiety took control, planting all sort of nefarious ideas in her mind. None of them answered the question shouting inside her—why was he standing behind her?

Edward was a master at making people cower with fear. She was no exception. He didn't speak, instead he let his presence, his nearness, the sinister machinations her own conscience compiled, do their worst. Mariana was no stranger to this particular ploy of King Edward's. She'd witnessed it at least a dozen times. But never, not once, had she been the victim of it. Until now.

The only way to beat Edward at his own game was to show no emotion. A task she excelled at. Although, doing so would put her in another predicament, and she might very well face his wrath.

Letting out the breath she'd been holding in a long, slow, silent whoosh, she reached for her goblet. Two could play this game. Sheer force of will made her fingers still their quiver as she gripped the stem and pulled the drink to her lips. A sip, the sweet tangy taste of fermented grapes, traveled over her tongue.

In all her days, however many she had left, Mariana was sure she'd remember the flavor.

A cold hand pressed to her shoulder.

"Perhaps, my lady, you would care to enlighten those present with the identities of our visitors."

The wine felt suddenly solid as dried bread as she swallowed down her constricted throat. Setting the goblet down carefully, she lowered her hands to her lap. Without looking at King Edward, Mariana answered softly, "Your Highness, I could not know."

He leaned low, his sour breath on her ear. "Ah, but you do, my lady, you do." His hand on her shoulder increased in pressure. "Tell them who it was."

Laced with venom, his voice sent a shiver of dread racing up and down her spine. Mariana was trapped. There was no getting out of this. He'd targeted her, wanted to punish her.

"Your Highness, I beg of you. I was but asleep in my room, recovering from my injuries."

"Liar," he whispered.

She hated when his voice got so low. When he spoke in hisses and through gritted teeth. Normally when a man raised his voice you could tell he was angry, but not so with Edward. The angrier he was, the quieter he got.

Just as she would try when gentling an animal, Mariana reached up and placed her hand on Edward's. She prayed that her light touch would send a spark of calm through him. But the king yanked away as though she'd burned him. Not for long however. The next moment, instead of squeezing her shoulder, his fingers were at the nape of her neck, tight and uncomfortable.

"Stand," he hissed.

Mariana did as he ordered. Not looking him in the eye. The king was much like a rabid dog and she had to move slowly, appearing docile, else he bite her.

"How did you come to be here?"

"Your Highness?"

"Don't play coy with me. Tell the people how you came to be here."

Mariana took a chance and glanced around the room, hoping to find a friend in the crowd. Most people looked away, embarrassed for her, uncomfortable to be witnessing the king's brutality against one he used to cherish. His new mistress sat gloating upon the dais. Mariana pitied her for not realizing that she would be in this same position one day.

"I was brought by Laird Ross."

The king growled low and menacing. "Tell them how you came to be in Ross' possession."

Mariana licked nervously at her lips. Telling the exact truth was likely to get her thrown off the nearest cliff. 'Twould only be Ross' word against her own... Then again, if the king already knew the identities of the intruders, he would know she lied, and she might find herself in a puddle of her own blood on this very floor.

There didn't seem to be any way of getting out of this mess alive.

"Laird Ross and his men—"

A loud bang from behind startled them all. Mariana whirled around to see a man dressed in tall leather boots, breeches that clung to his muscled thighs, and a metal-studded leather doublet over top a plain linen shirt. Her heart stopped, then kicked into an irregular drumming. Tall, muscular, perfectly gorgeous. Though his clothes were different, his intense eyes, stubborn square jaw and sensual lips were forever ingrained in her mind.

"Kindly unhand my wife," he drawled in a distinctly English accent.

"Pardon?" the king asked, eyes widening. For the first time she'd ever seen, he looked taken aback.

Brandon bowed low to the king, before straightening. "Your Highness, I have been searching high and low for the woman. I'd be glad to have her back."

"Your…wife?" The king's brow raised and he spoke slowly, Mariana guessed to regain his composure.

"Aye, Your Highness."

King Edward laughed, and gazed about the room. "How in the world did she become your wife, and whom may I ask are you?"

Brandon stared straight into the king's eyes, a bold move. "She became my wife when I found her amongst the burning village at Kinterloch. When we stood before God and professed to be each other's destiny."

Edward coughed, letting go of her. Mariana didn't move, though she wanted to run headlong for Brandon.

"Who are you?" King Edward demanded.

"I am Sir Whitley. My wife was stolen from me when men attacked our entourage."

"Is that so?"

"Aye."

The king continued to eye Brandon as if he were a fly he wanted to crush. "Why did you not seek my permission to marry?"

"'Twas a matter of life and death, Highness."

"The same situation you find yourself in now."

"I supposed 'tis a situation I often find myself in." There was an arrogant edge to Brandon's voice that bespoke of his power. Anyone in the room could hear it. But Mariana prayed the king did not take issue with it. There was no doubt in her mind, Brandon could easily dispatch Edward, but then he'd have the whole of the castle crashing down on him.

The king plucked at the sword at his hip. "I've not heard of you before, Sir Whitely. Why do you suppose that is?"

Brandon shrugged. "'Tis a shame we've not met before. I do apologize. I've not had the chance to come to court yet."

The king grunted. "And under whom do you serve?"

Mariana bit the inside of her cheek, sure that Brandon would unravel soon with the barrage of questions the king had. He couldn't keep the charade going for long. She stepped forward, intent on begging the king to let them go, but Edward held his arm out, stopping her from moving closer to Brandon.

He glared at Mariana. A lethal look that said he knew Brandon was lying and that he'd find out the truth of it soon. She clenched her teeth to keep them from chattering.

"Baron Berkeley."

Again the king grunted. Mariana couldn't be sure if he was displeased or not.

"Then you won't mind waiting for confirmation on that."

Brandon shook his head, his face turning solemn. "Unfortunately all of my men were killed in the attack. Berkeley sent us on our own to raid the next village over when we encountered the fire."

Brandon spoke with a straight face, as though he actually believed each word he spoke. Mariana wondered if he had not encountered a group of Berkeley's men and used one of the soldiers identities now. If he were to be found out…

"That is unfortunate." The king faced the trestle table to the right. He glanced back at Brandon, a menacing, smug smile on his lips, then returned his gaze to the table. "Baron Berkeley, can you confirm what this man has said?"

Mariana's blood ran cold. They would die here today, at the hands of a man who'd held her life in his grasp for years. There was no escaping him. She should have known that all along.

She stared imploringly at Brandon, but he wouldn't meet her gaze. Instead, he stared intently at the man who pushed back from the table behind her. Her throat itched with the need to scream.

King Edward whirled around. "Well, dammit, Berkeley, speak. A man and woman's lives are at stake here." The glee in his voice made Mariana's already roiling stomach lurch. His eyes were lit up like a devil staring at the next batch of loathsome souls he was going to consume.

She grew dizzy. Head pounding, legs weak. *Be strong*, she chanted to herself.

Brandon did glance at her then, his eyes filled with hope, promise. His lips moved into a small smile sending a rush of fresh emotion through her. She couldn't lose him. Not now.

He'd come back for her. Even if they died in the next few minutes, at least she knew there had been a chance at a future together, that all her feelings, her love for him, were returned.

Heart soaring, she smiled back.

Chapter Twenty

Sweat trickled an uncomfortable path down Brandon's spine. Their future lay in the very words the fumbling, drunken lord could not seem to muster.

Worst of all, Brandon was wearing breeches. *Breeches* for bloody sake. His meat and two veg were so jam-packed within the confines of the malicious garment he was ready to rip them off, forget the audience, and battle the entire great hall stark naked.

The wanton lass upon the dais, lounging in her chair as though drugged, gazed at him with a look he'd seen many times. She was a practiced whore, one who obviously got what she wanted—the king. How could he have ever thought she was Mariana? The woman lacked a distinct luster to her hair that made Mariana's glisten and shine in the light like the moon glinting off a darkened loch. The king's new woman was thinner, bonier, not as luscious. He recoiled at how wrong he'd gotten it.

Looking at Mariana only made his guilt and need to be out of this place worse. Her arm hung in a sling and slight bruises and scrapes marred her face. She looked battered, vulnerable. The lass tried to hide her fright, but the way her eyes widened and her lips were thin and white when they were normally plush and pink, gave her away. Still, her spine was stiff and she held her ground. Strength filled her. The lass had more bravery than she was probably even aware of. He tried to smile at her, hoped that it would make her feel slightly better, and it seemed to as she beamed a smile his way.

Mo creach, he hadn't had a clue what to do, how he was going to get her out of here until he'd crossed paths with the English maggot he'd stolen the clothes from. Lucky for him, the fellow had been nearly his size. Hence the extra tightness with the breeches. Brandon's cousin, Ronan Sutherland, oft dressed as an Englishman in order to pass over the border or come close to it without being bothered by the king's men. As children, they'd played Sassenach Whoreson—at least that's what he called it—and Brandon had gotten pretty damn good at it.

After stealing the guard's clothes, figuring out his identity was simple. Sir Whitely—a man who still actually lived. Brandon and his men had taken the fellow prisoner when the lout and his following had gone raiding near Eilean Donan about a month before. The man had spilled about Baron Berkeley. Fortunately, Whitely looked enough like Brandon for him to pass off.

Brandon's story would hold—if the inebriated lord could remember it.

Longshanks smiled, sly, just like a cat that'd cornered a mouse. The scoundrel wanted them to fail. Desired desperately to act out some vile punishment he cooked up in his mind. Brandon could feel it, sense it. King Edward wanted to hurt Mariana. But why?

"As I recall, there was a cavalry sent out in the Highlands several months ago," Baron Berkeley said, rubbing his thumb and forefinger along his long pointy beard. The man's face was covered in dark spots, and a mole the size of a rat turd stood prominently in the middle of his forehead.

"Oh, dear me," King Edward said, sarcasm dripping from his voice. He placed his hands to his face as though alarmed. "The Highlands you say? Dear God in Heaven save us all."

The room erupted into shouts of laughter, men elbowing each other. From the corner of his eye, he noted Mariana still stared straight at him and no other. She played the part of a wife very well, holding steadfast to her husband—or so he'd told everyone. With every ounce of his being he wanted her to be his.

Someone finally put the confused Berkeley out of his misery, elbowing the sot and informing him loudly that they, too, were in the Highlands.

Baron Berkeley cleared his throat and gave a nervous laugh. "Apologies, my king, I seem to have forgotten myself for a moment. Indeed, a few months back I did send out cavalry to scout out the Highlands for the major castles near waterways. Sir Whitely was among the men."

"Ah, I see." The king turned to face Brandon, his eyes narrowed. "'Twould appear your story holds up, Sir Whitely. I have an idea that it might have been different if our good Baron here was not so intoxicated."

Brandon bowed to the king, hoping to show that he was a loyal subject—and not that he wanted to slice him into a thousand jagged pieces. "I assure you, Your Highness, I am your most loyal subject."

That last part might not have been entirely a lie. It seemed from what Brandon had heard, that everyone was always climbing over top of each other, and not a one truly cared who their liege lord was, as long as they got a piece from his coffer of gold.

"As for you, Lady *Mariana,*" the king drawled, refusing to call her Lady Whitley. "I do hope we see each other again sooner rather than later."

Brandon refused to read into the king's veiled threat. Their story had passed muster and he wanted to get Mariana the hell out of there. However, it wasn't over yet, and he wasn't going to risk losing it now because he didn't follow some courtly rule. He waited for the king to dismiss them, a move that seemed unlikely to happen as the seconds ticked by.

When the crowd began to grow antsy, and Brandon was about to begin a brawl that ended with him stealing one of the nearby guards' sword, the king waved his hand in the air.

"Sir Whitely, take this woman, your *wife,* and leave my castle. Get back to your post and kill as many savages as you can along the way."

Rage burned in Brandon's chest, but along with it was the acute sense of relief. They weren't completely out of danger, but it was a start. He held out his hand for Mariana who rushed forward, limping slightly. Guilt at not protecting her made his stomach burn. He had to make it up to her.

Mariana's warm fingers slid against his, squeezing tight and a lightning current jolted up his arm. *Mo creach,* she felt good.

"My king," Brandon said with a bow.

Beside him, Mariana curtsied and murmured the same.

Kind Edward glowered at them. "We will meet again," he said.

"I shall look forward to it," Brandon replied.

The next time they met, he hoped it was in a dark forest where no one could watch as he cut the heart out of the English king.

"Let's go," he whispered to Mariana, tugging her hand.

There was no resistance from her. They hurried from the great hall, all the while, keen to hear if the king sent someone after them. No footsteps pounded toward them. No shouts of reprisal. Leaving Ion Dubh with Mariana was easier than he thought. Too easy.

Whenever a serious situation appeared to transpire stress-free, Brandon waited for the backlash. In this instance, they had to outrun whatever the repercussion would be.

When still no one intercepted them at the great doors, they pushed out into the courtyard. Rain still fell, though in less violent waves. He glanced toward Mariana, rain soaking her gown.

"Your cloak," he murmured.

"There is no time to retrieve it. I shall be fine." Her face was set, showing a stubborn streak he'd seen before.

"Wear mine," he said, tugging it from around himself.

"I couldn't."

"I've another." He wrapped the cloak around her, taking a moment to touch her cold, wet cheek. "I couldna bear to see ye suffer more."

Mariana leaned into his cheek, her blue eyes locking on his. "I've not suffered overmuch. Now that you are here, it is all fading away."

He wanted to kiss her. Wanted to look her in the eyes and know that what they were feeling was mutual, not a game played behind pretend names or in darkened rooms. He wanted to pull her into his arms and tell her that he loved her. He wanted to see her eyes when he pressed his mouth to hers, and see the emotion cross her face when he murmured her name against her cheek.

Mariana pressed her lips to his palm, then said, "We have to go. Before he changes his mind."

Brandon nodded. She spoke the truth. They'd only be tempting a bear if they didn't disappear now.

"I know."

A rain-soaked mount waited in the courtyard, the groomsman he'd tossed a coin to still holding the reins.

Brandon had taken the man's horse when he took his clothes, stripping it of anything discriminating.

"Our horse."

She raised a brow. "You truly did think of everything."

He winked at her, loving the shy smile she returned. "For ye, I would do anything."

Brandon lifted her onto the horse and tossed a second coin at the groomsman whose eyes were as wide as platters. "For your trouble. And your silence."

"My thanks, my lord, heartily." The boy took off at a run toward the stables.

Brandon swung up behind Mariana, making sure she was fully covered by the cloak. He urged the horse into a trot. They weren't going to walk out of this. The guard atop the gate studied him, suspicious. He looked behind Brandon and Mariana, perhaps expecting the inhabitants of the castle to come storming out, but when no one did, he opened the gates and let down the drawbridge.

Feeling as though Satan nipped at their heels, he didn't slow the horse, but galloped straight through the gate.

With Brandon's arms wrapped around her, the heat of his body warmed Mariana from head to toe. His hard chest was pressed tight to her back. Muscled thighs straddling her behind, and going the length of her legs. They were racing for their lives, but her heart sprinted for an altogether different reason.

When he'd leaned close, lips poised to kiss her, Mariana had desperately wanted to take him up on his offering. But to do so would only stall their departure and King Edward wasn't known to let people simply leave.

She feared his coming after them. Could imagine him in his great hall, turning to the guard and hissing, "After them!"

But now that they were gone, alone, and nearly safe, Mariana wanted to beg Brandon to stop the horse, to tilt her head back and claim a kiss that made her quake.

Obviously having no intention of slowing, Brandon pushed their horse hard. She recognized the path he took as the one she'd seen from her window. Over the road they flew until they disappeared into the trees. Brandon reduced the horse's speed then, but not to a complete walk. They trotted through the dimly lit woods. Small droplets of rain sprinkled down through the branches and leaves to trickle over them.

"Did you mean what you said?" Mariana asked, her stomach doing a little flip. If he said no…

Brandon gave her a quizzical look. "What did I say?"

"That I was your…wife?" She chewed her lip, suddenly very interested in how her mouth could take such abuse with all the chewing and biting she'd been doing lately.

"Well, lass, how could I? Ye are nay my wife."

Mariana couldn't help the gasp of surprise. For certain, he was right, but she hadn't expected him to be so blunt about it. She tilted her head back to look at him. He glanced down at her, eyes glinting with humor, and in complete opposition to what he'd just said.

"I…I…" What could she say? Heat suffused her cheeks. Lord, she wanted to sink far, far, far into the damp ground. The red of her cheeks had to rival that of a ripe apple. Did he jest with her or not?

Brandon chuckled. "Och, I but tease ye. In truth, ye are yet to be my wife, but that doesna mean I lied. Ye will be my wife, Mariana. My destiny."

She sagged against him, a heavy breath pushing past her lips. "I want you for a husband..."

"Why do I sense a but, there? 'Tis the truth I think ye could do better," he teased. Brandon tugged the reins, the mount coming to a stop.

"I have something to tell you. A matter which may change your mind about me." Her voice was whisper soft and her stomach churned. How could she confess to a man with a position like Brandon's that if he were to marry her, they would not be able to have a child? No heir to his clan.

He pressed a finger to her chin and turned her so that she had to face him. A soft, coaxing smile on his lips. "Tell me, lass. I swear, even if your plan is to kill me once we've wed, it will have been worth it, though I will put up one hell of a fight."

Mariana shook her head. "Murdering you is the last thing on my mind, I promise you."

"Then dinna fash. I would never harm ye."

Mariana took a deep cleansing breath, then blurt out the most horrifying words a prospective husband ever wanted to hear. "I am barren."

Brandon stilled for a moment, studied her closely, his eyes searching hers.

His fingers fell from her chin. "Barren? How do ye know this?"

Mariana glanced toward the ground, feeling tears burn behind her lashes. She breathed out again, hoping not to lose her voice to a sob. "You know my past… I've never been with child, even given that."

Brandon shrugged. "Maybe the men ye were with took precaution. Or 'haps they were barren themselves. 'Tis not always the woman's fault."

Mariana flashed her gaze up at him. "You don't understand. If you take me to wife, I will not be able to give you a child." She couldn't look at him, not now that she'd ruined everything. But keeping that truth was not an option. He had to know.

Brandon pressed a finger to her chin again and forced her to look at him once more. She moved her head, but kept her eyes lowered, not wanting to see the truth in his eyes. He would retract his offer of marriage.

"Look at me, Mariana," he said softly.

After several moments, she did indeed raise her eyes to his.

"I want to marry ye. I want to be with ye for the rest of my days. If that means we canna have a bairn together, then so be it. There are enough children within the clan, and I've enough cousins to give us heirs. Ye are what I want. Not your womb."

Mariana's mouth fell open, and though she tried to speak, no words came out.

"Aye. Ye." Brandon brushed his lips over hers. "Now, we've reached my things," he murmured.

He jumped down, her back instantly cold and Mariana mourned the loss of his touch and heat. Brandon lifted aside some brush and pulled out his plaid and weapons.

"You went into the castle unarmed?"

Brandon glanced up at her, and she lost her breath. He was ruggedly handsome, and oozed sensuality, even when rummaging in the bushes. "We'd not be here had I not. Kept these though." He slid up his sleeves to show the knives strapped to his forearms.

"How did you come by those clothes? And how did you know about Sir Whitely and Baron Berkeley?" In the confusion and urgency of escaping, she'd not asked.

Brandon explained quickly about coming across Whitely near Kinterloch, and the lone guard he'd stolen the garments from.

"We'd best hurry. The man will no doubt be wandering naked toward the gate of Ion Dubh any moment."

"Naked? You stripped him to the skin?"

Brandon laughed. "Had to. Couldna risk him chasing me in his braies."

Mariana smiled. "While the view is much more…revealing, I like you better with your plaid."

Brandon stood proud, his thighs and…other parts…outlined by the tight-fitting breeches. His gaze turned dark, hungry. "I like it that ye were looking."

Heart kicking up a notch, Mariana nodded. "I can't help myself. When I'm around you…"

Brandon took two large steps toward her, reached up and grasped her face between his coarse hands. He brushed his thumbs tenderly over her cheek bones, and they both searched each other's eyes for answers, for confirmation.

"Me too, lass, me too." His lips crushed to hers, claiming, taking, demanding.

Mariana grabbed onto his thick upper arm, leaning down into his fiery kiss. His lips were soft but firm, his tongue sweet and velvety hot as he slid it between her willing lips. She met each stroke of his tongue with one of her own. It seemed the last time they'd kissed had been so long ago. Too long.

Brandon wrapped his arms around her, and pulled her from the horse, making sure to be gentle with her broken arm. Her breasts crushed to his chest, nipples instantly hard, the crux of her thighs tingling. Love soared deep inside, and she wanted desperately to shout it out.

"Oh, Brandon… I dreamed of this. Prayed you'd come for me."

"Lass, I felt like someone had taken a piece of me when Ross carried ye off."

They spoke between fervent kisses, as though each one could be their last.

"I thought you might return, ye Scots swine." Mariana jumped at the sound of the voice behind them. "Give me back my clothes, then get down on your knees so I can kill you."

She opened her eyes and turned slowly. The man held a thin sword an inch or two away from her back.

"Don't hesitate you barbarian, else I gore your woman and you watch her guts spill at your feet."

Chapter Twenty-One

Brandon wished that this was the first time a situation like this had arisen. He wasn't proud to admit on the last occasion, the man on the other end of the sword was an angry husband intent on cutting his cock off. The woman he'd been kissing at the time was married—a fact he wasn't aware of, else he wouldn't have stolen her away for a rut in a hidden alcove.

In this case, Brandon actually felt lucky that the woman he was holding was supposed to be there, and the man on the other end of the sword was simply irked because he stole his clothes.

Brandon held up his hands, showing he was unarmed. Mariana did not move from his embrace, but did stare behind her at their threat.

"Apologies for leaving ye less than dressed, good sir. 'Twas an emergency."

A line of dried blood was on the man's forehead, from where Brandon hit him earlier with the hilt of his sword to subdue him. The bastard no doubt had one hell of a headache, which probably only made him more ornery.

"I don't give two shits about your emergency, Scots garbage. I care about you dying."

Well, it would appear reasoning wasn't going to work with this Sassenach.

"I shall willingly die, if ye but let the lass go."

Mariana gasped but made no comment, no move.

The man did exactly what Brandon expected him to do—he eyed Mariana like a piece of meat. Meat he could take a bite out of and savor slowly. Brandon was ready to knock the bastard senseless once more. His muscles tightened, ready to pounce.

As if sensing the man's interest, Mariana pushed out her chest, cocked her hip. What in heavens was she doing? Did she *want* the English prick?

"Oh, please have mercy. Don't hurt the Scotsman. He can't help it that he's Scottish," she pouted, her silky voice working its magic on them both.

Before he could grab her back she'd taken a step closer to the man, his sword blade sliding an inch into the air above her shoulder, but she didn't seem to notice or care. "Take pity on me, that I married him. Let me at least know he didn't die for my sake."

English licked his lips, having eyes only for the lass weaving him into her spell.

"A lady such as yourself shouldn't be shackled to that bastard," English said, anger in his tone. His eyes were filled with want.

Desire that left Brandon feeling physically ill.

His hands itched to reach out and grab her back. Force her away from the smelly, dirty, louse-infested arse.

Mariana did not appear to feel the same way. She reached out, traced a three inch line on the man's blasted chest. Brandon ground his teeth so hard he was afraid they might chip.

He'd clenched his hands into fists and was very close to sending one heavily into his opponent's eye. Give him another trickle of dried blood to match the other.

"Oh, I know…but King Edward insisted. I was his mistress until a few weeks ago."

The man's mouth gaped. "Lady Mariana?"

She nodded, the hair on the back of her head rustling with the wind. Brandon wanted to touch it. To reach out and twirl a glossy lock around his finger. Thought about doing so—until he realized where they were and what the significance of such a move might mean to the man who threatened their lives.

He was torn. At an impasse as to what to do. The Englishman was distracted enough that he could pull one of the knives from his sleeves. He could throw it, but worried that Mariana would move at the last minute and end up with a knife embedded in her face, rather than the blade hitting its intended target.

That was a risk he couldn't take.

So, he watched like a fool as she touched the man again. The bastard was mesmerized. Brandon could only imagine the captivating smile curling her lips, the way her eyes were probably a little wider than usual, not making her look surprised but rather intrigued.

Mariana was an expert with men. Taking beasts in hand. He was completely disgusted. Not with her, but how the tip of the man's sword fell toward the ground, as though he'd not just been holding it with the intent to kill. Brandon might as well put him out of his misery.

Too stupid to live. Any man could kill the bastard now, and do it with full warning given. English was so taken with Mariana, Brandon was pretty sure the man wouldn't have minded if a hundred armed Scots surrounded him right then and there.

Brandon had no fun taking a man's life when he didn't at least put up a fight. Slipping both knives from their sheathes in his sleeves, he then took one giant step forward. With Brandon's chest to Mariana's back, the bastard finally flicked his gaze away from her. Uninterested was the only way to describe the man's flat eyes when he set them on Brandon—well and irritated.

Flashing the man a satisfied grin, Brandon shifted his arms in quick fashion and pressed the blades against either side of the man's neck.

"Lass, I thank ye for distracting the fellow, but if ye would nay mind, could ye duck beneath my arms and take a step back?"

Mariana nodded slowly and bent at the knees, slipping from between Brandon and English.

"Ye might close your eyes," Brandon warned her.

He couldn't see her face, nor did he hear a response. The Englishman finally realized the threat he faced when Mariana no longer cast his spell over him.

"Please, don't hurt me," he begged. Actual tears glistened in his eyes.

This was no fun at all, but completely pathetic.

"Really, man?" Brandon whispered. "Ye'd cry about it?"

The man nodded emphatically. "I got me mum, and me sister, and…" He burst into loud, awful tears. His shoulders shook, head bobbed with the force of all the racket he made.

Brandon scowled. "Pull yourself together." He shook his head. "I willna kill ye, but I'm nay going to let ye go either."

The man was able to stop crying for a few minutes and glanced at Brandon with confusion. "You won't kill me?"

"Nay, ye sorry waste of human flesh. Put your hands behind your back."

The man willingly, and with eager quickness, put his hands behind his back. The stench of his fear permeated the beauty of the forest coming alive. Nature's own scent had a calming effect on Brandon. This maggot was messing with his equilibrium.

Brandon rolled his eyes. "On your knees," he said with a forced growl. Lord, he was close to laughing. "Scuttle over to that tree."

Brandon glanced toward Mariana, partly because he liked to look at her, but also because he wanted to gauge her feelings over the situation. A jolt of appreciation shocked its way through him. The woman was beautiful. Beyond beautiful, she was a vision. Her hair fell in waves around her face, dampened by the rain, and curled with the mist. Her eyes glowed in the light. Porcelain skin with arched brows and high cheekbones. She was a goddess, a seductress. No wonder she had the ability to charm men with a simply bat of her lashes or flash of her even pearly teeth.

With shocking clarity, he realized that he didn't simply love her, he was willing to give away his soul in order to spend the rest of eternity with her. If he didn't know better, he'd have thought he was under her spell. Enchanted like the rest of the men by fantasies that wouldn't come true. But his fantasy had already come to life. Damn, he wanted to kiss her.

"Ouch!" English cried out as his knee banged on a sharp rock. With his hands tied behind his back, he wasn't able to balance himself right, and he bounced on his good knee for a second before falling over on his side.

"Och, ye're a ninny," Brandon said under his breath.

Gripping him by his upper arm, Brandon hauled him up. The man shook beneath his fingertips.

"Come on now, at least try to save face before the lady," Brandon urged.

Seeming to still hold out hope that there was a chance for him and Mariana, English bucked up, straightening his spine and scurrying forward on his knees. When he reached the tree, Brandon pressed the man's chest against it.

"Normally, I'd put your back to the tree. But seeing as how ye stuck around to attack me the first time, I'll not make it so easy."

"But—"

"Dinna argue the point, English. I've already allowed ye to live."

The man whimpered and again Brandon rolled his eyes. Did the man have no pride? Well, the man was English. The whole lot of them seemed to lack any pride, at least that he'd ever known.

Making quick work of tying the sorry lout to the tree, Brandon returned to Mariana whose mouth was curved down in a frown.

"Will he die there?"

Brandon shrugged.

"I wouldn't want you to have his death on your hands."

"Would ye have rather he killed us both?"

She frowned. "I don't think he had killing me on his mind and he wouldn't be the first man I've had to subdue."

"Subdue?" He hated to think what that meant. The thought of her allowing any man to touch her threw him into a fit of jealous rage.

Mariana shook her head. "Toss him a weapon or something."

Brandon picked up a stick and put it into the man's hands. He leaned down close and spoke roughly to him. "Ye see now, I've let ye live and I've given ye a means to escape. Dinna come after me. Dinna tell anyone ye ever saw me."

The man nodded emphatically.

"Your ride, my lady." Brandon lifted Mariana onto the horse, then stuffed his clothes into the satchel at the side and his weapons in the saddle scabbards. There wasn't time to change his attire now. He'd have to bear with what was most certainly chafing.

After leaving the Englishman tied to a tree, Brandon rode his stolen horse ragged back to Eilean Donan Castle. Mariana rode in front of him, her back protected by the wall of his chest, but her mind left vulnerable and contemplative.

Brandon was not the savage she'd been led to believe all Scots were. She'd learned that when he found her outside Kinterloch. None of the men in his crew were barbarians, but men with passion, a fierce loyalty to their lands and people. They were good, wholeheartedly so. Guilt riddled a path throughout her for ever having believed such malicious rumors. If anything, her time with King Edward had proven that his lot were more vicious than any of the Scots she'd come across.

Sinking against his warmth and strength, she allowed herself to close her eyes for a moment. To breathe in his heady masculine scent and dream about what a life with him would be like. Finally free. She didn't have to worry over her future beyond what she and Brandon would do and where they would go.

Never would another man grace her bed, nor would she have to appease a stranger. At last.

Brandon's intake of breath, and the sudden stopping of his mount, had her sitting up straight, eyes open. Instantly, she knew what had made him gasp—just beyond the road, a body hung from the gate gracing the beginning of a bridge. Eilean Donan's bridge.

They'd made it back, but only to see this gruesome sight.

"Dinna look, my sweet. 'Tis not something a woman should have to see."

"But I already have," she whispered. This was not the first body she'd seen. King Edward had made the whole of his court witness countless deaths.

Brandon caressed her face, holding her tight to him. His comfort was calming, not something she'd felt before, and she closed her eyes to make it last.

She felt him squeeze the horse's sides with his legs and the mount trotted forward. Like a bee drawn to a flower, she couldn't help but open her eyes and stare at the man who hung lifeless and bloated from the top of the gate. She recognized him instantly.

Ross.

"'Tis a message," Brandon murmured. "To any English or Scots traitor who comes to find us, to find our rightful king. They will die."

Mariana nodded. The English had long passed their welcome here.

"We will nay find my men within."

Mariana shook her head, having guessed as much already.

"Night comes. We'll need to find shelter."

"Is it not safe within the castle?"

"My guess is, if the English are not already here, they will be coming soon."

Neither of them would be spared, nor treated with mercy.

"We shall make camp for the night elsewhere."

Brandon turned his mount away from the ghastly sight that'd greeted them, and urged it east, away from where they'd come.

Pressing a hand to hers, he lifted it and pressed it to his lips.

"I'm afraid, Mariana, that a life with me is not always going to be pleasant."

"No one's life truly is."

"But ye will be witness to so many things like ye've just seen."

"And as long as I have you beside me, I can overcome it."

Bringing her hand to his lips, he kissed her knuckles sending a shiver of warmth through her. "How did I get so lucky to meet ye?"

"'Twasn't luck, Brandon, but your compassion that brought us together."

"I never thought of myself as a compassionate man. But ruthless. Hard. My father was a brutal man, even to my mother. 'Tis in my blood. I fear it. Fear who I might become, what might already be inside me."

"The measure of a man is not in his blood." Mariana turned around in the saddle and pressed her hand to his heart. "'Tis here. And here." She slid a fingertip from one side of his forehead to the other. "What kind of man do you truly believe yourself to be?"

The intensity of Brandon's eyes locking on hers, held her captive.

"I want to be the man who is good enough for ye. The man who protects ye, honors ye, cherishes ye. Loves ye."

Love. Mariana's heart constricted. "Do you?" she asked. Waiting for his answer was enough to make her wish she'd not asked. The seconds ticked by like hours, and her stomach started to sink.

Brandon's lips were pressed so firmly together they were turning white. "Aye. I do."

"Moi, aussie. Je t'adore." I love you.

"Life with me will nay be like 'twas in a French court or an English court. I'm not as refined. Nor interested in gold, silver and jewels. But I will take care of ye. Love ye with every breath. Endeavor to give ye pleasure and joy."

"That is all I could ever ask for. You, Brandon Sinclair, are a true man. An honorable, compassionate, fierce warrior. I will never ask for anything more, save that you keep me as yours and yours alone."

"Ye were mine, the moment I first saw ye."

And then he kissed her, filling her with all the passion words could not express. Mariana wrapped her arm around Brandon's waist and returned his kiss with every ounce of love she possessed.

Above them, the sun had started to set, and all around them was quiet. Rain still fell, but in a mist that cooled her burning skin. Brandon led their horse into a private copse of fir trees where they were hidden from the outside world. Helping her down from the horse, he held her close against him so she could feel every line and ridge of his body, including his thick arousal pressed to her hip.

"When I make love to ye this time, I will call ye by your given name."

"*Oui,* and this time it will not be so I have a memory to savor, but a new beginning, a new life."

"Oh, my love." Brandon buried his face in her hair, his deep indrawn breath and whooshing out, tickling her neck.

His lips skimmed over her cheek and chin to find her mouth. Tenderly, he brushed his lips over hers, as soft as sigh. But Mariana didn't want him to kiss her softly, she wanted him to take possession of her, to thrust his tongue deep and show her the pleasure she knew he could give her. Taking the lead, she flicked her tongue over the crease of his lips. Brandon growled low in his throat and returned the movement with his tongue.

"Oh, *oui,*" she moaned, touching her tongue to his.

"I will never let ye go."

"Never." Mariana gripped her arm around his waist, her fingers massaging the muscles that connected with his spine. The throb she felt constantly in her broken arm faded, as though he healed her. She knew that he cured not only her body but her broken mind. He made her whole again, or perhaps whole for the first time. No one ever made her feel as cherished as he did.

Brandon wrapped his sturdy arms around her, his hands stroking over her back, her ribs, cupping her breasts. She arched into him, her nipples hard as pebbles, and aching for his touch. He teased her with small brushes of this thumbs over the turgid peaks, then pressed harder as he rolled each one between a thumb and forefinger.

"Ye have perfect breasts," he murmured against her lips. "Plush and round, they fit perfectly in my grasp, and your nipples… They respond to me with the slightest touch. I wonder what ye'll do when I kiss them, lick them…"

Mariana moaned at the thought. "Please," she whispered.

Brandon slid her gown over on shoulder, then skimmed his fingers over the top, reaching just inside to tease the bare flesh of her breast. Her breaths quickened, heart beat rapid. Brandon kissed her shoulder, slid his tongue down the top of one breast, teasing her with his hot mouth until she gasped for air.

He tugged her gown lower, her breast spilling free, and his lips brushed against her nipple. "Even more beautiful than I could have guessed. Pink and ripe."

Mariana forgot for a moment that they'd made love before in the dark and he'd yet to see her in the light. "Let me undress fully so you can see all of me."

Brandon stepped back, his eyes slightly wide and a wicked grin on his face. "I can honestly say a woman has never said that to me before."

Mariana smiled and winked. "You've never been with a woman like me."

"And well I know it."

With her good arm she untied the laces of her gown, then lifted the hem, gripping it with both hands.

"Let me undress ye," Brandon said. "I've been wanting to do that very thing since I saw ye all covered in soot."

Mariana smiled gratefully. He may have wanted to undress her, but he'd also seen her struggling. Brandon used care when tugging off her gown, and he tossed it over the horse's saddle so it didn't get wet on the moist earth. He removed her chemise next, and then just stared at her. His eyes wide, a wicked grin on his face.

"Good lord, woman, ye've a body made for a man to pleasure."

Heat burned her cheeks at his compliment. His words of praise were real, not like those she'd had before that whispered the same phrases to every woman. Brandon meant every syllable he uttered.

A shiver covered her gooseflesh, and she shuddered.

"Are ye cold?" he asked, suddenly concerned.

"Only a little," she said shyly.

"I suppose spring is not full upon us yet." He whipped off his cloak and wrapped it around her. "I'm sorry to miss the view, but wouldna want ye to freeze before I've the chance to set ye afire."

Mariana nodded. Suddenly shy, she was no longer the seductress, but a woman about to experience lovemaking with a man more precious to her than breath. Anticipation heated her blood.

"Let me see you," she said, her voice low and husky.

The seductress was back.

Chapter Twenty-Two

Brandon swallowed hard, internalizing a groan. His cock was swollen thick, pushing against the restrictive confines of the breeches he still wore—and Mariana's gaze was concentrated there, her eyes flashing with potent desire.

"As ye wish, my lady," he whispered.

Whipping off his shirt, he tossed the soggy piece of linen onto the horse. Mariana's eyes were wide as saucers as she took him in. If he didn't already know better, he would have thought she'd never seen a man in the skin. A thought occurred to him—'haps, she hadn't. 'Twas entirely possible that all of her previous lovers had bent her over fully clothed, or taken her in the dark. Winking at her with confidence, he decided that her appreciation stemmed from having never bed a Highlander before him. Never having seen what a real man looked like sans clothes.

Following his instincts, he grinned at her and plucked slowly at the strings tying his breeches in place. Mariana licked her lips, as though she watched a cook make a meal after she'd not eaten in a week. A woman starved for flesh, his flesh.

"Are ye satisfied with what ye see?" he asked, noting the way his voice sounded gravelly even to his own ears.

Mariana's gaze flashed toward his, a heady sense of passion filling their depths. Was it him or did her lips appear plumper? More red? Lord how he wanted to feel them wrapped around his—

"Very," she murmured. "Don't let me stop you." She stepped closer, the chill Highland air suddenly feeling sultry. Mariana's fingers skimmed along the waistline of his breeches, her nails scraping tantalizingly over the flesh of his hip. "Unless you want me to help you."

For the first time in his life, Brandon was speechless. The woman… Ballocks, but she was a siren. A faerie bent on seducing him and then claiming his soul. But he was powerless to move and every inch of his skin wanted to feel her touch.

"I'd never turn away a woman willing to assist me with undressing." Now, dressing was another matter. That meant he was either too old or she wasn't interested, neither case he wanted to be in at the moment.

Mariana smiled up at him, her eyelids lowered slightly, the curve of her lips sensual. Brandon dipped low, and kissed her. He slid his mouth over hers, licked at her lips, her tongue. Mariana eagerly kissed him back, not afraid of him in the least, but showing enthusiasm, desire.

He cradled her face in his palms, loving the taste of her, so fresh and sweet, along with her scent of flowers and passion. Mariana was like a sweet drink to a man dying of thirst. She opened up all the doors that had been previously closed to him. Made him realize that he was more than he once thought, that he could be more than he set out to be.

How could he possibly have lived before her, for he knew he'd never be able to live without her again.

Mariana slid his breeches low over his hips, his cock less than inch from being free. Once it sprang forth, he was sure to lose control, needing desperately to bury himself between the sweet folds of her sex, where he could find the ecstasy he'd sought there before.

"Och, woman," he murmured as he slid his lips over her chin to bite at her earlobe. "What are ye doing to me?"

"Exploring," she said breathlessly.

Exploring? He understood what she meant with a jolt when her fist wrapped around his cock, squeezing lightly and then stroking up over the tip and back down. Groaning, he bit her earlobe, and caressed the plush globes of her milky breasts. The woman tempted him beyond reason. Made his blood burn with a fire that would not be easily doused.

"I want to explore, too," he said. Hands massaging over her rear, he bent his head to her breasts, flicking his tongue in teasing swirls over her hard nipples. "I like what I've found."

Mariana laughed between moans. "Anything I have is yours to keep."

"Anything?"

"Anything."

"Even this?" Brandon slid his fingers over her damp cleft, sliding between the folds to gently massage the swollen bud. Mariana jumped a little at his touch. Precisely the reaction he was in search of. He suckled a little harder at her breasts, massaging her nub with the flat of his finger in a little circle.

The action had the exact effect he was looking for. Mariana stopped touching him, her forehead pressed hard to his shoulder.

"No man has ever…cared about my…" Her words were broken up by moans.

Brandon could feel her tensing against him. "Pleasure?" he asked, hoping that was the word she'd been looking for.

"*Oui*, pleasure," she panted. Her breathing was erratic, her heart pounding a beat against his own.

Brandon picked up the pace, rubbing quicker, a little harder. He kissed her breasts, suckled her nipples and continued ceaselessly with his touch.

Mariana writhed against him. His cock out of reach, she'd found a grip in his arms, massaging his shoulders between squeezing his muscles tight.

"Don't stop, please," she begged.

"I never would. Never."

"Mmm..."

The woman's reaction was so genuine, raw. Brandon could almost believe this was her first time—or that she was new at it. When they'd made love before it had been the same way. The shock, awe and beauty of pleasure for her.

"I want to feel ye finish on my tongue," he whispered in her ear.

Mariana's gasp was so deep, it sounded as though she choked on it.

Brandon didn't allow her a chance to negate his desire. He dropped to his knees, breeches still only partially down, and buried his face between her thighs. Heaven met his tongue. Glorious, slick heat. She'd washed with lemon soap, the scent still tangy on her flesh.

Nails dug into his shoulders as she cried out, her thighs quivered against his face. He loved her raw passion, her fiery nature. Slipping his fingers over her curves, he continued to lave at her cleft, flicking his tongue mercilessly over the bundle of nerves.

"No one...has ever..." Her panted words broke off as she moaned.

"No one?" For shame, she should have been devoured many times over. The woman was delicious, her response surreal.

Brandon gazed up at her, head thrown back in the fading light. Her chest heaved with each deep breath she took. She bit her lip, eyes wide and blinking up at the clouds, then she looked down at him.

A shudder took hold of him, delicious and wicked, it wound its way around his body before centering in his cock. He was the luckiest man alive.

Pleasure wrapped its stroking fist around Mariana. Pure decadence. She watched Brandon nuzzle between her thighs, his tongue making swirls in the place so many had used, but none had ever thought to indulge. Watching him watching her only heightened the wondrous sensations quickly taking over any control she might have once possessed. She was a woman in the throes of ecstasy. When Brandon thrust a finger inside her slick channel, she couldn't hold on any longer.

Her eyes widened, mouth formed an O and she cried out as her body shattered. He continued to nuzzle her until the waves subsided.

"Och, lass, ye're beautiful when ye peak." Brandon slid his hands over her hips and around her waist as he stood. "I want to see ye do so again and again."

She sighed, pressed her forehead to his chest and kissed the place over his heart. "Thank you," she murmured.

"For what?" he asked, sounding puzzled.

"For…that."

Brandon chuckled. "For tasting ye?"

She nodded.

"Dinna be shy with me, lass. I enjoyed every…last…drop." His words were separated by each slide of his fingers over her swollen nub.

Fire anew, ignited, and she moaned. "Brandon…"

"Aye?"

"I want you inside me."

"A need I canna deny, for I verra much want to be inside ye." He spread out his plaid on the ground and laid Mariana down atop it.

The soft wool caressed her back as his hard, hot body pressed down on her. She was instantly filled with the warmth of his body, the heat of her passion.

Wrapping her legs around his hips, she lifted up, her body searching for his. Wanting, needing, this intimate connection. Tonight, before the stars and moon, they were claiming each other. In this most natural state, they danced in the age old undulation of life.

Brandon kissed her softly, careful to keep his weight off her arm. His tongue was a soft pressure against her own, sliding back and forth. Tingles prickled over her skin, and unbidden, moans fell from her lips. This may have been one of the happiest moments of her life—indeed every moment in Brandon's arms, she felt cherished, honored, delighted in.

The softness of his shaft slid over the firing bundle of nerves, hidden by the folds of her sex. He opened her up, revealed her, treasured her. And she reveled in it. Wanted him to feel the same way. She massaged the muscles of his spine, down to his taut rear. He felt so good beneath her fingertips, as though made just for her.

Boldly, Mariana slipped her hand between them, gripping his shaft, she slid it between her folds, arching up against the wondrous sensations such a move elicited.

"Woman…" Brandon ground out, his jaw clenched tight as he met her gaze.

"Warrior," she tried to tease back, but her words came out a whimper.

"Good God," he moaned. He wrapped his hand around hers, so they both held his hard length, and he skimmed it lower over her opening, slick with natural essence.

Eyes locked, they both pushed him inside her, inch by precious inch. When he was buried to the hilt, Mariana didn't move her hand. She wanted to feel their union with not only him inside her, but sliding in her grasp.

Without questioning her, Brandon slowly pulled out then plunged back in. His cock was slick with her desire, and slid easily through her hand. The sensation was almost too much to bear. For her sensitive palm to feel him driving in and out…

Mariana bucked upward. Dear God, she'd never thought herself to be such a sensual woman, even with her position in the king's courts.

Brandon brought out this side of her, showed her what could truly happen between a man and a woman, especially when they felt so deeply for one another. This had to be magic, must be. Even her mind was afire.

"I love the way ye respond to me… Mariana, ye are so verra…sensual." Brandon's words were low, husky, whispered against her ear between his moans. "I love ye."

With his uttered confession, Mariana's world turned upside down and inside out. She cried out, her body quivering and trembling fiercely. Her thighs shook, her insides reeled with pleasure in tumultuous waves.

"I love you, too," she managed to say as the tremors of ecstasy slowed.

"Mariana," Brandon moaned. He thrust deep and hard and she clung to him, completely unprepared for the subsequent onslaught of another peak.

She cried out, nails digging into his rear, hips thrust upward in time with his. Brandon too, shuddered, his body tense above hers. Liquid heat consumed her, filling her.

They lay motionless for minutes, Brandon hovering above her, his eyes locked with hers. Mariana could see within his gaze that this moment had changed him as much as it had her. That lovemaking had never been so potent for Brandon. For either of them.

He collapsed beside her, pulled her into his arms and wrapped the plaid around them both.

"I meant what I said," he whispered.

"What did you say?" she asked, a smile covering her lips. Although she knew, Mariana wanted to hear it again, to forever ingrain that memory of him whispering those most sought after words against her cheek.

"I love ye."

"I love you, too."

Morning broke with golden beams of light filtering their way through the trees. Mariana hadn't slept so well in all her life as she did nestled in Brandon's arms with nature as their backdrop.

The tip of her nose was cold, but the rest of her was nice and toasty, snuggled beside him with his thick plaid cocooning them in body heat.

"Morning, love," Brandon whispered.

Mariana tilted her head back, resting her chin on his shoulder and smiled. "Morning."

"How did ye sleep?"

"Like a babe."

"Aye, me too."

Mariana leaned up on her elbow, fully aware that half of her breast was exposed. Brandon stretched his arms up wide over his head, his eyebrows wiggling.

"That's a lovely sight for a man in the morning." With his pointer finger, he tugged the plaid the rest of the way down. "Even better now." He tackled her back to the ground, smothering her neck with hot, wet kisses.

Behind them, someone cleared their throat. "A good morning to ye both."

Mariana gasped, covering her face with her hands. "Tell them to go away," she whispered frantically.

"I think your hands are covering the wrong part of your body," Brandon said with a chuckle, sliding the plaid further over them.

She was being silly, she was full aware of it, especially considering she'd been mistress to many, but somewhere along the line, she'd made a pact with herself that she belonged to Brandon and no other, not even for looking.

"Ho, there, Wallace. We came across the present ye left good 'ole Longshanks." Brandon managed to slide from beneath the plaid without exposing her further to anyone's eyes. Without his heat beside her, she quickly felt the coolness of the ground sinking through the plaid she laid on, chilling her to the bone. Gooseflesh covered her skin and she shivered.

Wanting to know just how many had seen them in such a compromising position, she peeked her eyes open and pulled the plaid up to her chin at the same moment. Only Wallace. Thank goodness.

But…oh, my…

Brandon stood directly in front of her, nude as a god. His rear tight and muscular just feet from her. She wanted to reach out and touch him. To feel him once more pushing against her, to have him shudder between her thighs.

Heat blasted over her cheeks, neck and chest. She sank further beneath the plaid, wishing to become one with the leaves and mossy ground, if only until Wallace left them alone.

What in blazes could be so interesting? Shouldn't Brandon be sending him away until they were decent? Tilting her head, she listened closely.

"Och, man, put some damn clothes on. I'm nay wanting to see your tallywag first thing in the morning."

Mariana bit her lip to keep from laughing.

"I'm nay the one who barged in," Brandon countered.

"How was I to know ye were with the lass?" Wallace whispered rather loudly.

"The men should have told ye I was going after her."

Mariana rubbed her good hand over her frozen thighs, and rubbed her feet together, hoping to create enough friction to keep her warm. It worked a little, but not as well as Brandon's body heat. Why wouldn't Wallace go away so she could at least get dressed?

Wallace's face turned hard. "That they did. Ye were lucky to come out of it alive. Dinna do something so foolish again."

"I canna promise ye that." Brandon's voice was filled with seriousness. "If my woman is being held by Longshanks again, I'll have no choice."

He called her *his woman…*

Mariana bit her lip to keep from singing with pleasure. Not that she truly would have done such a thing, but she was so pleased to hear him say it, her heart soared and energy burst like fire through her veins. With that feeling, she was capable of doing anything.

"Where's then new camp. We can meet ye there if ye're not of a mind to wait," Brandon said, turning toward his horse and throwing on his linen shirt—now dry.

Mariana wished he'd toss over her chemise, not that it would be easy to put it on with her arm in the sling, but she could manage it so as not to be so naked in front of the Guardian of Scotland.

"We've yet to make camp. For now, we've had a message that the English are choosing to fall back to England. The Bruce is going to give the majority of the men staggered leave for about a month."

Brandon nodded. Instead of grabbing the breeches he'd taken off the day before, he pleated a plaid around his hips and belted it.

"I dinna need to be one of the men taking leave."

"Aye, the Bruce wants ye to take your men back to visit their families. Let them know what they fight for. But keep them training. If he calls for ye, he wants ye to be ready."

"Where will ye be? The Bruce?"

"I'll stay with him. I've no family now. Those who have family have been given orders to return and see them safe. Same as ye. They will train and be ready when called."

Brandon gave a firm nod. "I will not let him down."

Wallace grinned broadly, flicked his eyes toward Mariana and she felt herself color again. "I suspect ye might want to be getting to the kirk."

"The kirk?" she blurted out.

Wallace peeked around Brandon. "Aye, lass, to become Lady Sinclair."

"Oh," she breathed, then choked on the lack of air intake. *Lady Sinclair.* Brandon's wife. He would be her husband. Forever. To wake up beside him every morning…

"Well, lass, what do ye say?" Brandon turned around and winked at her. "Ye did say ye've never seen a Scottish spring before."

Chapter Twenty-Three

Racing to the altar was not an activity Brandon ever foresaw himself doing. And yet, here he was, atop his horse, Mariana in his lap, surrounded by his men and Wallace. The Bruce and his set had remained ahead, looking for a new camp, and Brandon was glad to have at least a few weeks of reprieve.

They rode over hills, through glens and thick trees, until at last, they came to a small village.

And the kirk.

The small stone chapel had a tower with a diminutive bell that tolled noon. The priest burst from inside like he'd been chasing devils. He was a large man, his brown robes coming just barely to his ankles, like they'd been borrowed. A cross made of steel hung heavily from his neck on a thick chain. His head was shaved on the sides, and pulled back into a long braid. Sporting a long goatee, he looked more savage than Brandon himself. If not for the robes, Brandon might have drawn his sword.

"We'd like to be married," Brandon said.

The man nodded and waved them inside. He disappeared within, the oak door slamming ominously behind him.

"Odd looking priest," Brandon muttered.

Wallace stroked his chin and stared after the man. "He's got the look of a Mackay. I wonder if he wasn't sent into the priesthood as punishment for something."

"Like what?" Mariana asked while he tried to help her dismount. She batted away his hands and managed—awkwardly with her broken arm—to get down.

"I dinna know. We may never know." Wallace walked ahead of them into the kirk.

"Life with you is never without excitement, is it?" Mariana's eyes sparkled.

"No, I'm afraid if ye're looking for dull, I'm not likely to oblige, though I'd try my damndest."

She smiled, stroked Brandon's arm. "Why do I have a feeling you would have a hard time being dull? As long as we're together, that is all I need."

Brandon forced himself not to frown. There were going to be times he wasn't with her. When he was called to battle. Even with an iron will, he wasn't able to keep his brows from burrowing.

"I know what you're thinking, Laird Sinclair," she whispered, her fingers crawling a path up to his shoulder. "I won't begrudge you your position within Scotland. I won't beg you to choose between your duty to country versus your duty to me. I know what's at stake, and I support your country's need of your strong arm." She squeezed his upper arm, and leaned up to kiss his chin. "I only ask that you try with every ounce you possess, to make it home to me."

"On that, ye will never have to worry. My every breath and thought will be about finding my way back to ye. If I have to kill every damn Englishman in order to get it, then so be it, I will."

She presented him with a beguiling smile, grabbed hold of his shirt and tugged him closer. "Then kiss me senseless."

"Aye, lass, I will do that very thing." Brandon wrapped his arms around her and pulled her close. Their lips connected, hot, both of them trembling.

"I suspect that is what happens after the ceremony?" Wallace's voice broke their interlude, and they turned to find him poking his head from the door. "The priest is waiting, and he does seem to be an impatient sort. Is that not a sin, for a priest to have no patience?" He looked off into the distance as though trying to decipher that very thing, then disappeared again.

Brandon chuckled and shook his head. Wallace made all the blood, guts and pain of this war a little less horrific. When Mariana turned to go inside he held her back, his fingers twining with hers. "Wait."

She glanced back at him, a bemused look on her face. Lord, she was gorgeous. Brandon bent and picked a rather limp looking thistle. There did not appear to be more than sad flora in the immediate vicinity. He handed Mariana the purplish brown thistle with a smile. "'Tis not exactly the cut I would have given ye."

Mariana lowered her lashes, and pretended to sniff the thistle. "The most beautiful flower a beau has ever given me."

Brandon chuckled, glad she found humor in it as he did. "I dinna… This is…" Ballocks, but he couldn't seem to form a sentence. Nerves made him jumpy, and he was never this full of jitters. He was a warrior for heaven's sake.

"What is it?" she asked softly, coaxing him to answer.

Brandon thought he might just drown in the blue of her eyes, rather than say what he wanted. But if he didn't soon, Wallace was bound to poke his head back out of the church and drag them in.

"This has all happened to so suddenly. I simply wanted to make sure ye were all right with it."

Her brows knitted together. "Are you all right with it?"

"Aye." There was no hesitation in his answer. He was ready. "I love ye, Mariana. I'd have ye for my wife, to cherish for the rest of my days."

"Then get your blasted arse in here!" Wallace called from the door, then turned around and called inside, "Sorry, Father!"

Mariana chewed her lip, obviously trying to hold back a laugh.

"He's a feisty one," Brandon said with a smile.

"That he is." Mariana squeezed his hand in hers. "I love you, too. I want you for my husband, sudden or not."

Relief flooded him. He'd not truly thought she'd deny him, but mayhap deep down a part of him had thought that it might be too good to be true.

"Then, let us hurry inside." Brandon tugged her in, and they half ran, half walked into the kirk.

"Finally…" the priest muttered.

Mariana flashed Brandon a hidden smile.

"Apologies, Father, we were—"

"Och, I dinna want to hear it. I'll need to do your confessions and then I'll marry ye." The priest glowered. Truth be told, he looked more ready to go to battle than to take their confessions and join them in holy matrimony.

"This is Father Mackay," Wallace said with a raise of his brow.

The man flashed Wallace a glare, before turning toward Mariana who he watched like a falcon observed his prey. "My lady, shall we?"

Brandon was hard pressed to trust him, especially after hearing the name Mackay. They'd long feuded with his cousins' clan, the Sutherlands. He gave Wallace a questioning look, and the man nodded. If Wallace trusted the priest then he could too.

Though apprehension filled him as they man took Mariana behind the curtains of a covered alcove. He pressed a hand to the sword at his side. Seeing his movement, Wallace shook his head.

"He's fierce, aye, but the man took a vow, and a Mackay never goes back on their vows."

Brandon had to trust that the man standing alone behind the curtain with his woman was indeed loyal to the cloth.

Straightening her shoulders, Mariana forced herself to remain calm. The alcove was tiny to begin with, but was made even smaller by the presence of the warrior-like priest.

"Sit," he commanded.

Without question, she sat on the bench, hands folded in her lap. The bulky man sat opposite her, and looked at her with eyes the color of the sea. No longer scowling, he actually was handsome, in a rugged sort of way.

"Ye are to be married today?"

"*Oui*, Father."

"Are ye here of your own will?"

She nodded, wanted to ask him the same thing.

"I will hear your confession."

Mariana took a deep breath, for her sins were many.

"My, lass, 'that many, eh?" His lip curled in a half smile.

She shrugged and smiled back. "I used to be the English king's mistress."

Father Mackay's eyes widened and she feared he may not be a priest after all, and that he might take vengeance on her former lover through her.

Instead, his easy smile returned. "We all have our sins. If ye are not wanted by the Scottish law, then I can absolve ye of all your past transgressions."

"I assure you, Father, I am innocent of any wrong doing."

Father Mackay touched her forehead, stroking the sign of a cross. "Bless ye, my lady, ye are free of sin."

"Thank you, Father."

"Aye. Now let us get ye married."

Mariana stood as the priest did, but then turned around to gaze at him. "Why are you here?" she asked.

"Here? I am a priest and this is a house of God." He gestured for her to leave the alcove. "Go, we must see ye wed and on your way."

Mariana followed his directions. He was not likely to tell her anything about himself, and it was truly none of her business anyway.

The priest swiped aside the curtain, and every warrior piled within the small kirk sent their hands to their weapons.

"Och, put it away. This is a house of God for heaven's sake."

Mariana sucked her lip into her mouth to keep from laughing. The man was certainly a character, for sure. She met Brandon's gaze, and smiled. He was tense about the shoulders, his face pinched with something akin to alarm, but as soon as his eyes met hers, the lines disappeared and his lips curled. He looked her over approvingly, and heat spread through her.

This was her wedding day. A day she'd never thought to see come and here it was. Brandon held out his hand to her and she welcomed it, feeling the roughness of his fingers graze over her knuckles.

"Who gives this woman in matrimony?" Father Mackay called out, his booming voice echoing over the rafters.

"I do," Wallace said, his voice equally booming.

"Let us begin." The priest motioned with his fingers to step forward, and they did as one. "Kneel."

Mariana and Brandon knelt before the warrior priest, who fumbled through a tattered book. Finally, they recited their vows, but she could hardly remember the words, only thinking about the future and how her wish was coming true.

When they were finished, the men surrounding them cheered loud while Brandon bent her backward over his arm and kissed her. As always, the world around them seemed to disappear and she felt herself floating away into a realm that was halfway between a dream and a fairy tale.

"Well, Lady Sinclair, ye're stuck with me now."

"I can't imagine another place I'd rather be."

'Twas not until after the ceremony, and they'd ridden a good distance away, Mariana realized the priest had never heard Brandon's confession, *and* the gold and ruby ring King Edward gave her was missing from her finger. The latter, she thought a blessing, as it was a gift she'd rather not keep. But 'twould appear their priest had some confessing of his own to do. As for Brandon's lack of confession, she would pray daily for her husband's soul to make up for it.

Despite the possibility that English soldiers could attack, the men celebrated with great reverie that evening. They were going home for a much needed reprieve, one of their leaders had been wed in a love match—not too heard of. And besides, as one of the guards pointed out, the English were so damn loud, they'd likely hear them clinking down the road in enough time to sober up, or at the very least, ambush the bastards.

Mariana's face hurt, she'd been smiling so much, nonstop. The men had done toast after toast, for a happy marriage, down to enough bawdy well-wishes, her face had also long since burnt to a crisp blush. Having imbibed in more than her share of wine and whisky, she needed to excuse.

"Brandon, I need a moment of privacy."

He glanced up at her, merriment dancing around his eyes.

"I shall come with ye." He leapt to his feet and grasped her hand in his.

"I assure you, I'm in no need of assistance in this matter."

"Ah, a moment to relieve yourself, why didna ye say so?" He leaned in close, his lips touching her ear. "I thought ye meant for me to follow…so I might kiss ye behind the tree."

Mariana rolled her eyes, walked away, her hand slipping slowly from his.

"I'm still going to accompany ye. Dinna want any stray wanderers making off with my wife."

His wife. She loved the sound of that.

After making use of a private spot behind a bush, she exited the trees to see Brandon leaning his back against and oak, his arms folded in front of him. His eyes were lowered, and she almost thought him to be asleep standing, until her smiled at her.

"We're alone once more."

She looked about her, noting the way the forest was trying for spring.

"That we are."

"I like to be alone with ye."

Mariana sauntered forward. Brandon opened his arms and she easily stepped into his embrace.

"I dinna think anyone will bother us for a time," Brandon said seductively against her ear.

A tingle of awareness shot its way through her. "Are you certain?"

"Verra certain." This time, he skimmed his teeth over her earlobe, and then pressed his lips to that sensitive spot below her ear.

"Then we'd best make use of the time," she said breathlessly.

"Oh, aye." Brandon drawled out his words as his mouth dragged over the length of her neck to her shoulder.

Every inch he touched, and every inch he didn't, was suddenly hot, achy with need. Her nipples hardened, thighs quivered, and between them grew damp. Desire for him was potent, as it always was. Mariana didn't think she'd ever get used to it, for with each kiss, each look he swung her way, she shuddered all the more, as though it were the first time.

"Brandon," she crooned, pulling his mouth to hers. She kissed him feverishly, hoping to show him how much she desired him, wanted him.

"Och, woman," he growled, his hands skimming over her backside. He cupped her buttocks tight and tugged her against him, his hardened shaft pressing urgently against her middle.

Brandon tore his mouth away from hers, tugging at her gown until one nipple popped out. Must have been what he wanted, as his hot, velvet mouth flattened irresistibly to her sensitive flesh. His tongue was ceaseless, glorious torture.

Mariana threaded her fingers through his hair, tugging him away only to push him back. Her hips surged forward to meet his, grinding incessantly, until her breaths came in gasps.

"Mmm," she moaned.

"I canna stop, love, I canna." He lifted her into the air.

"Don't." She wrapped her legs around him, and with her good arm, yanked her skirts up around her hips.

"Oh, have mercy," he murmured against her lips as his hands came into contact with her naked flesh.

"No mercy." Mariana laughed seductively. "Take me, now."

Brandon growled, fiddled with his plaid, and seconds later was plunging hotly up into her. They both cried out as their bodies connected, as the stress of the world melted away and the heat of their passion united.

"Don't stop," she demanded. "Don't ever stop."

"Never." Brandon held her hips tight in his grasp, guiding her body as he drove in and out with fiery purpose.

She pressed a flurry of kisses over his face, before pulling his lower lip into her mouth with her teeth. Never had she made love with such urgency, such ferocity.

Driving his tongue into her mouth, laying claim to what she offered, Brandon twirled them in a circle and pressed her back up against a tree. One hand on her hip and the other bracing himself on the trunk, he continued to surge into her. Decadent sensations whipped through her, and both of their erotic cries sounded through the trees.

Without warning, Mariana's muscles seized as a potent release took hold, bursting from inside out in wave after delicious wave. Brandon's pace increased, only heightening her pleasure. He called out her name, dropped his forehead into the crook of her neck and shuddered against her.

They stayed like that, motionless, connected, breathing in each other's scents for what seemed like hours, until finally, Mariana said, "I think my legs are going numb."

Brandon laughed, and pulled her away from the tree, setting her on her feet. He righted her gown and fixed his plaid. "Are ye up for another drink of wine?"

"And then maybe some more privacy…"

"Och, lass, ye're a dream come true. Marriage to me suits ye," he grinned lopsidedly, and winked.

Oui, marriage to her Highlander suited her perfectly.

Chapter Twenty-Four

Ten months later…

"My lady, ye must lie down. Rest."

Mariana shook her head, glad for once her stubbornness could be put to good use.

There was no way on God's green earth she was going to give birth to this child without her husband present.

"My lady, please. 'Tis not safe."

Mariana whirled around. "Not safe?" she said with a near hysterical laugh. "What is not safe, is my husband's life. He promised he would return when the time came."

"Aye, but how was he to know ye'd be going to the childbed a week early?"

Mariana just glowered, and stalked as much as a woman heavy with child and experiencing labor pains could, to the nearest window.

She threw back the shutters, and glared out at the moon and stars and their reflections in the water. Nearing midnight, she was still not tired. And she was definitely not getting into that bed until Brandon returned.

After getting married, they'd traveled to Brandon's home—Castle Girnigoe, so far north, Mariana swore they'd forever be frozen. However much she'd believed spring would never come, it finally did, in abundance, and flourish. The most beautiful place she'd ever seen.

Mariana was welcomed to Girnigoe with open arms, and had immediately befriended his mother, becoming quite close, in fact. Beatrice was like a mother to her now and had been good company over the past several months that Brandon had been gone. As had Julianna, surprisingly. She'd apologized for her earlier suspicions. They had a lot on common recently, which helped in pushing them closer together. Both of their husbands were gone to war, and they were both with child. Julianna had probably already given birth to her babe.

With the English having returned to Scottish soil, the Bruce had called the Sinclair warriors to arms. News came to her every few weeks or so. He and his men had prevailed at the Battle of Falkirk, though the English had been victorious. Thankfully, all of his kin had also lived. They'd regrouped and struck hard again.

The last news she'd had was that he would have returned by now. Two days late he was, and for at least a day, she'd been forcing her body to hold in the babe, a feat in itself.

The door opened, and Mariana whirled around, expecting to see Brandon filling the expanse, but another more terrifying man did. The priest. Dressed in flowing black robes, the same steel cross. Obviously, the man had found something that fit.

"What are you doing here?" she asked, trying to put her hands on her hips, but her hips had been swallowed by her belly, so she dropped them back to her sides. She'd not seen him since the kirk.

"I've come to pray for ye and the bairn."

"Why?"

"'Tis custom."

"Custom for who and what reason?"

"For a mother and her bairn," he said with exasperation.

"Where is my husband?"

The man shrugged and let himself into the room, coming to stand in front of her. He gazed down at her swollen belly. A shudder of fear passed through her.

"How did they find you?" she asked, her instincts on high alert.

"I came to return this." He held out his hand, fingers slowly curling back to reveal her ring.

"Keep it," she said, tersely.

The priest raised a brow. "Why, my lady?"

"It means naught to me. I don't want it back."

He gave a curt nod and put it in a pouch at his side.

"Do ye wish to confess?"

"What?" Mariana frowned. "You came here to return the ring. Nothing more. I don't want it, so you can leave." She whirled around.

"My lady, I am here to comfort ye, as a man of God does."

"But you are only succeeding in annoying me. Now go away."

"If ye do not wish to confess, I cannot absolve ye of your sins and if I cannot absolve ye of your sins, they may be passed onto your unborn child."

Mariana groaned and turned back to the oversized priest. He wasn't fat by any means, but built of solid muscle, and she wished to throw his bulk right out the window.

"Fine, I shall confess. I stole a platter of sweet breads and a bowl of almonds from the kitchen. Hid them in my wardrobe and snacked on them the entire day today."

"My lady!" gasped the maid. They'd all told her she couldn't eat while in labor, else she might wretch.

Well, she was damned hungry.

The priest chuckled. "Anything else?"

"No," she muttered, crossing her arms over her chest.

"All right, then." He stepped closer, marked a cross on her forehead. "Ye are free of sin." His hand pressed to her belly. "And so are ye."

A pain clutched around her middle, and Mariana doubled over. The priest jumped back from her, and she watched his feet scurry over toward the door. Fast for a large man. He excused himself from the room, leaving her bent over in pain.

"Please come to the bed, my lady. Ye dinna have to undress, yet, if it doesna suit yet."

She shook her head. "No. I'll sit by the window."

"Fine, but at least let me put a blanket over your lap."

Brandon's servants were bossy. Well, not all of them, just the one assigned to her. She would have a serious talk with the woman when this was all over and done with.

The pains in her belly were coming quicker, and she rubbed her hands over her back and front to soothe herself. There was only so much she could do to keep the babe from coming. In truth, she didn't think her willpower had as much to with it as her praying and bargaining did. Brandon had to be here to witness the birth of their miracle baby.

She'd been certain that she was barren. Would have bet her life on it. But several months into their marriage, her woman's cycle ceased and she began eating like a horse. She never experienced the sickness most women complained of, and instead of being tired she was full of energy. A miracle, all of it.

And for that reason, Brandon had to be here. It wouldn't be right to bring in this gift of a child without him.

Another pain caused her to cry out. This baby was coming, no matter what she did.

The door creaked open again, and this time Beatrice tiptoed in, the blue of her eyes the same as Brandon's.

"How are ye feeling, lass?" she asked. "Why are ye not abed?"

"I am fine," she lied. "Just enjoying a bit of the night view."

Beatrice raised a brow. The woman's grey hair was pulled in a loose braid, and though she was nearing sixty, her face had few wrinkles. She dressed in plaid of brighter hues than most of those in the clan, colors that matched Brandon—deep yellows, greens and blues. The same plaid Mariana herself was wearing now.

"Then ye saw."

"Saw what?"

"Me." Brandon's voice boomed across the room.

"Brandon!" Mariana shrieked and jumped up to greet him, but the move proved to be too much. She slumped back into the chair and clutched at her belly.

The pain was intense and with it came a great pressure between her thighs. Brandon rushed forward, his hand on her belly. Are ye all right?

"I think I need to lie down now," she said, panting between words.

Brandon scooped her up and carried her to the bed, lying her down as gently as if she were made of glass and weighed no more than a feather—unlike the great sow she felt like.

"You're late," she murmured as he pressed his lips to hers.

"Ye're early."

She chuckled. "We waited—" But her words were cut short by another pain and more pressure.

"We must undress her," Beatrice said. "Get the midwife," she ordered the maid.

Brandon moved to leave, but Mariana clutched his hand. "Don't leave me."

"Ye want me to stay? Men dinna—"

"Stay," she cut him off.

Brandon nodded, went around the other side of the bed and climbed in beside her. "As ye wish, my love."

The midwife arrived and less than an hour later, Brandon and Mariana held their little miracles in their arms. A boy, Brandon after his father and a girl they named Mari.

Later that night, as they each held a bundle of pink, soundly sleeping baby, Brandon gazed at her, a smile of victory on his lips.

"Ye know, wife, I thought myself triumphant over Longshanks when I stole ye away. But now I have two more reasons to rejoice."

Mariana reached out and stroked the back of her fingers over Brandon's stubbled cheek, pure joy filling her heart. "I think 'twas me who did the stealing."

Her husband shook his head. "Nay, wife." He pressed a kiss to each babe's forehead and then one to her lips. "We *found* each other."

Mariana leaned onto Brandon's shoulder and gazed up into his eyes. "Finders keepers?"

"Aye, forever." He sent a slow wink her way, and Mariana's stomach fluttered.

"I love you so very much," she whispered.

"I love ye, too, my sweet."

Brandon brushed his lips over her forehead, then her mouth. They fell asleep, leaning against one another, all they ever needed, right there with them.

"The End"

If you enjoyed **THE HIGHLANDER'S TRIUMPH**, *please spread the word by leaving a review on the site where you purchased your copy, or a reader site such as Goodreads or Shelfari! I love to hear from readers too, so drop me a line at* authorelizaknight@gmail.com *OR visit me on Facebook:* https://www.facebook.com/elizaknightauthor. I'm also on Twitter: @ElizaKnight *Many thanks!*

AUTHOR'S NOTE

A note on Brandon's home. Castle Girnigoe, was not actually built until the late 15th century as the seat of the Sinclairs. For the purposes of its location, I pushed the building date up.

A noted on Ion Dubh Castle. This is a completely fictitious castle. I made it up, choosing a form of blackbird, in Gaelic.

I've included in this book, the past Author Notes from the first four books in the series, in case you missed them:

BOOK ONE: The *Highlander's Reward*

No author's note.

BOOK TWO: *The Highlander's Conquest*

In fiction, an author often takes creative license to bend fact around their story. I did so in this case with the Earldom of Sutherland. The original earldom was given to the Sutherland Clan in 1235, about 62 years before my story takes place. For the purposes of this family saga, it was important to shift this date slightly. Of additional note is that the family seat of the Sutherlands wasn't officially Dunrobin until the 1400's, however history shows that a castle stood on the site from the time of the earldom.

Hope you're enjoying the Stolen Bride series so far! I've certainly been enjoying weaving a tale around these fascinating characters.

BOOK THREE: *The Highlander's Lady*

A note on curse words. As you may have noticed, Myra has a bit of a foul mouth! In deciding that I wanted her to use this type of language I had to do a bit of research. Readers usually think that expletives are more modern, but they are in fact, quite old. Now, some of the words I've used aren't in written documents until the later medieval days, and there is no way to know just how long they were used before recorded. A couple of examples:

~F-word—first written documentation in the 1400's, so in essence could be much older than that.
~Shite - this is where the word shit comes from. It actually means excrement. Has been around since before 1508 when it was first documented to be used. Seen as a very taboo word however.
~Zounds - Actually a variation of God's Wounds.
~Damn - from the late 13th century.
~Mo creach - a Gaelic exclamation, meaning Good Heavens.

A note on hidden walls in Foulis. Foulis stands today with only shadows of its original self still in existence. The motte is still present, and a few stone structures such as arrow slit windows and a stone archway. The majority of the castle as it stands today was rebuilt in the middle of the 18th century. The hidden passageways were entirely my own creation—however, you never know.

A note on Murray's holding Blair. Not until several hundred years later did clan Murray hold Blair Castle. For the purposes of this story, I used creative license to move up the date, particularly because of location.

A note on the song Myra's mother used to sing to her. This is from the Scottish lullaby, Loch Lomond.

BOOK FOUR: *The Highlander's Warrior Bride*

Robert the Bruce (de Brus) did not have an older sister named Julianna—or that we know of. She is a fictional character I made up for the purposes of this family saga. Robert did have many siblings, including an older sister named Christina.

Eilean Donan was not, that I know of, used as a camp for Robert the Bruce in 1297/98. He did seek shelter there several years later. For the purposes of this story and the castle's mystery and location, I thought it perfect. Additionally, Kinterloch and the issues with Laird Ross are a product of my imagination—although it is known that Ross stirred up a lot of trouble during this time period.

The Saga Continues!

Look for more books in The Stolen Bride Series coming soon!

Book Six- *The Highlander's Sin* -October 15, 2013

He stole her away… But she set him free…

They called him The Priest. Maybe because of his billowing black robes and the steel crucifix that hung around his neck. Or perhaps it was because those who met him were compelled to pray. But Duncan Mackay was anything but a saint. He was a sinner—a paid mercenary. Until he met her, and she made him want to change his ways.

Lady Heather Sutherland, has never been compelled to follow rules. And this time, she's gone too far. Following in the footsteps of her brothers and cousins, she chooses to join the fight for Scottish freedom—and gets herself abducted by a handsome, rogue warrior, whose touch is sweet sin.

Duncan's duty was clear—steal Heather away from Dunrobin Castle. What he didn't expect, was to be charmed by her spirit and rocked by her fiery kiss. Now, he doesn't want deliver her to those who hired him, instead he wants to keep her all to himself.

****

There *were* six planned books in The Stolen Bride Series! BUT due to reader demand, I've decided to keep the series going! Following Book Six: *The Highlander's Sin,* will be *The Highlander's Temptation* - a prequel to the series. That's right! Lorna and Jamie's story.

If you haven't read the other books, they are available at most e-tailers. Check out my website, for information on future releases www.elizaknight.com.

ABOUT THE AUTHOR

Eliza Knight is the multi-published, award-winning, Amazon best-selling author of sizzling historical romance and erotic romance. While not reading, writing or researching for her latest book, she chases after her three children. In her spare time (if there is such a thing…) she likes daydreaming, wine-tasting, traveling, hiking, staring at the stars, watching movies, shopping and visiting with family and friends. She lives atop a small mountain, and enjoys cold winter nights when she can curl up in front of a roaring fire with her own knight in shining armor. Visit Eliza at www.elizaknight.com or her historical blog History Undressed: www.historyundressed.com

Made in the USA
Monee, IL
02 April 2021